KILL OR BE KILLED

Ben McCagg concentrated on drawing the Smith & Wesson. They'd started the fight and he had a right to defend himself. But the redhead's right fist came up so fast that McCagg caught it on the side of his face.

In the same split second the Smith & Wesson jumped into McCagg's hand and bucked and kicked as a metal cartridge exploded. One of the toughs, the one with a gun, folded in the middle and slumped to the floor.

The redhead was ready to hit again, but stopped when he saw his partner fall. "Don't shoot," he begged.

"Come on, you sorry son-of-a-bitch," McCagg hissed through his teeth. "You ain't fit to live!"

POWELL'S ARMY
BY TERENCE DUNCAN

COLORADO DESPERADOES

DOYLE TRENT

ZEBRA BOOKS
KENSINGTON PUBLISHING CORP.

ZEBRA BOOKS

are published by

Kensington Publishing Corp.
475 Park Avenue South
New York, NY 10016

First printing: April, 1989

Printed in the United States of America

Chapter One

He looked and felt good for a change, with clean clothes and a fresh shave and haircut. His pale blue eyes were clear and his hands were steady. He was proud of himself. Now was the time to see her.

Studying his reflection in the hotel room mirror, he ran a wooden comb through his thin dark hair and the dark moustache which curved around the corners of his wide mouth. Benjamin McCagg was tall, well over six feet, thin but straight, with high cheekbones, a square chin and a prominent Adams apple.

At forty-seven, he was too young to die. Too young to die of a bullet wound. Or of a bad liver.

But that was behind him. He had quit for good. Coffin varnish, some men called it. It was, for sure. It could kill a man as surely as a bullet. Maybe not as quick, but just as certain.

Exactly what he was going to do with the rest of his life he didn't know. But he did know what he was going to do now.

He walked down the uncarpeted wooden stairway with spurs chinking, carrying saddlebags over his left shoulder. A Smith & Wesson .45 with a five-inch barrel was cradled in a holster on his right hip. Engraved on the right side of the gun, under the lug, were the words: "Wells Fargo & Co." It was his gun. He'd earned it.

He paid his bill with a gold eagle, collected the silver change, smiled at the clerk in the striped shirt and sleeve garters, and headed for the livery barn. It was a beautiful summer morning, cloudless, with only a mild wind from the south. To the west were the shale hills covered with short cedar and piñon trees. To the east was the wide prairie of eastern Colorado. Colorado, a brand new state.

The town of El Moro, population six hundred and growing, was quiet. It was too early for the farmers and ranchers to come to town, and the railroad laborers were at work laying track over west. Spurs ringing, he walked past the Curly Wolf saloon and forced himself to look straight ahead. The smell of whiskey and stale beer was strong. A familiar smell. It pulled at him, a powerful pull. He yanked his new silver belly Stetson down tight like a man about to get on a bronc or into a fight. His jaw muscles bulged and his steps quickened until he was down the street and around the corner. Then a small smile turned up the corners of his mouth. He could do it when he had to.

The horse was a tall sorrel with stocking legs and a blaze face. Colorful, high-stepping. His saddle was worn but of good quality, made to order in Fort Worth, rimfire double rigged with a slick fork. Engraved on the skirts on the left side were the words, "Texas Rangers, Company D." It was his saddle. He'd earned it.

"Let's see now," he mused out loud, "go east to the Picketwire River, follow that northeast about two miles, and where it curves south, cut across to the east end of the curve. That's what she said in her letter. She said she wanted me to come see her and her husband. Said she'd always put another plate on the table for me. How long has it been? Five years? No, six. Yeah, six years. Wonder if she's changed much, now that she's married. Wonder if the move to free land in Colorado has been hard on her."

A frown crossed his leathery face when he recalled the times he had been near and wanting to see her, but was too

6

ragged, too hungover to be seen. Now—a smile wiped away the frown—he had gold in his pockets, new clothes and a handsome horse. Now was the time. It was going to be grand.

He rode over low hills and across dry, shallow arroyos filled with junipers. The Front Range of the Rocky Mountains was behind him, and Raton Mesa poked its flat top up to the south. The soil, he noticed, was red, drying, and covered with sagebrush, cane cactus, bluestem, gramma and buffalo grass.

"Step along, young feller," he said to the sorrel. "We've got people to visit."

That was when he heard gunshots.

He reined up suddenly and groaned. No. God, no. No more of that. But there it was again. Three shots, rapid, from a rifle. Two rifles. Then the pop of a pistol and boom of a shotgun. About a half mile away over a low hill near the river.

Indians? Naw. There hadn't been any Indian trouble for years. Hunters? Naw. The big herds of buffalo had been wiped out. More shots. White men were shooting at white men.

It was none of his business. Stay away. But the gunfire was coming from the direction he was going. He could either turn back or go on. The sorrel was shuffling its feet, pulling at the bit, wanting to move. He held it back for a minute, then reached a decision. Slacking up on the reins, he said, "All right, young feller, but let's be careful. No telling what's going on over there."

He rode to the top of a long, low ridge which curved away to the west. Below him was the Picketwire River, lined in places with big cottonwoods. Across the river was an adobe shack with a tin stock shelter. Goats grazed on a hill behind the shack, and row crops, green and close to the ground, grew between the shack and the river. A Mexican farm. Not a human in sight. He reined up and sat there, studying the scenery. To the north of the river, the prairie stretched as far as the eye could see. A few low hills broke up the monotony, but there wasn't a tree of any kind or even a bush north of the river. Just yucca and a little sagebrush. The short grass, the gramma and buffalo grass, was green but the tall wheat grass was ripe and brown. The country could use some rain. It looked a lot like West Texas.

More gunfire. It wasn't coming from the Mexican farm. Instead it was coming from farther east, around a bend in the river, beyond the cottonwoods. Right where he wanted to go. "Oh, Lord," he groaned aloud. "This ain't what I wanted to find." But he had to go on.

Following the river, he rode over another low hill and saw a cabin. The Picketwire cut a deep arroyo just ahead, and the cabin, built of rough lumber, sat on the north edge of the arroyo. A plowed field of about five acres lay east of the cabin. Two spotted cows grazed beyond the plowed field. They were milk cows with heavy bags and long tits. A calf lay in the sagebrush near the cows. Its head was up, but it wasn't moving.

He saw the riflemen. There were four of them, lying on their bellies about two hundred yards from the cabin, between him and the cabin. A man wearing a floppy black hat raised up on one knee, aimed a rifle and fired, then dropped onto his belly again. A pistol shot came from a window of the cabin followed by a shotgun blast.

It looked like a standoff. The people in the cabin were pretty well forted up, and the riflemen weren't about to get within pistol or shotgun range. The men on the ground began firing rapidly, working the levers on their repeating rifles, no doubt hoping some of their bullets would tear through the walls of the cabin and hit somebody. If they could get close enough it would probably work. A two-inch plank wouldn't stop a .44 slug fired at close range. But they were afraid to get closer. That pistol and shotgun were keeping them away.

Uh-oh. Now two of them were pouring fire into the window while the other two got up and ran at the cabin. They

8

intended to get closer. While the people in the cabin were busy dodging rifle bullets — or trying to — the pair of gunsels could run right up and pump lead through the walls. It was a one-room cabin. The people inside were about to be killed.

"Go on about your business, Ben McCagg," he told himself. "This ain't the place you're looking for and it ain't nothing to you. Men have killed men ever since time began and they always will. Go on about your business."

But while he talked to himself, he dismounted and hobbled his horse with a short rope he carried under the rigging rings of his saddle. Then he crept downhill on foot, keeping low, hoping he wouldn't be seen. Were they officers of the law, those four? Maybe the men in the cabin were cattle thieves. Cattle rustling went on all over the west. He came to a shallow draw where he could lie on his stomach and stay out of sight. He took his hat off so he could peer over the top of the draw without being seen. It wouldn't be long now. Two of the men were close enough to shoot through the walls. They were firing.

McCagg drew his short-barreled Smith & Wesson. It wouldn't shoot that far. But what would those two do if he fired a couple of shots in their direction? Just to let them know the people in the cabin had a friend outside. Muttering, "Well, we'll see," he squeezed off two rapid shots, aiming high, not trying to hit anyone. The .45 popped and bucked in his hand.

Everyone stopped suddenly. The shooting stopped. Even the wind was still. Peering over the top of the draw, he saw men's heads swivel in his direction, trying to see where the shots had come from. They moved only their heads. They saw him, finally. One pointed, but otherwise remained motionless. If they came at him, he wouldn't have a chance in a shootout, but he had it planned. He could back out of the draw and make it to his horse before they got close enough for their rifle slugs to reach him. Their horses were no doubt down in the arroyo, and by the time they got to them he'd have a good head start.

But they didn't come after him. While he watched, they suddenly broke and ran to the arroyo. They weren't looking for him, they weren't looking back at the cabin, they were just running.

McCagg went to his horse, untied the hobbles and mounted, ready to ride for it. He sat his horse on top of the hill in plain sight, believing the sorrel could outrun their horses if it came to that. It didn't come to that. When he saw the four men again, they were riding hard back toward town. They were giving up the fight. Lawmen, they were not.

The sorrel shuffled its feet and pulled at the bit, but Mc-Cagg held it there on top of the rise. He watched the four disappear in the direction of El Moro, then looked back at the cabin. A man came out, carrying a shotgun. Another man came out. Then a woman in a long dress. They saw McCagg. He waved. They waved back. Keeping his horse at a slow walk, he rode toward them, his Smith & Wesson in its holster. They didn't move, only watched him approach. The man with the shotgun was bareheaded with a full beard and baggy bib overalls. Middle-aged. He held the gun pointed at the ground, but in both hands so he could bring it up and fire in a second. The other man kept his sixgun holstered. He was average height, about thirty, strong-looking but not husky, with a smooth-shaven face. He wore denim pants and flat-heeled boots.

"Morning," McCagg said when he was close. He reined up but stayed in the saddle.

"Mornin'," said the man with the shotgun, eyes wary.

They stared at each other. The sorrel shuffled its feet.

"I'm, uh, I'm looking for the Kleagen outfit," McCagg said. "I've been told it's not far from here. William Kleagen."

The young man spoke next. "I'm Bill Kleagen."

"You are?" McCagg's face registered surprise. His gaze went over the young man, noted the intelligent blue eyes, the strong jaw. "It's been a long time. You could be him. Yep, you could be. Do you recognize me, Bill?"

A frown drew the young man's eyebrows together. He stared hard at McCagg, pushed his battered hat back on his head and continued staring. A brown cowlick fell from under the hat. Yep, McCagg thought, this is Bill Kleagen. And then the young man smiled. His whole face lit up.

"You're Ben McCagg."

McCagg smiled with him. "One and the same."

"Well, get down, Ben, and rest your saddle. Folks, meet Ben McCagg. I ain't seen him since I was a pup. Get down, Ben, so I can shake your hand."

Ben swung down, keeping his left knee against the sorrel's shoulder until his right boot touched the ground. The sorrel side-stepped away from him. The young man shook his hand, pumped it vigorously, then turned to the older man and woman. "This is Ben McCagg, a better man never came down the country. Ben, meet Harvey Arbaugh and Missus Arbaugh."

They all shook. The bearded man kept looking to the west, toward El Moro. "I don't think they'll be back today." He turned his head toward the cabin door. "You kids can come out now, but keep your eyes peeled."

There were two of them, a boy about eight and a girl about six. Towheaded and barefoot. The boy had holes in the knees of his pants, and the girl's long dress was ripped in the back. They looked at McCagg with eyes as big as saucers.

"Come in, Mr. McCagg," the woman said. "Have you had breakfast?"

"You can put your horse in that pen over yonder," the bearded man said, nodding to a wire corral on the east side of the house. "Bill's horse is in there."

"Yeah, I just sold a cow and calf to the Arbaughs and drove 'em over here. Got here just in time to help shoot back at those . . ." He didn't know what to call them in front of Mrs. Arbaugh and the kids, and his voice trailed off.

"Who are they?" Ben asked. "And what was the shooting all

11

about?"

Harvey Arbaugh answered, "Hired hoodlums, that's what they are. Tryin' ta take over our claim. They'll be showin' up at your place next, Bill."

"I expect they will. They've already served notice."

"I'm mighty happy you come along, Mr. McCagg," the woman said. "The stove's still hot if you need somethin' to eat."

"I sure do appreciate that, Mrs. Arbaugh, but I've had breakfast and enough coffee to keep me a while. And I am anxious to see Dawnmarie."

"I'll get my horse," Bill Kleagen said. "Dawnmarie'll be tickled pink to see you. She talks about you a lot."

Mounted, they headed east, away from a bend in the Picketwire. "It's only about five miles," the young man said. "Won't she be surprised." He was riding a small bay horse that looked like it had once run wild.

McCagg was quiet. He was troubled. Finally, he said, "Bill, what did Arbaugh mean when he said they'd be showing up at your place?"

"Aw, hell, Ben, I don't know. It's got something to do with the law. They said we ain't got legal claim to our land. Dawnmarie can explain it better than I can."

"Those gunsels weren't lawmen. They gave up too easy."

"Yeah, they ain't gonna get theirselves shot. They're just trying to scare somebody. I ain't worried about 'em. 'Specially, now that you're here." He shot a glance at McCagg and grinned. "When they find out you're an ex-Texas Ranger they'll go back to Denver where they come from."

"Uh," Ben grunted. He was silent again, and for a moment he forgot about Dawnmarie and how much he wanted to see her. All he could think about was gunfire, men dying, trouble. Trouble everywhere. He shook his head sadly. No matter where a man went there was trouble.

12

Chapter Two

They continued east, now out of sight of the Purgatoire River, better known as the Picketwire, a tributary of the mighty Arkansas. A small herd of antelope watched them until they got too close for comfort, then ran. They were the fastest running creatures on the American continent, and they skimmed over the sagebrush in a big circle. When the riders had passed, they came back to the spot they had started from. The land here was mostly flat with a few shallow draws. A mile ahead, the river curved back to the north, in a deep arroyo with only the tops of a few cottonwoods showing above the arroyo. They were headed for the north end of the curve.

"There's home, Ben. That's our place."

What McCagg saw was the same kind of cabin, two-inch boards with a split shingle roof. This one was bigger, probably two rooms. A stovepipe stuck up from the center of the A-shaped roof. There was a three-sided stock shelter made of more two-inch planks, a small garden in front of the cabin, and a half-dozen longhorn cows with calves. A pair of big horses grazed inside a small pasture enclosed with galvanized wire. The horses had work collar marks on their necks and shoulders. Next to the garden, a fire was burning under a black iron kettle. A galvanized wash tub with a corrugated wash board sticking out of one side was beside that, and two water barrels were next to the tub.

A strange-looking tripod, about fifteen feet high, had been erected near the cabin door.

"She's in the house, prob'ly sortin' out dirty clothes," Bill Kleagen said. "Tell you what, let's come up from the back of the house, and you wait there till I tell her to come out. Oh, won't she be tickled."

Ben agreed. "But hurry up, will you."

He held the horses while the young man walked around the house. He heard him call, "Dawnmarie. Hey, Dawn. Come out here. There's a man out here that says he knows you."

Heard her ask, "Who? Who's out here?"

He walked around the house and saw her. She saw him. She squealed.

"Uncle Benjamin!"

In four quick steps she had her arms around his neck, hugging him, patting him on the back. The top of her head came only to his chin. She stepped back, finally, and looked up at him, laughed and wiped a tear from her cheek. "Uncle Benjamin. I hadn't heard from you for so long. I was so worried about you. Oh, I'm just so happy so see you." She threw her arms around his neck again.

He had to clear his throat before he could speak. "I just had to come, Dawn. I think about you all the time. How are you? How's the homestead?"

She stood before him, a slender young woman in a long blue cotton dress, with shoulder-length brown curls. She had an oval face with a short straight nose, full lips and a firm, round chin. But what he was seeing was a child with the same long curls in a dress that couldn't be kept clean, following him around the ranch yard and always in his way. A child he was continuously scolding. But would have risked his life for.

Wiping her hair from her eyes, she glanced down at herself. "I look a sight, don't I. I didn't know you were coming. I'd have had a feast ready if I'd known. Come in, Uncle Benjamin. Bill will take care of your horse." Her hands were red and wrinkled from scrubbing clothes and bedsheets in hot, soapy water.

"Let the clothes soak till tomorrow, Dawn," her husband said. "You and Ben have got a lot to talk about. I'll go find us some supper."

Inside the cabin, the furniture was homemade of wood, a table, four chairs. A four-lid cooking range with an oven sat near one wall, and a shelf of dishes and cooking pots was nailed to another wall near the stove. He recognized some of the dishes. Fine china. They had belonged to her mother. On another shelf was a row of books. He recognized some of the books too, including the well-worn *Tales of the Arabian Nights*. He sat at the table and she sat opposite him with her hands folded. When she noticed the redness of her hands she quickly put them in her lap under the table.

"Where all have you been?" she asked. "We heard you resigned from the Rangers, and we lost track of you. I was worried."

"Oh, I've been around. Took a job on the Ladder outfit and helped move a few thousand cattle over to Dodge City. From there I went to Denver and worked for Wells Fargo on the railroad, guarding gold shipments. Things like that. I was surprised to hear you left Texas, but I shouldn't have been. A pretty girl like you was bound to get married and move away. But how come you moved up here?"

"Free land. Bill . . . you remember Bill, don't you?"

"Sure. When you mentioned him in your letter, I remembered. I always liked Bill. But somehow I expected you to marry a doctor or a merchant or somebody like that."

A small smile turned up the corners of her mouth. "A girl never knows who she's going to fall in love with. After you left, Bill and I got better acquainted. We talked a lot. He was born poor, but he's as honest as the day is long and a hard worker."

McCagg chuckled. "I recollect telling him once when he was a little kid to quit working so hard or it would stunt his growth." The chuckle died. "So you came up here for free

15

land."

"Yes. Bill never owned much. Uncle Benjamin, do you know what the opportunity to own land means to some people? It means everything. They'll do anything, suffer any hardship to be able to point at three hundred and twenty acres and call it their own."

Glancing around at the cabin, McCagg allowed, "Looks like you're doing all right. Bill did a good job of building a house."

"We lived in a tent the first eight months, but Bill hauled lumber from the railroad at El Moro and worked dawn to dark building this place. He works like that all the time. I'm afraid he's going to ruin his health working so hard."

"Got a crop of some kind in the ground?"

She shook her head sadly. "Yes, but it won't amount to anything. The first thing we were told when we got here was you can expect a good crop of wheat or oats or corn once in every five or six years. It just doesn't rain enough."

"I saw a few acres of irrigated crops on my way over here."

"Yes, if you can get some land on the flood plain you can irrigate a garden. But we got here too late. That land was already claimed. All that was left was the benchland. Our stock can go down to the river for water, but we have to haul water for the house. I managed to grow some potatoes and carrots and turnips by pouring water out of a barrel. There's plenty of wild game around here so we won't starve, but . . ." She shrugged.

"The future doesn't look too good, huh?"

She smiled suddenly, but it was a forced smile. "We're not giving up yet. Bill wants to go into the cattle business. He knows cattle. And there are miles and miles and miles of free grazing land north of here, between here and the Arkansas. Only trouble is, there's no water."

They were silent a moment, and somehow the vision of a bottle of whiskey popped into his mind. Swallowing a lump in his throat, he said, "Dawn, when I was on my way over here I

16

came on some men shooting repeating rifles at a cabin occupied by Bill and some folks named Arbaugh. Mr. Arbaugh warned Bill that they'd be over here next. What's going on?"

Her shoulders drooped suddenly, and she put her hands back on the table, forgetting about their redness. "It's a long story, Uncle Benjamin. We're in a tussle over who really owns this half section."

"It's open for homesteading, ain't it? And you did register a claim?"

Her fingers were clasped, twitching. "Yes . . . no. Well, we thought we did. I thought we did. It's ours morally if not legally, and I don't think a judge or jury would take it away from us. But," her face brightened with another forced smile, "tell me about your adventures. We read in the newspaper about the commendation the Rangers gave you. The newspaper said some of you had a gang of cattle thieves trapped near the border, but they were about to get away across the Rio Grande until you managed to get between them and the river. It said they would have escaped if it hadn't been for you. And," an accusing look came over her face, "it said you risked your life, Uncle Benjamin."

Grinning a wry grin, he said, "You can't believe everything your read in the newspapers. They like to make heroes of lawmen. It makes a good story."

"U-huh," she said, still accusing, "but I know you. You'd do something like that."

"I took an oath, you know."

"Uh-huh. We never did know why you resigned. Did something happen?"

"Naw." He shrugged. "It's a long story."

"Well." She put her hands back in her lap, and the bright smile returned. "You're looking fit and wealthy. Tell me what you've been up to. Did you strike gold, or something?"

Grinning, he answered, "Naw."

"What are your plans?"

"Oh, go back to Texas, maybe. Maybe move into the house

my mother left. Settle down."

"You ought to. Settle down, I mean. You know, if you tried, really tried, you'd make some lucky woman a darned good husband."

At that he had to laugh. "You've been trying to marry me off ever since I was old enough to vote. I told you you'd get hitched before I did."

"Yes. Bill and I have been married three years now, and finally, uh, well I found out just two weeks ago . . . I'm with child."

A broad grin split his face, and he slapped the table. "No. You mean I'm gonna be a grandpa? Or a grand uncle? Or whatever it is?"

She was somber. "You'll be the only grand whatever he has. He or she. Bill's folks were killed when he was only four, and I never really knew my folks either. And now Grandmother McCagg is gone." Suddenly, she reached across the table and put her hand on his. "But he'll have you and he'll be proud of you. As proud as I am."

He had to swallow another lump in his throat, and now he was forcing a smile. "He or she."

"I've got the written commendation you sent me for safekeeping. I wouldn't part with it for the world. And I've saved all the newspaper clippings. Someday I'm going to put it all in a book, the history of the McCaggs and all. You'll be the principal character."

"Naw. The principal characters ought to be my dad, your grandpa McCagg, and Tom, your dad. Your mother was a mighty fine woman too. They're the kind of folks that make the west a fit place to live in, Dawn. It ain't the lawyers and politicians. I hope you do write a book. Put 'em all in it."

She still had her hand on top of his when her husband came in, grinning. "I shot a big ol' tom turkey. We'll have a feast. I'd of butchered a calf, Ben. If I'd a known you was — were — comin'."

Dawnmarie stood. "I'll see what I can find for dinner. How

18

about some bread and butter? We've got plenty of butter, what with our milk cow. And buttermilk. You always liked buttermilk, Uncle Benjamin."

For a second, it came back—a vision of a shot glass fill of amber liquid, sitting on a polished bar. But only for a second. He swallowed and forced another grin. "I haven't had buttermilk for so long I forgot what it tastes like. But if you can make bread the way your grandma taught you, that'll be feast enough for me."

She unwrapped a loaf of home-made bread, went out to one of the water barrels and took out a pail of buttermilk. It made a good lunch. McCagg could remember when, as a boy, he had many times made his dinner out of nothing more than bread, apple butter and buttermilk. It brought back the good kind of memories, and he ate happily. After eating, the two men went outside and talked.

Ben nodded at the strange tripod and asked about it. "Oh," Bill Kleagen looked down at his boots and grinned sheepishly, "it's just an idea I got. It's a dumb idea."

"You're digging a well?"

"Yeah," still looking down. "Tryin' to."

"Wells have been dug before."

"Not around here. I'm down a good seventy feet now and all I've hit is dry dirt and rocks."

"Seventy feet?" McCagg rubbed his jaw. "That's pretty damned deep. How far are you going to go before you give her up?"

"Oh, I dunno. Not much further."

McCagg went over to the tripod, glanced at two lengths of steel pipe on the ground beside it, and allowed, "Can't go much deeper without more drill pipe. And that costs money."

"Yeah. I'm prob'ly just throwin' money away."

The pipes had coupling threads on each end, and the pipe that stuck two feet out of the ground had a steel cap fitted into the end. It was something that could be pounded on with a sledge hammer without damaging the threads. A chain wrench lay beside the pipe, and McCagg guessed it was used to turn the drill pipe when pounding got nowhere. "What kind of a well point have you got?"

"Oh, it's, uh, the usual kind, you know."

"One of those cone-shaped ones with grooves for drilling?"

"Yeah, one of those."

"Well," McCagg said, "if you hit water it'll sure beat hauling it from the river."

"Yeah."

"Bill," McCagg turned to face him squarely. "I asked you once and I asked Dawnmarie and I still don't know. Maybe it's none of my business, but I'm curious as hell. Why were those four gunsels shooting at the Arbaughs' cabin? Something's going on around here. What?"

The young man looked up at him and squared his shoulders. "They're tryin' to drive us off our land, Ben. They said we ain't got a legal claim to it. I don't know nothin' about what's legal and what ain't, but this is our land and we're stayin'."

McCagg absorbed that, and he knew the younger man meant it.

Bill Kleagen's shoulders sagged again. "They don't scare me none. It's Dawnmarie I'm worried about. Sometimes I've got work to do out of sight of the house. I'm scared for her."

"Listen," McCagg felt his face getting warm, "Dawnmarie is my niece. She's more than that, she's like a baby sister. She's the only family I've got left. They ain't gonna hurt her."

For a moment he wondered whether he'd said the wrong thing, whether he was taking on trouble. The shooting kind of trouble. He didn't want any more shooting. But the moment passed, and he clenched his jaws and spoke through his teeth:

"No, by God, they ain't gonna hurt her."

wrench lay beside the pipe, and the other gun
we tote the drill rigs, when pounding you
well of a —

Chapter Three

He slept on the floor in the kitchen. They offered him their bed, but he refused it. "I've slept on the ground and on the floor so many times I'll feel right at home," he said. They made him a pallet of two quilts, two blankets and a pillow, and apologized for not having an extra bed. "I'll go borrow a cot from a neighbor tomorrow," Bill Kleagan said.

"Yes," said Dawnmarie. "If we keep you comfortable, maybe you'll stay."

"I don't know how long I'll stay, but don't go to any trouble. If I'm any trouble, I'll saddle up and git."

Dawnmarie frowned at him. "Don't even think of it. We're just so happy to have you. While you're here with us, we know you're not dodging outlaws' bullets somewhere."

What she said stuck in his mind after the lamps were blown out and the cabin was quiet. Not about being welcome, but about dodging bullets. Yeah, he'd done his share of that. First with the Rangers and then with Wells Fargo. And what did he have to show for it? Everything he owned was right here with him. One change of clothes, a sixgun, a horse and saddle. And a few gold eagles.

If it hadn't been for Doc Bridges he wouldn't have that.

Ben McCagg smiled to himself in the dark when he remembered Doc Bridges. He'd liked the old sonofabuck. So he was a con man whose only goal in life was to "skin the suckers," as he put it. McCagg remembered what Doc had once said about himself: "I don't drink, I don't chew, I don't cheat poor people and I pay my debts."

Well, he'd paid his debt to Ben McCagg, and more.

They'd met in Denver on a day when McCagg thought he was going to die. It wasn't a gunfight that almost killed him, it was Demon Rum, Chain Lightning, San Juan Paralyzer, Coffin Varnish, or whatever anyone wants to call it.

Just remembering it brought a groan from his throat. He'd awakened in a Denver flophouse, and tried to make himself understand that he only imagined seeing big black spiders on the walls and snakes under the cots. But for awhile the D.T.s had him, and he sat up on the cot afraid to move. His head felt like it was about to blow up, his hands were shaking and his mouth was full of dry sawdust. He had to have a shot of whiskey. Had to have it. But the first problem was getting past those snakes. He felt for his sixgun. The holster was empty. For a horrified moment he thought it had been stolen, but then he remembered putting it in his valise. Smart move. Anything not fastened to him would sure as hell be stolen in those flophouses. Thank the Lord he hadn't taken off his clothes when he'd crawled onto that cot. But where in hell was his valise?

"Oh, Lord," he groaned. He couldn't remember. Got to get up from here, get outside. Find a saloon.

A coughing fit gripped him until he thought he was going to strangle. Someone yelled, "Shurrup." He coughed, hacked, swallowed and finally got unsteadily on his feet. No need to pull on his boots. He'd never taken them off. Step around those snakes. Where did they go? He could have sworn there were snakes on the floor. His hat had been flattened from sleeping on it, and he attempted without success to re-shape it. His hands wouldn't do exactly what he wanted them to. Trying to steady them, he shoved them into his pockets. Then another horrified thought came to him. His pockets were empty. No money, no folding knife, no wallet, nothing. Even the written commendation he'd gotten from Wells Fargo was gone. Stolen right out of his pocket. Or maybe that was in his valise too. The leather valise he'd had when he landed in Denver. Where was it?

On the street, he was only vaguely aware of where he himself was. He staggered down the brick sidewalk with his hair in his face, his hat out of shape and his shirttail hanging out. He didn't realize how close he came to being run over by a two-horse team pulling a carriage, and he didn't hear the man swear at him. Staggering into the saloon, he stood at the bar, inhaled the odor of cheap whiskey and stale beer, and ordered whiskey. The bartender eyed him suspiciously. "Two bits in advance."

"I'm, uh, I need whiskey terrible bad," he mumbled.

But the bartender had seen too many crumbums on the streets of Denver. "No jawboning in here, mister," he said, turning away.

Outside again, he leaned against the brick building, feeling sicker than he had ever felt in his life. He was going to die. Just fall down right here and die. Boy, could he use a friend.

And along came Doc Bridges.

He saw the polished black boots and the gray striped pantlegs stop in front of him, but he didn't look up. "Say there, partner," a man said, "you look like you're about to spill yourself all over the sidewalk."

"Uhhh," he said.

"Are you busted?"

"Uhhh."

"A drink of whiskey might help, but you need more than that. If I give you two bits what will you do with it?"

"Uhhh."

"Come on. I'll stand you for a drink."

He looked up then, and saw a tall man, as tall as he was, with a neatly trimmed gray beard, a homburg hat, fingerlength black coat, and a cravat at his throat. "Come on," the man said.

Back inside the saloon, the bartender shrugged and filled a shot glass with whiskey. The bearded man paid. McCagg's hands shook so badly he spilled some of the whiskey before he got it to his mouth, and he gulped the rest of it. It burned all the way down and hit his stomach like a rock. "Ahh."

Now that he was able to get a better look at the bearded man, he couldn't decide whether he liked what he saw. "Thanks, mister. I'm obliged." His voice was still shaky, and he cleared his throat, trying to put some strength into it. "Maybe I can return the favor some day."

"What are you going to do now?"

That required some thinking, and no answer came to his mind. "I dunno." He shoved his hands into his pockets again to stop the shaking. "Need another shot of booze to clear my head and then maybe I can think."

The bearded one nodded at the bartender and the shot glass was refilled. McCagg managed to get it all to his lips this time. It felt good going down and settling in his stomach. He could feel strength coming back into his legs and arms.

"A man can become addicted to that," the bearded one said.

"Yeah. I'm afraid . . . maybe I am."

"You're Benjamin McCagg, aren't you."

"Huh? Yeah. How'd you know?"

"I saw you on the street last night and I recognized you. I was there when Mr. Robert Carns gave you that commendation, and I read about you in the newspapers. They said you shot it out with some would-be train robbers and saved a gold shipment."

"Uh, yeah."

The bartender had been leaning his hairy arms on the bar and gazing idly out the big dirty glass window. Now he suddenly straightened up and studied McCagg's face. "Are you him? I read about that too."

"Yes sir," the bearded man answered. "this is Benjamin

McCagg."

"Well hell, if I'd knowed that, I'd have poured you one for free. Here." He reached for the bottle again.

"No, wait a minute," the bearded man said. "Mr. McCagg, are you sure you want another drink? You'd better think about it."

"Uh, well . . ."

"You're sober now, McCagg. Another shot and you'll be drunk again. Drunk and broke."

It was a tough decision to make. The two drinks had helped. He felt better and stronger. His hands weren't shaking so much. Broke, though. If he got drunk again he'd be on his ass for sure. But damn, another one would make him feel even better. All he could say was, "Uhh."

"I'll buy you some breakfast if you'll pass up that drink. Think about it."

"Uhh."

"Come on. There's a cafe around the corner. Some coffee and ham and eggs will do you a lot more good than another shot of whiskey."

He was right. No doubt about it. Hot coffee would taste good. But the ham and eggs could wait. His stomach wouldn't appreciate that. Yeah, some coffee would be good. Still, that whiskey would go down mighty good too. "Uhh."

"Mr. McCagg, we just met, but I'm talking to you like a friend. Believe me, you don't want another drink."

"Well, uh . . ."

"I'll pay for some breakfast." The bearded man's eyes were serious. He was sincere.

"Well, uh, all right." He couldn't take his eyes off the whiskey bottle until they were out the door.

Bill Kleagen was up at dawn, and Ben McCagg rolled out too. He didn't want his niece to come into the kitchen before he got dressed. Outside in the chilly morning air, he coughed and sputtered and wished he had a shot of whiskey, then was glad he didn't. Kleagen used a can of grain to entice a shorthorn cow to come to him. He tied her to a post and fed her the grain. Then he sat on a one-legged stool under her right flank and milked her. The cow kicked at him twice, but he was holding the milk pail between his knees, and she didn't succeed at kicking it away from him. When he was finished he poured half of the milk into another bucket, gave it to the cow's calf, and untied the cow.

"She gives enough milk for us and the calf too," he said. "We had two milk cows, but we only need one and I sold the other'n to the Arbaughs."

McCagg didn't know what else to say so he allowed, "Every family ought to have a milk cow. Nothing's better than fresh milk and butter." He chuckled. "I've worked for cow outfits that had several thousand cows and didn't know what fresh milk looked like."

Chuckling with him, Kleagen said, "We've got seven cows, but this is the only one I can milk. Them longhorns, you'd have to throw 'em down and tie 'em to get any milk out of 'em."

"And then it would taste like cactus juice."

"It'd prob'ly make you as wild as they are."

That brought another vision of a whiskey bottle to McCagg's mind, and his mouth went dry. He shook his head to chase away the vision.

Breakfast was pancakes with butter and thick blackstrap molasses. And coffee. Strong black coffee. Dawnmarie was bright and cheerful. She was especially pretty this morning with her oval face and slim figure. McCagg had to grin inwardly when he remembered her as a child. She never could keep from tearing her dress, and she never could keep her face clean. Always skinning her elbows. Always following him around asking questions about everything she saw, and always in his way.

"What are you grinning about, Uncle Benjamin?"

"Oh, just remembering. Good memories."

26

"It was wonderful, wasn't it? It was for me, anyway. Growing up on the ranch. Grandma and Grandpa McCagg were wonderful to me and so were you, Uncle Benjamin."

"Yeah." He ate silently as he remembered how her mother and dad, his older brother, were killed by a bunch of renegade Apaches, and how his folks had taken her in when she was only two — rather she was one year old and coming two — and raised her as their own. He was uncle and big brother in one package, but she always called him Uncle.

After breakfast, they went outside where Bill Kleagen resumed working on his well drilling. Dawnmarie built a fire under the big black kettle and heated water for clothes washing. Kleagen pounded on the steel cap that was fitted into the end of the pipe until it was ground level. He pounded on it with a twelve pound sledge. The he lifted off the cap and screwed another steel pipe into the top of that one. McCagg helped him pull a wagon up to the pipe where he could stand in it and pound on the top of the pipe. It was hard work.

When the well point hit rock and pounding got nowhere, Kleagen fitted his chain wrench to the pipe and turned it, walked around and around it. McCagg helped with that. Slowly, the well point ground its way through the rock, and Kleagen resumed his pounding.

"It's prob'ly all for nothing," Kleagen grunted, "but a man's gotta try." He pounded. "It's pure foolishness, I know."

Dawnmarie was wringing wash water out of a bedsheet when she looked up and saw riders.

"Bill," she said, apprehension in her voice, "someone's coming."

Chapter Four

The pounding stopped, and Kleagen squinted to the west. McCagg squinted too. "Two of 'em," Kleagen said. "Looks like that sheriff. Yeah, it's the sheriff."

No one spoke as the two rode up at a trot. Both men had silver stars pinned to their shirt pockets. Finally, one said, "Mornin'." He was plump, with a rider's high-heeled boots, a round red face, a handlebar moustache, and a dirty gray flat-brim hat. He looked like a cattleman.

"Mornin'," Kleagen said.

"Are you William Kleagen?"

"Yes sir, I am."

"I'm Sheriff Martin Gantt, Mr. Kleagen. I, uh, I'm afraid I've got some bad news."

"Yeah?" Bill Kleagen stood still and waited for the sheriff to speak further. McCagg said nothing, just stood with his hands on his hips. Sheriff Gantt looked him over carefully then turned his attention back to Kleagen.

"Fact is, Mr. Kleagen, a gent name of . . ." Gantt took a sheet of paper from a shirt pocket, unfolded it and read it . . . "O'Brien has filed a claim on this half section. The judge said he is entitled to it, and you've got to leave."

A gasp came from Dawnmarie. "The judge? What judge?"

"County Judge Clarence J. Topah."

"Have you got a court order?" Dawnmarie asked.

"No, ma'am. But the judge said he'll issue one. I came out to let you know what's happenin'."

"May I see that paper?" she asked.

"Shore, ma'am. I'm right sorry about this." Without dismounting, he handed her the sheet of paper. McCagg went up beside her and read over her shoulder.

"It's a permit under the Amended Homestead Act of 1864," Dawnmarie said as she read. "It has the land surveyor's description. And it names a Timothy O'Brien as claimant." Looking up at the sheriff, she asked, "Are you sure this is for our land?"

"Yes, ma'am. They've got a map at the county clerk's office. This territory has been surveyed by the U.S. Government, and there's no record of anybody named Kleagen having a legal claim on any of it."

"Then how did you know our name and where to find this half section?"

"Well, ma'am," the sheriff shifted in his saddle, "it's common knowledge that you folks have been here for a couple of years now, right where the river turns south, and this Mr. O'Brien knows where the land is he filed on."

"Oh, he does, does he." Dawnmarie was getting red in the face, and her voice was turning hard. "He has it all figured out. How to take advantage of us."

"I know how you feel, Mrs. Kleagen. I'm just doing my duty. This is a part of my job I don't like."

No one spoke for a moment, and the sheriff added, "Like I said, this O'Brien gent can get a court order."

"And then what?" McCagg spoke for the first time.

The sheriff's eyes passed over him again, paused on the Smith & Wesson then went up to the high-cheeked face and the new Stetson. "Well, I'm, uh, s'posed to order you off, uh . . ." He looked down for a moment, then looked up again. "They've got the right to run you off."

"Who?" McCagg was staring hard at the sheriff.

"This O'Brien and his pals."

"There's more than one?"

"I didn't catch your name," the sheriff said.

"McCagg. Benjamin McCagg. Mrs. Kleagen is my niece."

"Oh. Well, yeah, there's more than one. It seems like a bunch of them micks come down from Denver and started claiming some homesteads around here including two that ain't been recorded proper."

"A bunch of them, huh?" McCagg looked over the sheriff's head at the western sky, thinking.

"Seems like there's four or five." Martin Gantt squinted at McCagg. "Ain't I heard your name someplace?"

With a shrug of his shoulders, McCagg answered, "Not that I know of. You say they're pals?"

" 'Pears that way."

"Have they got a leader?"

"Now, that I don't know. They do seem to know what they're doing."

With the sheriff's apology, Dawnmarie's attitude had changed. "Won't you gentlemen dismount? Would you like a drink of water? I can put the coffee pot on."

A sigh came from Sheriff Gantt as he stepped stiff-legged from his saddle. The other man stayed horseback. "That's sure nice of you, Mrs. Kleagen, but we don't want to bother you none. I'm sorry I have to be the one to bring you the bad news."

"We've been expecting it," she said. "Mr. O'Brien and some of his pals have been here. Only a week ago. They . . . weren't very nice."

"They're boozers, and they don't look like farmers or stockmen or anybody that'd work a homestead. But they knew how to record a claim on it."

McCagg asked, "Who else's homestead have they filed on?"

"The Arbaughs, and they claimed some half sections that nobody else has claimed."

"Well . . ." Dawnmarie was puzzled. "If they're not farmers, what do they want with the land?"

30

Shaking his head, the sheriff answered, "That's something else I don't know. All I know is the judge said they did it legal."

"And Bill and my niece didn't?" McCagg directed his question at the sheriff, then at Dawnmarie. She glanced at her husband and didn't answer. Bill Kleagen looked down at his boots. He hadn't spoken a word since he'd greeted the sheriff.

They were quiet until the sheriff spoke again, conversationally. "Looks like you're drilling a well."

"Naw," McCagg said. "Just experimenting."

"It's been tried before. Old Man Jackson over near El Moro dug down sixty feet and didn't find a drop."

"Yeah, well."

"Anyhow," the sheriff mounted his horse, "I just came out to let you know what the deal is. I hope there's no trouble."

For the first time, the other lawman spoke. "If they don't git, there will be." The inscription on his badge read Deputy Sheriff. He was wide in the shoulders with a thick neck and smooth-shaven face.

"Now wait a minute, Joel," the sheriff said, "we don't threaten honest folks."

Joel was staring at McCagg, and his eyes were not friendly. "I'm just tellin' 'em."

"We'll go now, " Sheriff Gantt said, turning his horse around. "I wish you folks the best of luck." Joel followed, but continued staring at McCagg until his horse was turned around and he had to look ahead.

Dawnmarie and Benjamin McCagg watched them go, but Bill Kleagen walked away. He walked by himself to the arroyo and disappeared down the path to the river.

When McCagg looked over at his niece, he saw she was near tears. "Dawn . . ." He didn't know what to say. She hurried into the cabin. He started to follow, hesitated, wondering whether she'd want to talk to him, then went after her. She was his baby sister. They'd talked about a lot of things. Personal things included.

31

She was sitting at the kitchen table, hands clasped in front of her, fingers twitching. When she heard him come in, she looked up. Tears were in her eyes. "It's my fault, Uncle Benjamin. It's not Bill's fault. Bill is not to blame."

"For what, Dawn?" He sat opposite her.

"For . . . for anything. He's a good man, honest, hard-working, caring, considerate. He's not to blame for anything."

"I know that."

"Then you won't blame him for . . . for not doing what I should have done?"

"If you say so."

"It's my fault. I should have gone with him. To the land office. I knew, I mean I should have known. He has his pride, but I thought he'd . . . oh, I should have done it."

"Are you saying, Dawn, that this half section is not recorded in Bill's name?"

"That's right. It isn't. I thought it was. Not until that O'Brien and his cohorts came around did I go to the land office and check on it." She wiped tears from her eyes with the palms of her hands. "He built this house. He . . . he did all this work."

"I don't get it, Dawn. Didn't he go to the land office and sign the papers?"

"Uncle Benjamin." There was pain in her face. "Grandma McCagg taught you to read and write. She taught me too. She made sure we went to school. I've always been a reader, and you like to read too. But Bill . . . Bill was a hired hand, an orphan like me. He wasn't Grandma McCagg's family. No one sent him to school."

"Oh."

"It's my fault. I saw Bill go in the land office, but I didn't go with him. He . . . he didn't deliberately lie, Uncle Benjamin, but he had his pride. He didn't sign. He became embarrassed and left without signing. I assumed he signed an X, which is perfectly legal, but he didn't sign at all. I didn't know until that O'Brien came around. He told me then. He's terribly ashamed and embarrassed. It's my fault. I should have gone with him and signed for him."

"Oh. Hmm. Well, ain't there, uh, I don't know much about the law, but ain't there such a thing as squatters' rights?"

"Apparently not. Not in this territory. Not on land that has been opened for homesteading."

"Hmm."

"There are others. Men who believed squatters' rights would become homesteaders' rights, and failed to do the paper work. Some of them are like Bill and can't read or write, and some of them just didn't think it was necessary."

"Uh-huh. And now some gunsels from Denver who know the law are trying to cash in on their labor."

"That appears to be it." She wrung her hands. "I had no hint that we were here illegally until O'Brien came around and threatened me. Bill was working somewhere out of sight of the house. I should have suspected. Some strange men were here last summer. I didn't see them. Bill told me about seeing them, first in the river bottom, then on the banks, looking through a spy glass on a tripod, looking north between those two low ridges. They wore campaign hats. When Bill asked what they were doing they were very secretive. Polite, but secretive."

"This O'Brien threatened you?"

"He said we get out or there would be violence. I asked Bill to go to the sheriff, but I'm afraid he has no faith in the law."

He studied the table top, studied her hands, his hands. Her hands were rough and red from the work. He cleared his throat. "I've been an officer of the law and I know the law ain't—isn't—always fair. But I can't believe . . ."

He was interrupted by hammering outside. Standing, he went to the door, looked out and saw Bill Kleagen pounding on top of the pipe, driving it a fraction of an inch at a time into the ground. He went out.

"I take it you're not planning to leave."

"No," Kleagen grunted between swings with the sledge.

33

Then he stopped, let the hammer drop, and turned to face McCagg. "I'm too damned stubborn to let 'em run me off. But . . . Ben, I wish you'd do somethin' for me. For me and Dawnmarie. I wish you'd take her to town and keep her there 'til this . . . I don't want her to get hurt. I'm worried about her."

"Well, sure, Bill, if . . ." Again he was interrupted.

"I heard that," Dawnmarie said from the doorway. "If you're staying, I'm staying. I can shoot. Uncle Benjamin taught me how to shoot. And we've got your pistol and that old rifle. I'm staying."

"But, Dawn, honey, I . . ."

"That is that." She stepped back inside and shut the door.

The two men looked at each other, a worry frown on the younger man's face. Ben McCagg ran a hand over his jaw, pushed his hat back and scratched his thinning hair. Then he smiled. "She's a McCagg, Bill. Us — we — McCaggs are so stubborn we'd make a balky mule look plumb agreeable. The last thing I want is shooting. I've had enough of that to last me a hundred years."

"But if you folks will have me, I'll stick around too."

Chapter Five

It was nearly noon when McCagg caught and saddled his sorrel horse. "I'm going to the land office and the county clerk's office and maybe I'll go see that judge too. I'll try to find out exactly what kind of jackpot we're in the middle of here, then maybe we can figure out what to do about it."

"I'll fix some dinner pretty soon, Uncle Benjamin. As soon as I wring out this tubful."

"If I'm going to see everybody today, I'd better get going."

Bill Kleagen was pounding on the steel cap, swinging his heavy sledge. He looked up as McCagg rode past. "Hurry back, Ben. We'll wait supper for you."

"No, don't wait. If I don't get to see everybody today I might stay in town tonight and try to catch them in the morning."

"Uncle Benjamin."

He reined up a moment.

"They've shot at houses without caring whether they hit anyone inside. They're dangerous. Don't risk your life for us."

Grinning a wry grin, he said, "Don't worry about that. I've dodged all the lead I care to."

As he rode he looked to the north and saw the pitiful plowed field, a field of what was supposed to be wheat. Only a few inches of green showed above the ground. Weeds were outgrowing the crop. "Wouldn't feed a family of jackrabbits," he muttered to himself. Glancing at the cloudless sky, he continued muttering, "Only a fool would try to grow a crop around here. Hell, this ain't farm country. No man can make a living on three hundred and twenty acres of dry dirt. Prob'ly take sixty acres to graze one cow and calf, and with water so scarce a herd of cattle would probably hang around the river and starve. No wonder the government is giving it away."

Another look at the sky, and, "Probably colder than a witch's tit in the winter and drier than a piece of hell in the summer. This half section ain't worth fighting for. But like Dawnmarie said, some men would go to hell for a piece of land they could call their own."

Silently, Dawnmarie was glad she didn't have a family of four or more to wash, cook and keep house for. By noon she was tired, but she had the bedsheets and clothes for her and her husband washed, rinsed and hung on a line of smooth wire stretched from a corner of the cabin to a tall post Bill had set in the ground. Her one remaining good gingham dress was clean, but would have to be ironed. That meant putting two of the flat irons on the stove to heat, spreading the dress over the kitchen table, and using the irons one at a time to press the wrinkles out. That would make the dress good for one trip to town. A ride to town and back in the wagon would leave it dirty and wrinkled. No use ironing Bill's denim pants and cotton shirts. They would look good for only a couple of hours anyway, not much longer than it would take to iron them.

She dumped the rinse water out of the tub and straightened her back with a small groan. Bill, she saw, had finally pounded the pipe down close to ground level. He had one more pipe to go and then he would have to give up. The pipe cost money and they had just enough money to buy groceries for the rest of the summer. If they hadn't had an extra milk cow to sell to the Arbaughs they would be broke. Both had avoided the subject of what they would do when that money was gone, but they would have to talk about it, make some plans. She dreaded it. Bill would be heartbroken when he had to admit, finally, that they couldn't make a living here.

Her garden helped. She had some potatoes, carrots, lettuce and turnips growing. But Bill had to haul water by the barrelful up the arroyo from the river, and it took a lot of water to irrigate even a small plot. Glancing at the sky, she silently prayed for rain, but she didn't expect her prayers to be answered. It would be too late for the wheat anyway. It was dying, and the weeds had taken over. No use cultivating a field that wouldn't grow a crop.

"I'll fix some dinner, Bill," she said. "Can I help you with that?"

"No, this is the easy part," he said, glancing up at her. "It won't take long and then I'll be in."

He had a length of twine in his hands, heavy twine with an iron bolt tied to the end of it. He began lowering the twine down the center of the pipe, hoping that when he pulled it back up there would be moisture on the bolt.

Dawnmarie went into the house. Now, she thought, is the time. Now, while Uncle Benjamin is in town, is the time to talk it over and make a decision. She dreaded it, but a decision had to be made.

The sorrel horse had been in the El Moro livery barn before, but still it had its head up and its ears twitching as it stepped warily inside, snorting at every unusual sight and smell. When it balked at the sight of a wheelbarrow loaded with manure, McCagg grinned. "Come on, young feller, you've seen plenty of that stuff. It doesn't nowise resemble a bear."

"I'll give you forty bucks for 'im, cash money," the barn owner said. He was a short man in bib overalls, lace-up shoes and a bill cap on his head. "Gold money. None a that government paper."

Still grinning, McCagg said, "That's what you offered two days ago."

"Forty two. How's that? That's more'n I ever offered for a horse before."

"If I sell him I'll have to buy another. I wasn't cut out for walking."

"Trade you a good horse, and give you cash to boot. How's that?"

"Naw. I'll pay you two bits silver for enough hay to feed him today and maybe tonight. How's that?"

"Hay's gettin' scarce. Have to haul it from up there on the Picketwire."

"How much?"

"Got to make it forty cents a day and night."

McCagg unsaddled the horse and led it into a stall. "Don't get to liking this, young feller," he said to the horse. "When we get down to Texas you might never see another barn."

With the livery owner paid, he hitched his new wool pants up higher on his lean hips and walked, spurs chinging, out onto the street, looking for the land office.

El Moro didn't have any sidewalks yet, just dirt streets and dirt paths beaten along the storefronts. It was a railroad town, platted by the Denver and Rio Grande, but the cattlemen and homesteaders found it a handy place to buy supplies, and merchants found it a good place to attract customers. So did the saloon owners. But it wasn't the boom town the railroad builders had hoped it would be. They deliberately tried to ignore the older town of Trinidad to the south, seeing an opportunity to start their own town and sell lots on land given to them by the U.S. Government. That scheme had worked up north at Colorado Springs, another town built by the railroaders who bypassed Colorado City. Up there the new town was rapidly outgrowing the older community. But here it wasn't working so well, possibly because the railroad's rival, the Santa Fe, was building towns all along its route to Trinidad from the east.

Still, the railroad financiers used their considerable clout with the politicians in Denver and got El Moro designated the county seat of the newly created Trinchera County. A courthouse was under construction, being built with bricks and green lumber hauled from the refractory and the sawmills at Trinidad. Meanwhile, the county offices were scattered around town, set up wherever vacant rooms could be found.

The U.S. Land Office sign was easy to see, and McCagg stopped there first. Closed. But he found the county clerk's office in the same two-room, clapboard building. "Howdy," he said, stepping through the connecting door.

"Yes sir," said a small, thin man with a green eyeshade and red suspenders. He had been bending over a desk, turning pages of a book that was almost as big as the desktop.

"I, uh, would like to check the validity of some homestead claims east of here, along the Picketwire."

"Do you have a legal description?"

"No. But I can probably pick them out on a map. They're on both ends of a big bend in the river."

The little man picked up the book, which was about as much as he could carry, and lugged it to a long table near the door. "That land has all been surveyed by the U.S. Government, and I keep records of who has recorded claims on it. None of it that was opened up for homesteading has been proved up on yet. It was only opened up three years ago."

"Well, uh." McCagg flipped through a few pages, recognized nothing. "Could you tell me which pages show the river bend about eight miles northeast?"

"You're not thinking of homesteading over there?" The little man's eyebrows went up under the eyeshade.

"I might be. Why?"

"I don't know." He shook his head. "Way I hear it, homesteaders have starved out over there, and still there seems to be a lot of interest in that territory."

"There is, huh? Do you know who is showing interest?"

39

"A Mr. O'Brien has been in here looking over these maps and surveys and writing down a lot of information."

"Any idea why?"

Shrugging, the clerk answered, "No idee a-tall. He wouldn't say anything. Just studied the book and wrote it down."

"Can you pick out the half section claimed by William Kleagen?"

"Sure." He turned four pages and tapped a page with a forefinger. "Right here. I know right where to look 'cause that's one of the homesteads this O'Brien was interested in."

"I sure do appreciate you telling me all this, Mr. uh . . ."

"Jones. Orville J. Jones. I'm, the county clerk of Trinchera County."

"I sure do appreciate your help, Mr. Jones, and I need more information, such as, does William Kleagen have legal right to his half section?"

"Well, sir, I'm not sure. I make up my maps from the Land Agent's records, and I, uh, with information from his books I recorded that territory as unclaimed. But, uh, now I hear that Mr. Kleagen and a Mr. Arbaugh have made some improvements and are claiming it. I've also been told that their claims aren't legal."

"Who told you that?"

"I got the information from the U.S. Land Agent, a Mr. Bruce Thiede, and he said he received a note to that effect from Judge Topah."

"A note? Not a judicial order, or anything like that?"

"No, but if the judge went to the trouble of writing a note, he could write a legal order."

"Hmm. Yeah, he could at that. A judge can do almost anything."

McCagg studied the floor a moment, then, "I know you've worked hard, Mr. Jones, getting the records straight about who owns what land. It's a job that has to be done. The citizens of this county are in your debt."

Orville Jones wasn't used to getting compliments, and his face turned red. He didn't know what to say. McCagg turned to leave, paused, "One more question, do you know where I can find this Judge Topah?"

"He holds court in a building right behind the Curly Wolf saloon. I don't know whether he's there now."

"I'm much obliged to you, Mr. Jones."

The Curly Wolf saloon. He remembered seeing that place. He remembered how much he had wanted to go in and try some of that Taos Lightning he'd heard about. He also remembered that he didn't want to. When he walked past the saloon, the door was wide open and the odor of whiskey and beer was strong. Men laughed inside. Haw-haw. Ben McCagg tugged his hat down tighter and with all the will power he could muster walked past without turning his head. Once past, he cut through a vacant lot to the alley and saw a log cabin with a sloppily painted sign that read: "Trinchera County Court. Judge Clarence J. Topah, presiding."

He'd seen county courts before. Too damned many of them. He knew the judges were well-fed by collecting fines from drunks. Drunks the lawmen brought in. Some of the money collected went into the county coffers, but some of it went into the pockets of the judges and the town marshals. Arresting drunks was profitable. And the damned judges had the gall to lecture the citizens about their responsibilities.

Justices of the Peace, they were called in Texas. "Huh," McCagg snorted out loud. Justices, hell.

Oh well, they weren't all bad. Like lawmen, there were good ones and bad ones. McCagg had been a lawman and was proud of it. The judge deserved to be treated with respect.

He tried the door. Locked.

Hell's hooks. He walked a half-block before he found someone to ask. "Pardon me, do you know where I can find Judge

41

Topah?"

"Yonder." The man in railroader's overalls and a bill cap pointed to a frame house a block north. It was the only house on the block.

"Obliged."

Spurs chinging, he walked up to the front door and knocked. His knock was answered by a plump woman wearing a long, lacy apron. Her gray hair was tied behind her head in a knot. "I beg your pardon, ma'am. I'm looking for Judge Topah, and I was told he lives here."

"Wait right there," she said, closing the door in his face.

He waited. He stood on first one foot then the other. Finally the door opened again and an overfed middle-aged man with a neatly trimmed gray beard stood in the door. "Yes?"

"Judge Topah, my name is Benjamin McCagg, and I'm related to William Kleagen who is homesteading about eight miles northeast on the Picketwire. I understand you have ruled that the homestead is not legally his. Would you please tell me . . ."

The judge interrupted, "My court will be in session at eight o'clock tomorrow morning. If you wish a hearing, I suggest you appear before me then."

"Well, sir, I'm not asking for a hearing right now, I'm only trying to find out what the situation is."

"Do you have legal counsel?" Judge Topah had thick gray eyebrows and thick gray hair that grew low on his forehead.

"No sir, I only . . ."

"If you have a legal question, I suggest you retain legal counsel."

"Well, sir, I . . ."

The judge was accustomed to having the last word. "My court will be in session at eight o'clock tomorrow morning. Good day." Again the door was closed in his face.

Chapter Six

"Well, hell," McCagg muttered. "That's fine. Just fine." He walked back to the street. "I haven't learned a damned thing, and it looks like I'll have to hire a lawyer to even get to talk to the damned judge. A public servant. Huh. Probably serves himself more than anybody else."

Back on the main street, he wondered what to do next. He wondered if there was a lawyer in El Moro. To find out he walked the two blocks of businesses, past two general stores, a laundry, a blacksmith shop, a barber shop, the Curly Wolf. He crossed the street to keep from passing in front of the saloon. No lawyer sign. Probably have to go to Trinidad to find a lawyer. Maybe all the way to Pueblo. It would cost a month's pay to get a lawyer to come to El Moro, look over the land records and represent Bill Kleagen in court. And then there was no guarantee it would do any good.

Well, it had to be done. There seemed to be no other way. A few years ago land disputes were settled with gunfire. But Ben McCagg had had enough of that. Going to court was better. Supposed to be, anyhow. A wry grin turned up the corners of his mouth under the moustache. Better for the lawyers.

He decided to go back to the Kleagen homestead and tell them his plan. He'd pay for the lawyer himself. Dawnmarie would object and her husband would too, but this had to be settled and he couldn't leave until it was. They could pay him back some day.

With that in mind he walked past the Curly Wolf without seeing where he was going. The odor hit him in the face like a damp, smelly rag, and he stopped. He was thirsty. He could spit cotton. A shot of whiskey would sure go down good. Naw, Dawnmarie would smell it on his breath. A beer? Sure. A glass of cold beer was what he needed. No harm in that. He went in.

After being outside in the bright sunlight, he had to stop in the doorway a moment and let his eyes get accustomed to the dim interior. He made out a short bar that was nothing more than a long twelve-inch plank. A row of whiskey bottles and a beer keg sat on another plank behind the bar, and a man with muttonchop sideburns and a dirty white apron around his middle stood between the two planks.

"Draw one," he said to the barman. Blinking, he looked around the room. A half-dozen men sat at plain wooden tables, staring at him. The floor was wood, splintery, looking like it had never been swept. A glass of beer was set in front of him, and he picked it up. It was warm.

"Ten cents. Three for two bits."

McCagg paid and took a swallow. It would never take the place of whiskey. Out of the corner of his right eye he saw a man get up from one of the tables and walk his way. He took another swallow.

"McCagg, ain't it?" It was the deputy sheriff named Joel.

"One and the same."

"Have you moved off that piece of land yet?" Joel's voice was threatening.

McCagg tried to ignore him. "Nope."

"I want you off in twenty-four hours. Get it? I'm goin' out there tomorrow and youall had better be gone."

"We won't be." Another swallow.

"Then we'll bury you there."

"We? Who is we?"

44

"Me, myself and I."

This was leading to something McCagg didn't like. This was the way a lot of gunfights started. Men had died over conversations that started like this. He decided to leave. After he finished his beer, that is. This time he picked up the beer mug with his left hand, leaving his right hand hanging free near the butt of the .45. He drained the mug, set it down, wiped his moustache with the back of his hand and turned toward the door. He didn't get far.

The deputy grabbed his right arm and spun him around, muttering, "No goddamn squatter turns his back on . . ."

He shut his mouth so quick he bit his own tongue as he felt the bore of the Smith & Wesson pressing the end of his nose. The gun had appeared from nowhere. Just appeared.

Joel's eyes crossed as he tried to look down at it. He gulped and stepped back a step. The gun followed him. His eyes moved up to McCagg's face. The face he saw was as hard as granite. The eyes in the face were cold. "Don't twitch a muscle," the face said. Joel gulped again and froze.

For a long moment they stood that way. No one spoke. No one moved. The only sound was the deputy's quick nervous breathing. Then, finally, McCagg lowered the .45. With his eyes locked onto the deputy's eyes, he let the hammer down and holstered the gun.

"Tell you what, Mr. Deputy Sheriff," he said, trying to keep menace out of his voice, "you go on about your business and I'll go on about mine."

"Fair enough." But the words didn't come from Joel, they came from behind McCagg.

Sheriff Martin Gantt stepped around McCagg and faced him. "I was just about to walk through the door and I saw what happened. You threatened an officer of the law, but it looked to me like he started it." To his deputy, he said, "Go on, Joel. Go on home now. I don't want to see you again tonight. Savvy?"

Joel's face was still white. He gulped again and headed for

the door with rapid steps.

Sheriff Gantt was studying McCagg's face. "I don't know where I heard your name before, but I heard it somewhere. One thing's for sure, you're a professional with a gun."

Voice dry, McCagg said, "I've survived where some men didn't."

"Well, I'll tell you something, Mr. McCagg. It doesn't matter how fast you are with a gun, you start shoving folks around and you'll end up in jail. Or dead. If I can't arrest you by myself, I can get plenty of help."

"I didn't come here to shove anybody around."

"Why did you come here?"

"To visit my niece and her husband."

"And how long are you planning to stay?"

It occurred to McCagg that how long he stayed was none of the sheriff's business. But why antagonize the man? "I don't know. It appears they're having some trouble over who owns what piece of land. I intend to help every way I can."

"Even if it means shooting, huh?"

"Yeah."

A pause while the sheriff digested that, then, "Well, you're lucky — everybody's lucky — I heard and saw what happened just now. Joel's a little hot-headed."

McCagg silently agreed with him. He'd known too many hot-headed lawmen, men who were so full of authority they just couldn't contain it. But the sheriff didn't seem to be that kind, and McCagg kept this mouth shut.

"Well, nobody was hurt so go ahead and have another beer, but keep that pistol in its cradle." Martin Gantt left.

Without thinking, McCagg looked over at the barman and spoke one word: "Whiskey."

The decision they had to reach was even more complicated now. Bill Kleagen was excited, almost as excited as he was when he'd picked a half-section and declared it his. His and

Dawnmarie's. Now he'd done something else, something they said couldn't be done. But what the hell to do next?

"I wish Uncle Benjamin would get back," Dawnmarie said as she cleaned up after the noon meal. "We ought to hitch up the team and go to town ourselves, Bill, instead of leaving it up to Uncle Benjamin to find out what's happening."

"Aw, Dawn, you know I cain't. I'd have to stand back and let you do all the readin' and writin' and talkin'."

"You can read. You're getting better all the time. And you can sign your name now."

"Yeah, but I cain't read fast enough. They'd know. If they watched me tryin' to read they'd know."

He was right, and she couldn't argue about it. She had been teaching him, but he was still slow. Painfully slow. He was trying, reading a little every night, and he really was getting better. But if they went to town, to the land office and to see the judge, she would have to do the reading — and the talking — while he stood there getting more and more embarrassed. It was good that Uncle Benjamin had come along. He could do it for them. She wished he would return, and she hoped he had good news.

"How do you go about borrowin' money, Dawn? From a bank, I mean. The McCaggs borrowed from a bank to buy land and cattle. How do you do it?"

That brought a wry grin to her face, and a dry chuckle. "It was easy. Too easy. That's why the McCaggs don't have a red cent now. That and Grandpa McCagg's death. He borrowed so much and agreed to pay so much interest that after he died Grandma McCagg had to sell the ranch. Uncle Benjamin was gone from home then looking for adventure."

"Yeah, but sometimes, if you borrow for the right things, it pays off."

"Sometimes it does. However, Grandma McCagg, if she were alive, might not agree with that."

"We're in a real pickle, ain't we, Dawn?"

"What do you think we should do, Bill?"

47

Shaking his head sadly, he allowed, "We ain't givin' up. As long as I've got two good hands, I'll find a way. Maybe we can move to Trinidad for a while and I can get a job in the coal mines or on the railroad. That'd give us enough money to buy some pump rods and some more drill pipe. And it'd keep us eatin'."

"It might come to that. We've got another year to prove up on this land, and if I understand the law it doesn't say we have to have a harvest, just cultivate a crop. We can plow up the wheat and plant another crop. Who knows, next spring it might rain."

Bill Kleagen got to his feet. "That's what we'll do, then." He went to her and put his arms around her from behind. "I ain't quittin', Dawn, honey. Don't give up on me. Please."

Turning, she put her arms around his neck. "Wouldn't think of it."

The Curly Wolf didn't nowise resemble the pleasure palaces of Denver. There was one saloon in Denver — McCagg couldn't remember the name of it — where the bar was of polished oak and the mirror behind the bar was thirty-five feet long. The walls were covered with what looked like red velvet and pictures of naked and near-naked ladies hung on the walls. No common ordinary lamp shades there. Nothing but the finest etched glass. The place was so elegant that soft cotton cloths were attached to the bar for wiping beer foam off gentlemen's moustaches, and steel mesh covered the floor near the bar to keep the floor from getting slippery with spilled beer.

That was where McCagg had started his drinking spree, his high lonesome bout with Anheuser's, which went from there to Kentucky bourbon, which went downhill from there to Forty Rod, so-called because it could kill at that distance. He must have covered all of Denver, spending his Wells Fargo bonus money, before he woke up in the flophouse flat broke.

Doc Bridges probably saved his life, rest his soul. A crook? Naw. A con man? Sure, but an honest one. After meeting Doc Bridges, Ben McCagg believed there was such a thing as an honest con man. Doc's mission in life was "a fair and legitimate business," he had often said, and McCagg believed him.

"Why," Doc once said over a steak supper in one of the best restaurants in Denver, "if you could see men as I see them, surrounded by the glistening pile on the counter or table which they hope so soon to be theirs; if you could see the cold, selfish, cruel glitter in their eyes you wouldn't hold it against me for skinning them."

McCagg listened as he ate.

"Why, anyone who thinks I am a crook has only to see the keno and faro rooms rob poor laboring men. Many of the losers come to me for help and I always help them."

Doc Bridges was such a good talker that he talked McCagg into helping him skin a sucker, and damned if McCagg didn't enjoy it. The sucker was a Congressman from Kansas who came to Denver to patronize the palaces of pleasure far away from his wife and his constituents. He spent taxpayers' money freely, as freely, or even more so, than McCagg had spent his bonus money.

It was the legal lotteries in Colorado and the state-operated policy shops that gave Doc Bridges the idea. His scheme needed three men and a rented hole-in-the-wall office. The third man was a well-dressed, well-groomed gent introduced as Dave. McCagg didn't think he could do his part. He'd never put on an act in his life. But as soon as he saw the fat-faced, cigar-smoking, corn fed, puffed up Congressman, he fell into the role as naturally as a professional actor.

Dave started it. He accidentally-on-purpose met the Congressman in the lobby of his hotel, and somehow the sucker agreed to accompany Dave to a policy shop to see if he had a winning ticket. On the way they met McCagg, who had shucked his gun, but held onto a ticket which he declared was

49

a winner. He had figured out how to beat the game, McCagg said. He couldn't lose.

Inside the shop, behind the counter, was Doc Bridges, frowning at anyone who thought he could win with anything other than pure luck.

"We'll just see about that," McCagg said, producing his ticket.

It paid fifty bucks. Dave's ticket was a loser.

"Hah," said McCagg. "I can do it again, too," and he did. "Now," he said, "what I need is a pile of money. If I keep winning these little pots, the state is gonna get wise to me and change the rules. I've got to win a pile before they get onto me. Anybody want to lend me some money? I'll split the pot. Say, sixty-forty."

"How much are you allowed to win?" asked the Congressman.

"There's no limit," Doc said, "But," he said to McCagg, "I'm not so sure I can sell you another ticket, sir. The state is losing too much money here. I'll have to report this."

"Now just a minute, my good man." The Congressman had a fine booming voice. "This is a game of chance and if the state loses that's the state's misfortune." Turning to McCagg, he asked, "How about fifty-fifty?"

"Well, all right. Have you got a couple hundred on you?"

Opening his calfskin wallet, the Congressmen counted out ninety-two dollars. "That's all I have on my person," he said, "but I can get more. My bank note is as good as cash."

"Well hell, that's better than nothing."

Within forty-five minutes their winnings had pyramided to over two thousand nine hundred dollars. The shopkeeper slapped the counter. "That's all. I can't sell you another ticket. I've got to report this."

"Now see here, my good man, we have been playing your game in good faith, and we want our winnings."

"Oh you do, do you. How do I know you could have paid if you'd lost? You've been gambling here with paper. You started with less than two hundred, and now you say I owe you almost three thousand. You say you could pay with a bank draft? Oh yeah? Let's see it."

The Congressman wrote a check for two thousand nine hundred dollars, and was advised to come back that afternoon. If the check was good, he'd get it back plus his share of winnings. If not, he'd get the check back and absolutely nothing more.

"I'll be back," the Congressman said, "and I might bring the authorities with me. We'll see who pays whom here."

He was no more than around the corner when the shop was closed and the three con men were out the back door. Doc cashed the check at a small discount and they split the money.

But the next day the Congressman got revenge. He hired an assassin.

Chapter Seven

Doc Bridges took the bullet in the chest. McCagg still wasn't carrying his gun, and all he could do was chase the shooter down the street and lose him in an alley. Back in the restaurant, he found Doc sitting at the table as if nothing had happened, even though blood was spreading across his white shirt.

"I'll go fetch a doctor," McCagg said.

"No. Just go with me to my hotel. I want to die in bed with my boots off."

"You're not going to die if we can get a doctor."

As usual, the older man out-talked McCagg, and walking with little difficulty made it to his hotel room. Once there, he collapsed on the bed, and his breathing became ragged. McCagg unlaced his shoes and pulled them off. "I'm going for a doctor."

"No. Listen." Blood was coming out of Doc's mouth now. "I want you to take my money, and there's something else I want to give you."

"I can't take your money. You'll need it to pay the doctor."

"Forget the doctor. Take the money. You're my best friend and I have no living relatives that I know of. Take it. If you don't, the state will."

"I'll get a doctor." McCagg headed for the door.

"No. Wait." He raised up on one elbow. "It's too late. I know a mortal wound when I see one. Listen, there's something else." A coughing fit brought up more blood, and he fell back. McCagg wiped his friend's mouth with a hotel towel. "In that drawer there is a gold brick. It's yours."

"A gold brick?"

"It's not really gold. A chemist made a couple of them for me of lead and brass filings. He mixed some molten glass with it to give it the ring of gold. Cost me a hundred bucks apiece. But . . ." Another coughing fit. Doc's voice was getting weak. "They're the standard thirty thousand dollar size, and I got ten thousand for the other one." The bearded man's chest was heaving and his heart was pounding. Blood came from his mouth with every cough, coloring his beard. Still, he talked on, sometimes in whispers.

And then he stopped talking, and his eyes closed. A few seconds later the heart stopped pounding, and the eyes re-opened, sightless.

It wasn't much of a funeral, but not for a lack of money. The casket was of hand-rubbed mahogany with brass handles and a silk lining. The mortician supplied the pallbearers — for a fee. He also supplied a preacher for a fee. The preacher read from a Bible, said "Amen," and Doc Bridges was buried in Denver's best-groomed cemetery.

Benjamin McCagg went back to his hotel feeling like he was a hundred and ten. He had lost a good friend. He felt empty, lonely. Terribly lonely. He thought again of his niece.

A long groan came out of him when he opened his eyes. His head throbbed, and his mouth tasted like dry cow dung. He tried to sit up, fell back, tried again. Where the hell was he? Were those bars on the window? In jail? Wiping a hand across his eyes, he blinked and tried to comprehend. It was a jail, all right. One window with bars. A door with bars. But

. . . he blinked again . . . the door was open.

With another long groan he got up off the wooden bunk and walked with shaky steps to the cell door. From there he could see a desk, old, scarred, and wanted posters on the wall. On another wall was a gun rack holding two rifles and a short-barreled shotgun. The sheriff's office. But how did he get here? And why wasn't the door locked?

The outer door opened and Sheriff Martin Gantt came in, with his plump round face and handlebar moustache. "See you're still alive," he said pleasantly.

McCagg mumbled, "You sure about that? I'm not so sure." He smacked his lips and swallowed with a wry face. Gawd, what a taste.

Chuckling, Gantt said, "You're standing. I never saw a dead man stand up."

"Uhh," McCagg muttered. What a head. He leaned against the cell door and rubbed a hand over his face. "I did it again, didn't I?"

"You sure got stinking. But you were a friendly kind of boozer. Didn't start any trouble. I brought you over here to keep you from falling on your face in the street."

"Uhh. How come this door's not locked?"

"I can't lock up everybody who drinks too much. The judge thinks I ought to, but, hell, if I did I'd have half the men in town crammed in there."

" 'Preciate it." He took two steps, paused, two more. "My hat. Where's my hat. And my gun?"

"Right here." Gantt opened a desk drawer and took out the holstered Smith & Wesson. "Your hat's hanging on that peg over there."

Hands shaking, he buckled on the gunbelt and put on his new Stetson.

"That's a right interesting pistol you've got there." The sheriff leaned back in his desk chair and propped his feet up on the desk. "I couldn't help reading the engraving. Now I know where I heard your name before. Read it, I mean."

54

"Uhh. Yeah."

"If you want to you can wash up in back there. Does your niece know about your drinking?"

"Naw. I hope she never knows."

"I won't tell. But you'd better get washed up before you see her again. You can borrow my razor."

"Yeah. Thanks. 'Preciate it."

Outside, the early morning sun hurt his eyes, but he managed to peer up the street and see a hand-painted sign that said El Moro Cafe. He turned his feet unsteadily in that direction, grateful that it was in the opposite direction from the Curly Wolf Saloon. He had coffee on his mind when he shuffled past the Pinon Mercantile, the larger of two mercantiles in town. Then he had something else to think about.

"Oh, Mr. McCagg. Mr. McCagg."

Half-turning, his bloodshot eyes took in a middle-aged woman with a round pleasant face and a plump body in a long, gray cotton dress. She was standing on the one step that led from a dirt path into the store.

"Mr. McCagg, you left without your package yesterday. I have it for you."

"Package? Uh, what . . . ?"

"I'll get it for you. Just a moment, please." She turned and disappeared inside the mercantile, a two-story, wood-frame building. He went to the step and stood there, wondering what the hell he'd gone and done now. In ten seconds she was back, handing him a small neatly wrapped package with a red ribbon around it.

"What . . . ?" It was all he could say.

"It's the bracelet you bought for Dawnmarie. Remember? The little silver bands?" Her pale eyes went over his face, his soiled clothes and his shaking hands. "You were a little, uh, shall I say, under the weather when you came in yesterday and bought this. You paid for it, and when I went to wrap it you left. Mr. McCagg, I hope you're all right now."

"Huh? Oh, yeah, I'm fine. You say I paid for it?"

"Yes. You don't remember, do you? When you came in you said you are an uncle of Dawnmarie's and you wanted to buy her a present of some kind. Dawnmarie and I are good friends. I've known her and Bill ever since they came here. She's such a nice young lady and Bill is such a hard worker. I know she's going to like this bracelet. It just came in from Denver yesterday morning."

"Well sure, and I thank you, Mrs., uh, thanks a lot."

"It's Mrs. Brown, Ada Brown. Are you going out to see Dawnmarie this morning? If you do, give her my best regards and tell her to come for a visit as soon as she can."

"I'll sure do that, Mrs. Brown." He turned to go, then, "Uh, Mrs. Brown, I, uh, don't know how to ask this, but . . ."

"Dawnmarie doesn't know about your drinking." It was a statement, not a question.

"No, she, uh, doesn't know."

"I had a brother with the same problem. Some say it was a weakness, but I'll always believe it was an illness. Dawnmarie won't find out from me, but you'd better have some coffee and some breakfast. I have a small kitchen in the back room. Would you care to come in? It's too early for customers."

"Thanks a lot, Mrs. Brown, but I don't want to trouble you. Don't worry, I'll get over this right soon."

"Dawnmarie told me about you. She thinks you're the greatest. Are you sure I can't help you some way?"

"No, I appreciate it, but I'll be fine. I really will. Thanks again." He walked away.

"Take care of yourself, Mr. McCagg."

He swallowed two cups of black coffee and gulped down two pancakes, and was happy to know that his stomach wasn't threatening to heave them back up. He felt better, steadier. It wasn't as if he'd been on a long drunk. Thanks to the sheriff, he'd sobered up overnight. The sun was well above the eastern horizon and the street traffic had picked up considerably by the time he left the cafe. Most of the men on the street looked to be railroaders, in their bib overalls and bill caps. A cowboy rode down the street at a slow jog, loafing in the saddle, and a man and woman went by in a horse-drawn buggy with a canopy to keep the sun off. They "Whoaed" at the mercantile, got out and tied the horse to a hitch rail.

What to do next? The only thing he'd learned was there was a dispute over who was entitled to what land northeast of town. It was a dispute that had to be settled by law. A few well-placed bullets might settle it for a while, but not for long. Eventually, it would have to be done legally. That meant going to court. Would the judge look at the land transaction records in the county clerk's office? Probably not unless the records were brought to him. Would the county clerk lug that big book to the courtroom? And how about the U.S. Government land agent? His records were important too. The easy way to do it was to hire a lawyer. McCagg had had enough experience with the law to know that a lawyer could subpoena any records he needed. He could get the judge to order the county clerk and the U.S. land agent to bring all their records into court. And he could argue the law better than any layman.

Well, all right, if that's what it took. Dawnmarie and Bill probably didn't have the money to hire a lawyer, but he had some of Doc Bridges' money left. He couldn't think of a better way to spend it. Yeah, he'd do the civilized thing and hire a lawyer. If he could find one. Sheriff Gantt ought to know.

But the sheriff wasn't in. Instead, it was Deputy Joel who sat in the sheriff's chair with his feet propped up on the desk. His feet came down with a double thud when McCagg walked in, and his thick neck seemed to swell. McCagg stopped suddenly too when he saw the deputy.

"Whatta you want?"

"I was hoping to find Sheriff Gantt here." McCagg didn't take his eyes off the deputy's face.

"Well, he ain't here."

With sarcasm, McCagg said, "Well, would you be so kind, Mr. Deputy, as to tell me where I might find him?" He couldn't abide a bully lawman.

"Don't get smart aleck with me. I'm not taking any shit from you or anybody else."

"Are you going to answer my question or are you going to just sit there like a big-assed bird?"

Deputy Joel jumped up, his hand over his gun butt. But when he saw McCagg's hand over his gun butt, he stopped. His voice was shaking with anger when he said, "You got by with threatening an officer of the law once. By God, you can't get by with it again."

Still sarcastic, McCagg said, "Officer of the law, huh? Hell, I wore a badge when you were still dirtying your diapers, and I arrested better men than you every day before breakfast."

Suddenly, the deputy's attitude changed. His face softened, and his right hand went to his jaw. He scratched his jaw while he pondered what he'd just heard. Finally, he asked, "You did? Where?"

"Texas Rangers. Company D."

"Well, uh, that don't give you the right to talk smart aleck."

"All right." McCagg forced himself to relax. "Let's start over. I'm trying to find out who has legal claim to the Kleagen homestead. And if the Kleagens don't have legal claim to it, why?"

"They don't. I can tell you that for sure. Sheriff Gantt has already told you that. Timothy O'Brien has registered for that half-section and has legal right to it."

"But the sheriff doesn't have an order from the court to force the Kleagens off."

"No, but it's coming. Prob'ly today."

"That's something I want to see the judge about. And I want to do it the right way. What I came in here for was to ask the sheriff where the nearest lawyer is."

"In Trinidad. He's the only one this side of Pueblo."

"What's his name?"

"Haddow. Michael Haddow." The deputy grinned a lopsided grin. "Yeah, you ought to go see Mr. Haddow. He'll set

58

you straight on who has legal claim to what."

He was walking to the livery barn to saddle his sorrel horse when he saw a light wagon coming from the east. The road was so dry the two horses were kicking up puffs of dust with their feet. The woman on the spring seat wore a bonnet, and the man beside her wore a black hat. When they came closer, he recognized them. Dawnmarie and Bill Kleagen.

Quickly, he looked down at himself. His new wool pants were dirty and wrinkled, and his boots had lost their shine. He held his hands out in front of his eyes. At least they were steady now. Maybe she wouldn't suspect. Bill Kleagen stopped the team in front of him, and Dawnmarie said, "We were worried about you, Uncle Benjamin."

"Morning, Dawn. Bill. I hope you didn't make a trip to town just to see what I'm up to."

"Naw, Ben," Bill Kleagen said. "I kept tellin' Dawn you could take care of yourself anywhere. But we decided we ought to come to town and do what we can and not leave it all up to you."

"Well, tie up somewhere and I'll tell you what little I've learned, and then we'll figure out what to do."

"Bill's got some news for you, Uncle Benjamin. Good news."

"Dawn, honey," Bill Kleagen said, "I'll tie up in the alley. Why don't you go on to the store and visit with Mrs. Brown. We'll be in in a couple minutes."

McCagg helped her out of the wagon, and watched as she crossed the street and went into the mercantile. Then he climbed up beside Bill and they rode down the street and around the corner to the alley behind the mercantile.

"What's this big news, Bill?"

Kleagen glanced at him and grinned. "I hit water. Sure as shootin', I hit 'er."

"Well, I'll be damned. Where can we get a pump?"

"I think Ada Brown's got one for sale. I hope she's got enough sucker rods. But . . ." His smile vanished. "I don't think we've got enough money right now."

In the alley, they climbed down and tied the team to a hitching post. "Well hell, Bill, I've got a few bucks. I'm good for a loan."

"Aw, I don't wanta do that, Ben. I don't know when I could pay you back."

They didn't see the three men come down the alley toward them until they turned to leave. The three blocked their way. They carried sixguns in holsters tied low.

"You're Bill Kleagen," said the biggest one, a red bearded, red headed gent in baggy bib overalls. "I've been lookin' fer you."

"Yeah, I'm Bill Kleagen. Who are you?"

The redhead was as tall as McCagg and broader, thicker. His face looked like it had once stopped a rock slide. McCagg pegged him as a brawler. "I'm the man that's gonna kick your sod-bustin' ass all over town. My name is Tim O'Brien."

Chapter Eight

Bill Kleagen's face froze. His shoulder muscles bunched and his hands balled into fists. "You're O'Brien, the man who threatened my wife when I was away from the house?"

"That I am. And it's lucky you are that you wasn't at home. I'd of kicked your ass plumb outa the county. You're squattin' on my land."

McCagg stood spraddle-legged, his hand near the butt of the Smith & Wesson. He watched the three, watched their gun hands. Two of them watched him.

Bill Kleagen hissed through clenched teeth, "I wanta tell you somethin', mister. If you ever threaten my wife again, I'll kill you."

"Haw-haw," the redhead said. "You ain't even packin' iron."

"I am," McCagg said, voice hard.

"There's three of us and we always carry guns."

McCagg's blood had turned cold. "I'll get at least two of you."

"Haw-haw. You can't even get one. But anyways we don't want no killin'. Not unless you start it. That sheriff don't take kindly to killin'. But if you wanta shuck that hogleg and fight with your dukes, we'll teach you who's boss."

"Like you said," Kleagen hissed, "I'm not armed, but if you'll drop your gun I'll take you on."

"Wait a minute, Bill, he's got fifty pounds on you."

"Fifty pounds of shit."

This was a side of Bill Kleagen that McCagg had never seen. Quiet, serious Bill, the orphan who worked for his keep at the McCagg Ranch, the most inoffensive kid McCagg had ever known. But back then he didn't have a wife to protect.

"Shit, eh? You ain't gonna be nothin' but shit when I git through with you." The redhead unbuckled his gunbelt and handed it to one of his partners. He balled his fists. His fists were as big as hams.

"Hold on, Bill," McCagg warned. "He's a lot bigger and a lot more experienced than you."

"No sonofabitch is gonna threaten my wife."

"Haw-haw." One of the big fists suddenly came up from the redhead's knees with enough power to fell a mule. Kleagen saw it coming, and stepped back. But that blow was immediately followed by another, and it caught Kleagen on the side of the head. The big man could move fast.

Kleagen staggered sideways but didn't go down. He got his fists up and landed a punch on the redhead's jaw. That slowed the big man, but only for a second.

McCagg wasn't watching the fight. He was watching the other two men, daring them with his eyes to go for their guns. They made no move toward their guns.

There was grunting, straining and the smack of fists on flesh. Bill Kleagen hit the ground on his back. Scrambling up immediately, he continued throwing punches. A few landed and he was strong enough to make them hurt. But the redhead was stronger and his punches hit harder. Kleagen went down again. McCagg had to look.

"That's enough," he said. "One more blow and I'll put a .45 slug through your goddamn head."

"No, Ben," Kleagen mumbled through split lips. "It's my fight." He was on his feet again, fists up in front of his face.

"You haven't got a chance, Bill. You're fighting his way. Let me do it my way."

"No." He swung his right fist and it connected with the

redhead's chin. For a few seconds, as the big man staggered back, McCagg had hope. But only for a few seconds. Growling like a bulldog, O'Brien put his head down and charged. Kleagen managed to step aside and punch again, but he only hurt his fist on the big man's head. Whirling around with surprising speed, O'Brien threw punches fast and furious. Two of them caught Bill on the head, and Bill fell. He got to his hands and knees and shook his head, trying to clear his vision. Slowly, he got up, then let out a long groan and collapsed.

Dawnmarie's scream caused McCagg to jerk his head around in her direction.

She had come around the corner looking for her husband and her uncle and she saw the last flurry of blows that felled her husband. She ran to him, dropped onto her knees beside him.

"Stop it. Stop it." Bending over her husband, she moaned, "Bill, oh Bill." She looked up at McCagg and pleaded, "Uncle Benjamin, can't you stop it?"

The Smith & Wesson was in McCagg's hand then. He stepped in front of the redhead. "That's it, mister. Get gone or I'll drop you like a pole-axed steer. Get. All three of you. Get."

The other two made no moves. McCagg was calm, now. His blood was cold. His voice was full of death. "If the three of you aren't out of my sight in five seconds, I'll take the big sonofabitch first then the other two."

The only sound was Dawnmarie's moaning and the redhead's heavy breathing.

"You can't take all of us," O'Brien gasped.

"Maybe not, but I'll get you. One wrong move from anybody and you're dead." He meant it and they knew it.

"Let's go." The redhead turned on his heel and walked away. His two partners followed. McCagg watched them until they were around the corner out of sight.

Dawnmarie had her husband's head in her lap, hugging him. "Bill, oh Bill. Why, Bill?"

Through bleeding lips, he mumbled, "They scared you, Dawn. I couldn't let 'em get by with that."

She was still pleading as she looked up at McCagg. "Uncle Benjamin, what are we going to do?"

"There are ways of dealing with that kind, Dawn. Let's try the legal way and if that doesn't work, we'll . . ." He didn't get to finish what he started to say. The back door of the mercantile opened and a woman's voice interrupted.

"Oh, my. What happened? Dawnmarie, what happened to Bill?"

"He was fighting, Ada. He was fighting a man much bigger. It was the man who threatened me last week."

"Oh my. Is he hurt bad? Bring him in here, and let's see what we can do for him."

With McCagg on one side of him and Dawnmarie on the other, Bill Kleagen got to his feet and stood drunkenly. His left eye was closed with a deep cut under it, he had a knot on the right side of his head, and his lips were cut and swollen.

"Bring him in here."

"All right, Bill?" McCagg said. "Here we go."

They got Kleagen seated in Ada Brown's small kitchen in back of the store. A water faucet hung over a steel kitchen sink. The kitchen had running water from somewhere. No doubt from a manmade dam somewhere uphill from the town. McCagg wondered whether the pipes froze in the winter. Ada Brown turned the tap and wet a wash cloth with the small stream of water that came out.

"Now let's see," she murmured. "Let's get you cleaned up, Bill, and then I've got some tincture of iodine that will keep infection out. Some of Dr. Madison's salve will help the healing. How do you feel?"

He managed to grin with one side of his mouth. "Like I've been run over by a buffalo." To Dawnmarie, he said, "Reckon I don't know much about fightin', but I had to try."

"I understand, Bill, honey. You men think you have to do these things."

64

Ben McCagg could only stand there helplessly. At first he wondered why Dawnmarie let the older woman work on her husband, then he knew why. Ada Brown seemed to be an expert. She worked swiftly and gently, murmuring softly all the time.

"This is going to sting, Bill, but it's necessary." She applied the iodine, and a tear came to Kleagen's one good eye, but he made no sound. "A cold compress will help the swelling on your head." She held the cloth under the water tap until it was wet and pressed it against the purple bruise.

While she worked, McCagg looked around the kitchen. Neat. Only one dirty dish and that was a coffee cup. Only one cup. He wondered about that.

A bell tinkled in the store and Mrs. Brown left to wait on a customer. Dawnmarie wet the cloth again and held it to Bill's head.

"Uncle Ben," she said, "we came to town to find you and to see the land agent, and hopefully to see the judge too. But Bill's in no condition to do anything for the rest of the day. Did he tell you that he struck water?"

"Yeah. That's good news. Now you can pump water right in front of your house without going to the river for it."

"Yes. We'll, uh, we'll buy the pump rods and a pump as soon as we can."

"Bill told me you're a little short on cash right now. I've got money I haven't spent yet. It's yours."

"Oh no. Thank you very much, Uncle Benjamin, but Bill doesn't want to borrow from anyone. Except maybe a bank. And we have practically no collateral. But Bill is planning to get a job here in El Moro or in Trinidad and save enough money to buy the equipment we need."

"Yeah," Kleagen mumbled. "Thanks, Ben. But if we don't get title to the land, we'd be fools to spend money improving it."

"Can't argue about that. And speaking about that, I was sort of planning to go to Trinidad and hire a lawyer. I'll bet a smart lawyer can figure a way to keep those gunsels off your land."

"Yes," Dawnmarie said, "but we're back to the problem of . . ."

"Yeah, I know. No money. I'll pay."

"Uncle Benjamin . . ."

"I'm going to do it, Dawnmarie. Personally, I think it's a h—heck of a note when a feller has to pay to get justice, but maybe it's better than shooting it out. Maybe."

"How can we ever repay you?"

"You don't, that's how. Uh, how deep is that well?"

Kleagen mumbled, "Seventy-two feet."

"That'll take a lot of sucker rods."

"I'll leave the drill pipe in the hole for casing. All it takes is seventy-two feet of rods and a pump. And," Bill Kleagen managed a grin, "a strong arm to work the pump handle."

"And," Dawnmarie added, "title to the land."

"I'm gonna start working on that right now," McCagg said. "Maybe I won't go to Trinidad today. I want to see that you two get home all right, what with Bill not having a gun with him. But I think I'll go and try to see that judge, then I'll come back here."

He left through the front of the building, through the store packed with merchandise of all kinds, including sacks of flour, sugar and cornmeal. A long counter was piled with clothes and dress materials. Galvanized steel buckets and wash tubs hung from the walls, and shovels, picks and crowbars leaned against the walls. Another room opened from the east side, and McCagg guessed it held more merchandise. He wanted to ask Mrs. Brown if she had any pump rods, but he didn't want Dawnmarie to hear him ask. He didn't get a chance. Mrs. Brown had three customers standing around while she waited on a fourth.

Walking past the Curly Wolf brought a terrible thirst, and he couldn't help thinking about how good a shot of whiskey would taste going down. He could almost feel it settling in his stomach, bringing a warmth that would spread to his whole body. It would make him think better and put him in the right frame of mind to talk to a judge. A glance back at the mercantile showed him that Dawnmarie was not in sight. One quick one, and then he could do whatever he needed to do.

The saloon door was open, and the odor reached him and pulled at him. He approached the door, shot another quick glance over his shoulder and saw her. Dawnmarie had come out onto the step that led to the mercantile.

"Huh-uhm," he said, clearing his throat, and making an abrupt change of directions. He swallowed a dry lump, swallowed again as he cut through the vacant lot and went to the alley and the log cabin that served as a county court.

Chapter Nine

Inside the courtroom, he found two rows of wooden planks for seats. A platform with a heavy desk and a chair on it was at the far end of the room. The desk looked to be big enough and heavy enough to stop a freight train. Otherwise, the room was empty. McCagg walked to the far end, his boots thumping on the wooden floor and his spurs ringing, and found nobody.

"Now what the hell," he mused aloud. "Reckon the justice business is slow today. The sheriff didn't lock anybody up last night." He walked back to the one door and stepped outside. "Dammit." Then he saw the judge coming.

Judge Clarence J. Topah swung a walking stick as he walked, and he moved sprightly for an overweight man. He was bareheaded, and his thick gray hair matched his trimmed gray beard.

"Oh, judge, I was looking for you," McCagg said.

"Very well, my court will be in session directly." He entered and walked briskly to the platform, mounted it and seated himself in the chair behind the desk. McCagg followed, and held his hat in his hands.

"Is there something you wish to bring before the court?"

"Yeah, judge, it's the same thing I mentioned last night. I . . ."

"You will address me as Your Honor while you are in my

court."

McCagg was tempted. He wanted badly to address him as Your Satchel Ass Honor, but he didn't. He had to pause, think, and swallow another dry lump. A court, to win the respect of the citizens, had to have prestige. There had to be dignity in the court.

"Well, speak up."

"Your Honor, it seems from what I was told by County Clerk Orville Jones that a half-section of land east of town that was settled on by Mr. and Mrs. William Kleagen is now being claimed by a man name of O'Brien."

"Well?"

"Mr. Jones told me that the U.S. land agent got a note from you saying O'Brien is legally entitled to the land."

"So?"

"I'd like to know if that's true."

"You are saying that Mr. Jones told you something he heard from the U.S. land agent?"

"Yes sir."

"I believe you told me last night that your name is Benjamin McCagg, is that correct?"

"Yes sir."

"Well, Mr. McCagg, what Mr. Jones may or may not have said to you is hearsay. As a matter of law, everything you said here just now is hearsay. First, you are telling me something that Mr. Jones said to you. Further, you are telling me something that the land agent said to Mr. Jones. You can't be certain of what anyone said to Mr. Jones, and I can't be certain of what Mr. Jones said to you. Do you understand that?"

"What you mean, Your Honor, is I have to bring both Mr. Jones and the land agent into court so you yourself can hear what they have to say."

"That is correct."

"Well, can you tell me, are squatters' rights, and the rights of discovery legal?"

"I am not in the business of dispensing legal advice."

"I see. Then to find out I'll have to go to Trinidad and ask the only lawyer this side of Pueblo?"

"That is what I would suggest."

"And since there is only one lawyer this side of Pueblo, does everybody who comes into this court have to bring him along?"

"In criminal matters, no. In civil matters, such as disputes over the ownership of property, it is the best way."

"Is it necessarily the only way?"

"Mr. McCagg, any ruling I make without hearing arguments from members of the bar representing all litigants is subject to being overruled by the district courts."

McCagg rubbed his jaw and turned his hat around in his hands. "This gets more complicated all the time."

"Again, I suggest you consult an attorney."

"Yeah. I mean, yes sir, Your Honor." He started to leave, then thought of something else. "Uh, Your Honor, I've been told that you are going to sign a paper ordering William Kleagen and his wife off their homestead. Hearsay or not, surely you can tell me whether that is true."

"Have you seen such an order?"

"No sir, I haven't."

"Until you do, until such a directive is presented to Mr. Kleagen, he has every right to remain on his homestead."

"Are you going to sign an order?"

"I have been asked to, and I have not ruled it out."

"Who asked you?"

"A Mr. Timothy O'Brien."

"Has he or anybody else asked you to order Harvey Arbaugh off his land."

"You're asking a lot of questions. Mr. McCagg."

"Yes sir. I'm a relative of the Kleagens and a citizen of the United States of America, and I believe I have a right to know what is happening in the courts."

"Very well, I believe the gentleman's name is Cannon.

George Cannon."

"And he says he has filed a legal claim to the Arbaughs' homestead."

"That is the matter to be resolved, yes."

"But it's not resolved yet?"

"I have issued no instructions to anyone."

"But Sheriff Gantt went out to the Kleagens and said you are planning to issue an order."

"Then the sheriff has misconstrued my comments."

McCagg turned his hat around in his hands again, and pondered that. "Your Honor, would you please tell me what your comments were?"

With an exasperated sigh, the judge said, "Very well. You do have a right to know. Mr. O'Brien and Mr. Cannon came into this court and said they have filed a claim under the United States Homestead Act as amended to two half-sections of land. I disremember the legal descriptions, but the land is on the Purgatoire River northeast of El Moro. The sheriff, or rather his deputy, happened to be here on a criminal matter, and he overheard. They advised me that the land is now occupied but the occupants have no legal claim to it. They showed me a U.S. survey map and pointed out that no one has legal claim to those two parcels. It happens. Some folks just don't think they need to comply with the law."

"Some folks don't know what the law is. They believe if they settle on the land, work it, it's theirs."

"Unfortunately, the law has to be complied with. Mr. O'Brien and Mr. Cannon showed me that they have followed the law to the letter, and they asked me to direct the sheriff to order Mr. Kleagen and Mr. Arbaugh off the land in dispute. I merely said it appears they do have legal claim, and a court order could be forthcoming."

"Surely, Your Honor, you wouldn't order two families out of their homes and off their land without a hearing."

"I have not done so. I merely said a directive could be issued. I also said the defendants have a right to be heard."

71

"I see. Hmm."

"But if the defendant cannot show a legal claim, I have no choice under the law but to order an eviction."

"Uh-huh. Well, sir, what I've learned here is very interesting. The fact, as I understand it, is nobody has authority to force the Kleagens or the Arbaughs off their land. Not yet, anyway. And if anybody tries to force them off, or even threatens them with bodily harm, they could sign a complaint and have them arrested. Is that right?"

"That is where the matter stands at this time."

"Then the Kleagens and the Arbaughs can challenge any order you issue?"

"If they ask for a hearing, a hearing will be conducted. But if they ignore an order from the court, they forfeit their legal privileges."

"Thank you, Your Honor. 'Preciate it."

Outside, McCagg couldn't help grinning and speaking to himself, "Whether the old fathead meant to or not, he has been a hell of a big help. Maybe the law will work after all. Maybe."

Walking back through the vacant lot with his head down, he pondered his next move. Let's see, the sheriff seemed convinced that a court order is coming. He ought to be set straight about that. McCagg directed his steps toward the sheriff's office and jail. Again the odor from the Curly Wolf pulled strongly at him, but he clamped his jaws tight, forced himself to look ahead and walked on by.

Sheriff Gantt was in, rummaging through papers on his desk. He looked up when McCagg entered. "You still in town? In town's where men get in trouble."

"Not always, sheriff. There's trouble out in the tulies too." McCagg folded his lean frame into the one other chair in the room. "For instance, shots have been fired at one house and a woman has been threatened at another because a couple of gunsels are trying to take over somebody else's homesteads."

"I heard about that. Shooting at folks is against the law, and

72

if the Arbaughs can identify the shooters and will sign a complaint I'll arrest the hell out of them. Threatening somebody is no crime. Not around here, anyway."

"The Arbaughs probably don't have any faith in the law, and won't even report it. My niece is trying to be civilized, but she doesn't expect any help from the law either. As far as proving a right to the land goes, it's going to take a lawyer to convince the judge of anything, and who the hell can afford that?"

"They don't work cheap."

"What I came to see you about, sheriff, is the judge told me he hasn't signed any kind of court order and isn't even sure he's going to."

"He told you that?"

"Just now."

Sheriff Gantt leaned back in his chair and studied the ceiling a moment, then said, "Joel told me the judge promised this O'Brien feller he'd sign an order any day now. That's why I rode out to the Kleagen place. To give them fair warning. Joel wanted to go along and I let him."

"So it was Joel who misunderstood the judge?"

"Yeah." He studied the ceiling again. "I'm glad you stopped by. That's good news. I don't want to drive honest folks off their land."

"You already said you have no idea why O'Brien and a feller named Cannon want those two half-sections?"

"No idea a-tall."

"Hmm." McCagg stood. "Well, it sure is a puzzler. The land ain't worth a damn for farming, and water is too scarce for grazing. Bill Kleagen built a good strong two-room house, but they can't live in it if they can't make a living there."

"It's a puzzler, all right."

McCagg considered telling the sheriff about the fight behind the mercantile, but decided not to. Bill Kleagen didn't try to avoid that fight. The judge would probably blame him as much as anybody else. Besides, Bill was not the kind of man who would go to the law when he got the worst of a brawl. No use even mentioning it.

"Anyway," he said to the sheriff. "I reckon we'll just go on about our business and see what happens next. The judge said that if he orders you to drive those folks off, they can demand a hearing and argue their case."

"Yeah. And in the meantime, maybe this O'Brien and his pals will lose interest in the whole thing and go back to Denver where they came from."

"Yeah. Maybe."

But as he left the sheriff's office and went out onto the street, spurs chinging, he knew the redhead wouldn't lose interest. Somebody wanted that land and they weren't about to give up without a fight. He could only hope that the dispute would be settled by law and not by gunfire. There was hope that it would be. But not much.

Chapter Ten

As sore as he was, Bill Kleagen just had to show McCagg proof that he had struck water. He lowered the bolt on the end of his twine into the drill pipe. When the twine went slack he pulled it out hand over hand. Sure enough, the bolt and two inches of the twine were wet.

Through split lips, Kleagen grinned. "There's sure enough water down there. And it can be pumped up."

"Yeah." McCagg had to grin too. Then he turned serious, "Uh, Bill, I don't want to do anything against your wishes, or anything, but I asked Mrs. Brown to order some sucker rods from Denver. She didn't have any on hand. There's been no demand for them around here."

"You did that, Ben?"

"Yeah. I know you didn't ask me to, and Dawnmarie didn't ask me to, but I did it because I wanted to. You don't have to pay me back or anything."

"You already ordered 'em, huh?"

"Yeah, it's done."

"Does Dawn know?"

"Not yet. Mrs. Brown said it will take a week. She can order the stuff by telegraph, you know, and it doesn't take the railroad long to get it down to El Moro."

"Well, I'll be damned." Kleagen shook his head. "It's done, and that's all I can say. I'll just be damned."

After supper, while Dawnmarie washed the dishes, they talked about it again. "You can maybe pump enough water to irrigate a little garden, but not enough to grow a field of grain. It takes a lot of water to do that. So what's next, Bill?"

"Aw," Kleagen said, "I'm no farmer anyhow. All I know is cattle, what I learned on the McCagg Ranch." He was silent a moment, and McCagg waited to hear what he'd say next. "I know a spot about seven miles north of here where the ground is low and water stands on it for sometimes a couple of weeks during the rainy season and when the snow melts. I'll bet I could hit water there too."

"Drill another well?"

"Yeah."

"Then what?"

Kleagen glanced at Dawnmarie and back at McCagg. "You got me there, Ben. I can't claim that piece of ground, or buy it, so it wouldn't do me any good to drill a well there."

"And even if you could claim it, then what?"

Dawnmarie wiped her hands on a towel made from an empty flour sack, and sat at the table with them. "Bill wants to go into the cattle business."

McCagg mused aloud, "I reckon that's all free range to the north."

Kleagen nodded. "Nobody's settled on it because it's worthless. Too far from water to graze cattle and no good for farming."

"Has it been surveyed?"

"I believe most of the state has been surveyed," Dawnmarie put in.

"Then it's open for homesteading."

"Probably. But we can only homestead one half-section, and we've got that."

"Hmm." McCagg got up and poured himself another cup of coffee. "If you hit water there and wanted to work yourself to a frazzle pumping water, you could graze a couple hundred cows between here and there and a few miles beyond there."

"I figure there's enough grass to graze four hundred head."

McCagg chuckled, "You've got it figured out, haven't you, Bill?"

Dawnmarie answered with a smile, "I told you he's a dreamer." She reached over and patted her husband's arm. "Tell him about the rest of your dream, Bill."

Kleagen suddenly stood and went to a wooden trunk against a wall. Opening it, he took out a thick catalog, brought it to the table and turned to a well-worn page. "There. See that?"

What he pointed to was an engraving of a windmill. It stood on four wooden legs and towered twenty feet over a pump. Beneath it all was a wooden trough where a horse, two cows and a dog helped themselves to water.

"I can read it," Kleagen said. "Dawn taught me to read. It says Empire Windmills Manufacturing Co. Uh, Sy . . ." Here he had to study the words. "Sy-r-a-cuse. Syracuse, New York."

McCagg knew he had memorized the message, all but one word it was obvious that Bill was learning to read. He held out his hand. "Put 'er there, Bill. You're not just a dreamer, you're a thinker and a doer." They shook hands.

"I don't know how he's going to do it," Dawnmarie said, pride in her voice, "But he'll think of a way."

"Would you show me that spot tomorrow, Bill? The spot you've got picked out to drill a well on?"

"Sure, I'll show it to you."

"But right now," said Dawnmarie, "I've got a present to open." She took the small package with the red ribbon off a shelf and, sitting at the table again, carefully opened it. She let out a squeal, put the bracelet on her right wrist, and squealed again. "It's beautiful. I've never had anything like it. Oh, Uncle Benjamin." The silver bands gleamed from the lamplight as she held her wrist up.

***

77

The U.S. land agent was in. A short, thick man with muttonchop sideburns and nearly bald head, he looked up when Benjamin McCagg opened the door to the Land Office and stepped inside. McCagg had to duck his head to get through the door, and inside he had to remove his hat to keep from bumping the ceiling.

"Are you Bruce Thiede?"

"I am."

"My name is Benjamin McCagg. I'm interested in homesteading on a piece of ground due northeast about nine miles. Is that country open for homesteading?"

Bruce Thiede leaned back in his wooden chair and laced his fingers behind his head. He studied McCagg, from the thin dark hair to the Smith & Wesson to the spurs on his boots. "That's free range. It's public domain. You don't have to homestead it to graze cattle on it."

"I want to own as much of it as I can, and I understand I can claim a half-section under the homestead laws."

"You can if you pay a fifty dollar registration fee."

"I'll pay."

"All right." He leaned forward, opened a desk drawer and pulled out a roll of maps. Spreading them out on a desk, he said, "Can you point out the spot?"

"Well, there aren't any landmarks to go by, but, uh . . ." McCagg leaned over the map, studied it, saw the big bend in the Picketwire, and pointed with his finger. "Right here. I think this is the spot."

"You'll have to have it surveyed, and that will cost you too."

"Whatever it takes."

"Mr., uh, McCagg, you said? It's none of my business, but I'm curious. There's no water for at least ten miles from there. Cattlemen tell me that's too far for a steer to go for water. Would you tell me why you want that piece of land?"

"I don't mean to be disrespectful, but I'd rather not say right now."

The land agent was suddenly exasperated. He plopped

down in his chair and frowned at McCagg. "What in God's name is going on? Men have been coming in here and claiming some of the most worthless land in the country and won't say what they want it for. What's going on? Did somebody find gold or silver out there?"

"Not that I know of. Who else is claiming land out that way?"

"Why, the most rag-tag bunch of hardcases I ever saw. Six of them have come in here and picked out land."

"In the same part of the country?"

"They've picked out a string of half-sections to the south of the spot you just picked out." He stood and put his finger on the map. "They've got a string of land running east and west here that's probably five miles long."

McCagg rubbed a hand over his sparse hair. "That is a puzzler, ain't it?"

"It certainly is. They're so damnedable close-mouthed about it."

"Any idea at all?"

"None whatsoever."

"Well hell, at least they're south of where I want to settle."

"All right, all right. Mine is not to wonder why, only to see that the law is followed. You have to make certain improvements, you know, to gain title. Grazing livestock is not what the U.S. Congress had in mind."

"I understand."

Shaking his head, the land agent said, "Well, if you want to pay the registration fee and pay for the survey, that's your business."

"Who does the surveying?"

"I'm the only qualified land surveyor in Trinchera County. You can go to Trinidad or Pueblo and get another surveyor if you wish to."

"You get paid for surveying land and draw government paychecks at the same time?"

Bruce Thiede's face turned red, and he stood again. "I have

a right to supplement my meager government salary."

Grinning, McCagg said, "All right. Maybe you have at that. I meant no offense. The sooner this is done, the better. When can you get to it?"

"Day after tomorrow. You'll have to go with me and show me the spot."

"I'll meet you here at seven o'clock day after tomorrow."

His next stop was the Pinon Mercantile. Mrs. Ada Brown was busy measuring some gingham for a woman in a sun bonnet, but she smiled at him and said, "Good morning, Mr. McCagg. I'll be right with you."

He noticed for the first time that she had a nice smile, and her plump body inside the long dress looked to be filled out in the right places and not too much so in the wrong places. Plump but neat. Did she have a husband? He decided he wanted to find out. Dawnmarie could tell him. No, on second thought that wasn't a good idea. Dawnmarie would ask why he wanted to know, then tease him about finding a good woman and settling down. That is, if Ada Brown didn't already have a husband.

Mrs. Brown promised to order the drill pipe right away, and said she had already ordered the pump rods. "They should be here in a few days. Whatever are you good people planning out there?" And as soon as she asked, she knew she shouldn't have. "You don't need to answer, Mr. McCagg. It's none of my business."

He grinned, but at the same time he realized that a general store was a good place to pick up the latest news — and gossip. It was obvious that Dawnmarie hadn't told Mrs. Brown about Bill's well, but Mrs. Brown could easily guess. A well was the only place pump rods could be used. His grin widened when she said:

"I haven't mentioned it to anyone. If Dawnmarie didn't mention it, as good friends as we are, I won't talk about it either."

"You're a good woman, Mrs. Brown."

He untied the sorrel from a hitchrail in front of the land office and started to put his foot in the stirrup. He paused when his eyes fell on the Curly Wolf. Standing on two feet now, he fought with the impulse. One drink is one too many. Well, maybe a beer. Hell, the damn beer is warm anyhow and will look and taste like horse piss. That would cure any man's drinking problems. Yeah, but the water around here doesn't taste too good either. Just a beer, then go back to the Kleagen place and see if I can earn my keep. Just one.

As soon as he stepped through the door he wished he hadn't. Redbeard and his two pards were seated at a table, and they saw him. He couldn't back out. That would be running. Trying to ignore them, he went to the bar and ordered a beer. The bartender's wise eyes remembered him, but he drew a mug of beer from a keg and said nothing.

"Haw-haw. I'll bet that bucko's from Texas."

"What makes you think so, Timothy, me boy?"

"He looks like he was fetched up on cow shit, that's what."

"He does kind of smell like cow shit, don't he?"

McCagg took a swallow of beer and pretended he didn't hear.

"That's all Texas sends up here, cowboys, cowgirls, cowhorses and cow shit."

"Haw-haw. I'm bettin' if you poked a hole in 'im cow shit'd come out."

"Hell, let's go see."

Chairs scraped the floor as the three stood up. The bartender leaned over the bar, close to McCagg's face. "Git out of here, mister. Git out before you git hurt."

A strange thought went through McCagg's mind. The beer was warm. It didn't taste good at all. The redhead's name was O'Brien. One of the others was probably George Cannon. They're about to start a fight. In spite of law and order, a man had a right to defend himself. If he could draw and shoot fast enough he could end the land dispute right here and right now. He concentrated on drawing the Smith & Wesson.

Three fingers around the butt, one finger on the trigger and his thumb on the hammer. Draw, cock and fire, all in one motion. He'd practiced it a thousand times. It was as much in the mind as in the hand. He concentrated, and he was ready.

He turned to face them.

Chapter Eleven

But it wasn't shooting the redhead had in mind. Big fists balled, he stopped in front of McCagg.

"I whupped your partner and I can whup you too."

McCagg didn't speak, just looked the redhead in the eye. The other two started to fan out. McCagg spoke then.

"One more step and he gets a .45 slug in the middle of his ugly face."

They stopped.

"Whup 'im, Timothy, me boy."

"Why don't you take off that shooter, cowpoke, and fight like a man?"

McCagg said nothing, but his eyes and the set of his jaw warned them that one more move on their part and the lead would fly.

"I can whup you anyways, gun or no gun." But the redheaded one made no further move.

He was standing close enough to reach McCagg, and McCagg expected to see a big fist aimed at his face. Let him. He could draw and shoot faster than that big sonofabitch could hit. He concentrated on the .45 in its holster, on his right hand, and on O'Brien's big middle. Now he wanted to fight. Come on, you big tough ugly sonofabitch. Let's end this right here. But his mouth remained clamped tight.

The bartender pleaded, "Now wait a minute, gentlemen,

it's three against one. He has a right to use his gun to defend himself. He . . ."

"Shut up."

The bartender shut up.

"Hit 'im, Timothy. If he reaches for that smoke pole, I'll drill 'im through the gut."

Now McCagg moved his eyes toward the man who had spoken, the man on his left. He changed his plan. This man was the most dangerous. If Timothy hit him, his first shot would have to take out this man before this man could draw and shoot. The redhead would be next. He might have to shoot the redhead from flat on his back, but he could do that if he had to. Come on, you sonsofbitches.

"Hit 'im, Timothy."

Timothy didn't move. No one moved. For a long moment, no one moved. McCagg remained tense. He didn't dare relax. Any second now. And then it came.

The redhead's right fist came up fast, so fast that McCagg caught it on the side of his face. In the same split second, the Smith & Wesson jumped into McCagg's hand and bucked and kicked as a metal cartridge exploded. The man on McCagg's left buckled in the middle and slumped to the floor.

The explosion and the smell of burned gunpowder stung ears and noses.

The redhead was ready to hit again, but when he saw his partner fall, he suddenly dropped his hands. "Don't shoot. Don't shoot."

McCagg's jaw hurt where he'd been hit. He raised the .45 until it was pointed at the middle of Timothy's face. He hissed through his teeth, "You goddamn, rotten, sorry sonofabitch. You ain't fit to live."

"Don't shoot. Please." Timothy O'Brien was a scared man now. His face didn't look so tough. "I only wanted to duke it out. I, we, didn't mean to kill anybody."

"You sonsofbitches ain't gonna beat on me or any of my friends. Not ever." His trigger finger tightened a fraction of an inch.

"Please, don't shoot."

The bartender spoke again, "Go ahead and shoot the bastards, mister. I'll go to court and testify on your side."

"Please. Don't shoot."

He wished the sonofabitch would quit begging. He wished he would hit him again. "Come on," he hissed. "You wanted to fight."

"No." O'Brien was backing up now, hands out in front of him. "No shootin'. I didn't mean for anybody to get killed."

"Then git."

"Wait a minute," the bartender said. "Don't let 'em leave yet. I'll fetch the sheriff." He whipped off his dirty apron, hurried around the bar and out the door.

McCagg kept the .45 in his hand. "Go ahead and move," he said. O'Brien and his one standing partner didn't move. The man on the floor let out a long gasp, shuddered once and was quiet. His sixgun lay on the floor near his fingers.

"He's dead," O'Brien said. "You killed 'im."

"Too bad. Give me half an excuse and I'll put a slug in you too."

"We didn't mean to kill nobody."

"Is that why you shot at a cabin over east with a man, a woman and two kids in it?"

"We didn't hit nobody, just wanted to scare 'em."

"You could've killed one of them."

"They're trespassin'. The law says we got a right to run off trespassers."

"Who told you that?"

"Mr. H—." Suddenly, O'Brien clamped his mouth shut.

"Mr. Who?"

"I ain't tellin'."

"Well, whoever he is he told you wrong. The judge hasn't decided yet who has a legal claim to that land. If I see any of you over there I'll shoot you for trespassing. Get that?"

Two men in railroaders' overalls and brogan shoes came in,

stopped, stared, jaws open. One said, "Wha . . .", shut his mouth and backed out the door. The other followed. McCagg kept his gun pointed at O'Brien and his pal and waited.

It wasn't the sheriff who came running in, it was the deputy, Joel. He had a sixgun in his hand when he came through the door. "All right, drop it. Drop it right now."

Instead of dropping his gun, McCagg slowly, deliberately let the hammer down and holstered it.

"Now what the humped up hell is goin' on here?"

The bartender answered, "They started a fight. That one on the floor, he . . ."

"I didn't ask you, I ask him." He pointed with his gun at McCagg.

"He told you right. Why didn't you let him finish?"

"Did you shoot that one?"

"Yeah."

"You're under arrest."

"No, I'm not. I shot in self defense."

"You say. The fact is, a man is dead. He is dead, ain't he? And you killed 'im. You're under arrest."

"How about them? They started it."

"You're the one that done the killin'. Get your hands up."

"Look." McCagg pointed to the gun on the floor beside the body. "He had his gun out and was about to shoot me. I shot faster. That's all there was to it."

"We'll just lock you up and let the judge figure out what happened."

"That's the way the law works, huh? They started the fight and they go free."

"Killin' is against the law around here and we enforce the law."

"Shit." But he knew there was nothing he could do about it. He might catch the deputy looking away, draw and put a bullet through his heart, but that would be dumb. A lawman could be the sorriest sonofabitch in the world, but no excuse for killing one would be accepted. He either allowed himself to be arrested or be a fugitive from the law. He shook his head sadly and muttered again, "Shit."

This time the cell door was shut. It was slammed shut with a loud, ringing "Clang." A long key was turned in the lock.

"Where's the sheriff?"

"Out of town."

"When do I get to see the judge?"

"When I'm ready."

They had attracted attention walking from the saloon to the sheriff's office, and that was embarrassing to McCagg. Not to the deputy.

"What'd he do, Joel? Did I hear a gun?"

"He shot a man. I'm takin' 'im to jail. I don't allow that kind of hooligan stuff." Joel's chest was puffed out.

McCagg had been afraid to look around at the curious, afraid he might see Mrs. Brown. And now, two hours after he was locked up, his fears were realized. Mrs. Brown came to see him. The deputy stayed beside her, watching her.

"I hope you don't mind," she said by way of apology. "I heard what happened, everyone has heard, and I want to know if there's any way I can help you."

He was irritated. Help him? Hell, he didn't need any help from a woman. Especially a woman he barely knew. "No, there's nothing you can do."

"Do you want me to send word to Dawnmarie?"

"No," he answered quickly. "I'll, uh, there's a court here, and I did no wrong. They can't keep me here long."

"Whatever you say, Mr. McCagg. Word spreads quickly around here, and everybody I've overheard talking about it is glad somebody made believers out of those men. They've been bullying people here for two or three weeks now. I'm sure the judge will find you innocent of any wrongdoing."

"Yeah," McCagg said, glumly, "if I ever get to see him." It was a long day. He walked back and forth nervously.

Where the hell was the sheriff? Why didn't he get to see the judge? In Texas, he recalled, the john laws could lock a man up for three days and nights without taking him before a judge. Three days and nights. They could lock a man up that long just because they didn't like his face. That was the law. The goddamn law. He couldn't stand being locked up for three days and nights. He walked, sat, walked.

Ada Brown brought him his supper. Deputy Joel lifted the clean dish towel off the plate, took a long look at the roast beef, mashed potatoes and gravy and the plum pudding, then unlocked the cell door.

"Stand back," he ordered, the plate in one hand and his sixgun in the other. McCagg stood back. "You're a lucky feller. I'm s'posed to get your supper at the cafe, and if I did you wouldn't be gettin' nothin' as good as this."

"Thanks, Mrs. Brown."

"I went to see Judge Topah," she said. "He said he'll send for you tomorrow. I couldn't get him to send for you today."

"Thanks for that too."

It was a long night. He walked, sat, walked, and finally slept a little. At daylight Ada Brown brought him his breakfast, ham and eggs and thick slices of toast. And coffee. Hot, black coffee. He wished she hadn't, but he appreciated it too. All he could say was thanks.

"If the deputy doesn't take you to see the judge today, Sheriff Gantt will. He'll be back today. Everybody in town knows what happened. Nobody is blaming you."

Yeah, he thought after she left, but a feller can spend a long time in jail before he ever gets a chance to prove his innocence. Damn the goddamn law anyway.

It was the sheriff who took him before the judge. "If I'd been here you wouldn't have stayed the night in jail," he said. His round face was screwed up with worry and his handlebar moustache was twitching. "I had to go see the district attorney down to Trinidad and just got back. Hell, I no more than unsaddled my horse when people were telling me all about the shooting."

In the judge's court, McCagg was surprised to see a dozen men and women sitting on the wooden plank benches, waiting to see what would happen. Among them was the bartender from the Curly Wolf. Redbeard and his pal were not among them.

Judge Topah strode through the room with a stern look on his face, climbed the platform and seated himself behind the desk. He looked out over the spectators with a frown. "It is customary for everyone to stand when the duly elected judge enters the courtroom," he scolded. "Everyone stand."

Everyone stood.

"All right. Now then, the county court of Trinchera County is in session. Be seated. Mr. Sheriff, do you have a matter to bring before the court?"

It didn't take long. The bartender was the only witness, and when the judge learned that the other witnesses were not present, he frowned again. "It is the sheriff's responsibility to see that the witnesses are present."

"I, uh, Your Honor, I was in Trinidad and just got back. I couldn't find the other witnesses. I've been told that they left town."

"Very well, I find there is insufficient evidence to keep the defendant in custody. But," he peered down his nose at McCagg, "settling disputes with gunfire will not be tolerated in my jurisdiction, and if the district attorney, when he hears about the shooting, wishes to refile charges against you, you will have to stand trial in the district court. Next case."

"He won't," Sheriff Gantt said as they left the courtroom. "He always goes along with my recommendation, and I don't arrest anybody unless I've got the goods on them." He chuckled. "Clarence Topah practiced law in Denver before he came down here. When the citizens had to elect a judge he was the only man in the county qualified to sit on a bench. Now that he's the Judge he wants to preside over a trial so bad he can't stand it."

***

He wanted to get out of town as soon as possible now. He hated having to tell Dawnmarie that he'd killed a man, but he had to do it. She had always disapproved of fighting, but she understood that human nature being what it was men sometimes had to fight. When her own husband had been beaten up in a fight, she had only sympathized with him. McCagg believed she would sympathize with him too. Still, he dreaded having to tell her.

The livery owner took his half-dollar and warned him that O'Brien and his pals had left town yesterday afternoon, saying they would be back to settle the score. The sorrel was glad to get out of the dark barn and into the sunlight, and McCagg was about to put his foot in the stirrup when he heard his name called.

"Oh, Mr. McCagg. Yoohoo."

He wished she would leave him alone. Sure, he appreciated her bringing him some good food while he was in jail, but he wished she would leave him alone now. He forced a smile anyway. "Yes, Mrs. Brown?"

Hurrying up to him, she handed him a roll of newspapers. "These just came in yesterday. Dawnmarie likes to read newspapers. Would you be so kind as to take these to her? You are going to see her, aren't you?"

"Sure, I'll take them. Uh, I want to thank you again for the chuck. I know the county doesn't feed jail prisoners anywhere near that good."

"You're welcome, Mr. McCagg. Give my regards to Dawnmarie and Bill."

Finally, he was mounted and out of town, following a wagon road between the sagebrush and cane cactus. A hot, bright sun beat down on his shoulders, and perspiration ran down his face from under the new felt Stetson. One of those wide-brimmed, high-crowned straw hats the Mexicans wore would have been more comfortable. He brushed flies off his

90

horse's neck and shoulders as he topped a low hill, rode down a draw and up a long, low rise. The river was on his left, with a few tall cottonwoods. The farm he'd seen before, with an adobe hut, a tin shed and short green rows of something growing, was across the creek. At the top of the rise, the hair on the back of his neck tingled a warning, and he reined up, twisted in his saddle and looked back. Five horsemen were on the hill behind him. From that distance he wouldn't have recognized them had it not been for the red beard. The bearded one raised a rifle, and two seconds later McCagg heard the POP. The distance was too great and the bullet fell short. But McCagg got the message.

The fight wasn't over.

Chapter Twelve

Dawnmarie took the news calmly. She said she had been worried about him, and was thankful that he was all right. He could tell by the tight expression on her face that she wished to God it hadn't happened, but nothing more was said about it. He told her and Bill about arranging to meet with the U.S. land agent first thing in the morning, and he'd have to roll out of bed early. He'd leave without breakfast, he said, but Dawnmarie wouldn't hear of it. "You're not going to leave my home on an empty stomach, Uncle Benjamin. I wouldn't treat a stranger that way, much less my only relative."

"Ben," Bill said after supper, "I'll drill the well on your half-section, and if I hit water I'll build a shack and plant somethin'. That way you can prove up on it without bein' there."

"If you hit water and you do the proving up, it's yours. I've got no use for it."

Dawnmarie busied herself reading the newspapers Ada Brown had sent. She had to turn the lamp wick up, pull the lamp to the edge of the table and sit close to it to read. "Hmm. Says a stage was robbed in the San Luis Valley on its way to Trinidad and three gold bricks were stolen. Four men did the robbing, all wearing long rain slickers to cover their clothes and masks to cover their faces.

"Hmm. Here's an article in the *Trinidad Gazette* about two more families moving off their homesteads. It quotes one man as saying President Grant was right when he called the land between the Missouri River and the Rocky Mountains nothing but a desert where nothing can grow. Too bad." She put the paper down and was deep in thought a moment. "Why, I remember reading that. Why, that was a long time ago. Way back in 1873, or thereabouts." She read on quietly a while, then, "Oh, they've got some new sewing machines at a store in Trinidad. Oh well, I don't have a lot of sewing to do anyway."

Finally, she put the paper down, rubbed her eyes with the heels of her hands and reached for another newspaper. "I like the Trinidad paper, but the Denver papers carry more national news. This one is the *Rocky Mountain News*. Sometimes it's kind of funny. People in Denver think we're still shooting buffalo and fighting off the Indians down here. They think we can't read, I guess."

"Some of us can't," her husband put in.

"You can. Look." She pointed at a big headline. "What does it say?"

He read, haltingly, painfully. "S-T-A-G-E R-O." He guessed the rest. "Stage robbed. That's what it says."

"See. You just need more practice. It's the same story as the one in the Trinidad paper. They must have telegraphed it to Denver. That telegraph is a wonderful service. Tomorrow when the light is better you can read some more."

Before the husband and wife went to the bedroom for the night, she said, "Don't worry about oversleeping, Uncle Benjamin. Bill never oversleeps."

Chuckling at that, McCagg blew out the lamp, took off all but his shorts and crawled between the blankets on the pallet on the floor. He kept the Smith & Wesson on the floor beside the bed. But for a time, sleep wouldn't come.

It was that headline: STAGE ROBBED. It reminded him of a robbery on the train from Leadville to Denver. An attempted robbery, rather. He'd killed two men then. Now he'd killed another.

The whole thing came back as if it had just happened. The explosion, the gunfire, the bodies.

He was in the express car, his usual place, when the train stopped with a shuddering, jerking grind, a screeching of iron wheels on iron rails. Then he heard pounding on the door between the mail car and a passenger car. "Open up in there. Open 'er up or we'll blow 'er open."

He squatted behind the big iron Wells Fargo safe and said nothing, just kept his eyes glued to the door, the .45 in his hand.

A shotgun boomed and a splintery hole appeared in the door. Another blast and the lock shattered. When the door opened, he was ready for them. The .45 popped and bucked in his hand, and drove them back.

"Throw down your gun and come out of there. Come out or we'll blast you out."

Still, he said nothing. Just waited.

It was quiet for a few seconds, but he knew they hadn't given up. Fingers moving as fast as he could move them, he punched out the empty shell casings and reloaded. He saw the stick of dynamite come through the door and land on the floor not far from where he squatted. With a groan and a curse, he dove to the other side of the big safe and got there a split second before the explosion.

It deafened him. The safe teetered on one edge and fell over, missing his legs by inches. Mail sacks were ripped apart, and the air was thick with flying papers. His head was full of church bells. His vision was muddy.

They were coming.

Only vaguely aware of what he was doing, McCagg rolled. He rolled behind the overturned safe, aimed at the door and fired. A half-dozen shots came his way. They smacked against the safe and thudded into the wall behind him. He fired four more shots, aiming at dim figures among the smoke and papers.

Then it was quiet again. Except for the bells in his head.

The car was full of smoke, and papers still swirled around him. He waited, shaking his head, trying to clear his vision and stop the ringing. Waited, Smith & Wesson ready. One bullet left. Waited.

Gradually the papers settled on the floor and the smoke cleared enough that he could see the door. It stood wide open, vacant. The door in the next car was open too, also vacant. Two men lay on the floor near the door.

"Hey," a man yelled. "Hey in there. They're gone."

Head ringing, he waited and watched.

"They're gone. Are you hit? We're comin' in. Don't shoot. Don't shoot."

Mr. Robert Carns, regional manager for Wells Fargo, made a small ceremony out of it when he handed McCagg two fifty dollar bills and a commendation printed on a sheet of paper decorated with fancy gold scrolls. He delivered a small speech, praising him for bravery above and beyond the call of duty. The Denver newspapers were represented, and two reporters tried to interview McCagg. No use.

"He's drunker'n a lord," a reporter said. "He doesn't know where he is or what he's doing."

"He's tanked up on stagger soup, all right."

Sleeping was impossible. It wasn't the hard floor, it was the shame. Demon booze was ruining his life. It had cost him his job with the Rangers and it had cost him his job with Wells Fargo. Got a commendation and a bonus and was fired all in the same day. Shame, shame. He lay awake hoping Dawnmarie never found out. The shame would be hard to bear if she ever found out.

By noon the land was McCagg's. The U.S. land agent had paced off a half-section, driven official stakes in the ground, and given McCagg a receipt for his fifty dollar registration fee. A half-section of prickly pear and sagebrush, but with some good gramma and buffalo grass too. With a well, it would be good grazing land, but worthless for farming. In fact, a plow would ruin it.

In El Moro, McCagg had a meal in the Trinchera Cafe and pondered his next move. If he had the drill pipe he'd go to work drilling a well on his land. Or, if he had the pump rods he'd go to work installing a pump on Bill's well in front of the Kleagen house. He had neither, so what to do?

He'd ride down to Trinidad, that's what he'd do. Hunt up that lawyer, pay a fee and find out whether squatters' rights meant anything. If it was, he and Bill would defend to the death the Kleagens' right to the land. Hopefully, they'd get some help from the sheriff. If it wasn't, well at least they'd know where they stood. Maybe Bill could take down the house and put it up again on McCagg's homestead. It would be better than nothing. McCagg would help.

On his way to Trinidad, he looked to the west at the shadowy, blue mountains. They raised the horizon so high he had to tilt his head back to see it from under his hat. Looked cool. Good country. In the summer. Cold and snowy in the winter. Rocky. Down here under the Rockies, the land was cut by deep arroyos with wide valleys, piñon and cedars. The railroad from the north paralleled the wagon road, and carried most of the traffic nowadays. He would have taken the railroad, but the train had already gone through El Moro and there wouldn't be another until early next morning. Then he would have had to wait another day to make the return trip. It wasn't far, and a horse traveling at a steady trot could make it in a few hours. He'd get there before the lawyer closed his office for the day. He hadn't decided whether he'd wait until the next day to come back. If he came back tonight he'd have to give the sorrel some rest and feed and ride back in the dark. Oh well, he'd done his share of night riding. A horse, when he knew where he was going, could find his way easily in the dark.

Trinidad was an older, bigger town than El Moro. Before he got there, McCagg could see the smoke rising from sawmills and the coal mines over west. He passed a refractory where bricks were made and shipped to other parts of the state. Bricks were a good building material. Lasted longer than wood and didn't erode like adobe. Wind and rain had no effect on them.

The sorrel's head was up and its ears were twitching, catching all the sights, sounds and smells of a big town. Wagons of all kinds and sizes crowded the streets, and horsebackers wound their way between the wagons. Wooden sidewalks lined the streets downtown, along Commerce Street, past hotels, restaurants, businesses of all kinds, and saloons. Pedestrians were almost shoulder to shoulder on Commerce Street. Men in soot-covered overalls, faces black with coal dust, gentlemen in fine wool suits with vests and cravats on their throats, kids in ragged clothes with holes in the knees, ladies with corsets pulling their stomachs in tight and allowing the long dresses to flare out at the hips. McCagg had to turn around and ride back north a way to find a livery barn. He made sure the sorrel was fed some good hay, then went looking for the lawyer's office.

He found it on Commerce Street, on the second floor of a two-story brick building. Wooden stairs creaked under his boots as he climbed, and a wooden floor creaked in a hall until he stopped in front of a door with a thick glass pane. Painted on the glass was the message: Michael T. Haddow. Attorney At Law. He tried the door knob.

Locked.

For a moment he stood there, wondering what to do. Finally, he walked down the hall to the next door. The floor creaked and his boots thumped. A sign on that door told all interested persons that a land surveyor occupied the office. He tried the door knob. It turned and the door opened. A narrow-faced man in a striped shirt looked up from a desk and frowned as the door opened. McCagg quickly apologized.

"I beg your pardon, sir. I didn't mean to bother you. I'm looking for Mr. Haddow and I wonder if you can tell me where I might find him."

The frown disappeared and the man answered civilly, "Out of town. Took the train this morning. Said he'd be back tomorrow."

"Oh." McCagg suddenly felt drained. He'd made a long ride for nothing. "Tomorrow for sure?"

"That's what he said, but I can make no promises. His affairs are his own."

"Uh-huh. Uh, could you tell me, is there another lawyer in Trinidad?"

"Not that I know of. But business and professional people come and go."

"I see. Well, I'm obliged." He backed out the door, closed it and stood in the hall a moment. "Damnit," he muttered.

Outside on the plank walk, he had to sidestep to keep from colliding with a well-dressed gentleman, and he backed up against a building out of everyone's way while he tried to figure out what to do next. He could go back to El Moro and the Kleagens, but if he did that he would have accomplished nothing. If he didn't, Dawnmarie would worry. All right, he'd sent a telegraph message to Ada Brown, and if Dawnmarie and Bill went to El Moro to look for him, she could deliver the message.

Locating the United States and Mexico Telegraph Co., he wrote: "Mrs. Brown, if Dawnmarie asks, I'm in Trinidad waiting for a lawyer. Ben McCagg."

It cost seventy-nine cents, but it made him feel better. A good bed in a hotel would be welcome after sleeping on a floor and in a jail cell. He picked the Trinidad Hotel, checked into a room on the second floor and flopped down on the bed. After lying there a few minutes he felt restless and decided to buy some new pants and a shirt and take a bath. The pants were cotton duck, brown, and the shirt was light blue muslin,

98

soft and comfortable. A bath in a long, tin tub in the men's room on the first floor was relaxing until someone knocked on the door. It reminded him that other men had to use the room. As he walked out, a man in business clothes was waiting by the door. He scowled at McCagg.

A Trinidad newspaper told him the stage robbers still had not been caught. The stolen gold bars were worth thirty thousand dollars each. Yeah, he remembered Doc Bridges telling him about the value of gold bricks. The robbers, if they weren't caught, would be rich. For a while, anyway. That is, if they could sell the bricks. He sat in his hotel room, turned the page and read on. Another big hunk of land that was once part of the old Maxwell Land Grant had been sold to a rancher from Texas. He grinned to himself when he remembered someone once saying Texas was going to take over Colorado without firing a shot. Texans were getting control of some of the real estate, all right. What they couldn't homestead they bought.

Restless again, he went back to the street. A steam whistle somewhere signaled the end of the work day for some company's employees. Soon the single men would be heading for the cafes and then the saloons. That's all a single man had to do in his spare time, drink and gamble and get in trouble. A man with a family had other things to do. McCagg grinned a wry grin and shook his head sadly. Which was worse, drinking and carousing or working your heart out to support a family? That was something every man had to decide for himself. A family man he wasn't and never wanted to be. But that drinking and carousing was getting old too. Nope, he'd had enough of that.

He sat in the hotel lobby for a while and listened to a drummer complain about how bad business was. Nobody wants to work any more, the drummer groused. There just ain't a market anymore for sewing machines. Those factories back east were making clothes so cheap and so fast that women nowadays didn't care much for sewing. Every mercantile he went to had sewing machines in stock already and didn't need any more. Well, by God, if that's the way things were he'd go into ready-made clothes. By God, people couldn't go naked. Yep, he'd go back to Denver and get in with some company that sold clothes. There'd always be a market for clothes, by God. "What line are you in, mister? Cattle?"

McCagg didn't want to get into a long conversation, and he politely excused himself and went back to the sidewalk. It was dark by then, and street lamps were lighted. A ricky-tick piano sounded somewhere. Listening, he determined that it came from a saloon down the block. Good music. "Oh, Suzanna." Somebody was working up a storm on that tune. Idly, he walked in that direction and stopped in front of the door. The piano player was pounding out "Camp Town Races" now. Men were stomping their feet in rhythm. Inside, the cigar and pipe smoke was thick, and the smell of stale beer was strong. Men and women were dancing on a small dance floor in front of the piano. Men were laughing and slapping each other on the back.

"What'll it be, mister?"

"Oh, uh, whiskey," McCagg said.

Chapter Thirteen

Smelled like horse manure. He ought to know, he'd smelled enough of it. But who cared? Thinking about it was too much work. Easier to just lie there. Yeah, just lie there.

"Hey, mister." The toe of a boot nudged his hip. "Hey. You got to git up. You can't lie there. Hey."

Groaning, he opened one eye. He'd been dreaming about horse manure. Some dream. Gawd, what a head. Someone was hammering on his head. He closed the eye and groaned.

"Mister. Come on, mister, git up. I got work to do."

"Uhhh, quit it. Quit it, will you." He forced the eye open again.

"You got to git up, mister. You can't lie there."

"Uhhh." The other eye opened.

"You want I should git the law? They'll lock you up if I do."

He raised his head. "Uhhh." It was horse manure. Gawd, he was lying in it. Old straw and horse manure. "Uhhh. What . . ."

"You're in my barn. You got to git up."

"N-o-o." He sat up. His head pounded and his eyes burned. "What, uh . . ."

"It's my livery. I know you 'cuz your sorrel horse is here. But you got to git up. I don't wanta git the law."

"The law? Uhhh." He got to a sitting position and looked around. "Only wanted to see about my horse."

"You must of been so tanked up you didn't know where you was."

Both eyes open, he cranked his neck and looked up at the livery owner, a short man in shapeless denims, flat-heeled boots and a black hat. "Uhhh." Painfully, taking care not to jar anything, he got to his feet and leaned against the wooden wall of a horse stall. He rubbed a hand over his sparse hair, over his head, and looked around for his hat. The livery owner picked it up and handed it to him.

"Can you walk? Where're you stayin'? Go stick your head in that there water tank. That'll help."

"Yeah. All right. I'll, uh, do that." With staggering steps, he made his way to a steel tank the size of a wash tub, dropped onto this knees and put his hands in the water. Cool. He splashed water over his face and put his hat on. Standing, he said, "Did I really sleep in horse shit?"

That brought a grin to the livery owner's face. "You sure did. I've seen some drunk men, but not drunk enough to do that. You really been up Fortication Creek. Nobody'll believe me when I tell 'em."

Fumbling through his pockets brought another groan. No wallet. "No hotel room key. No nothing."

The livery owner's grin faded to a frown. "No? I'm not surprised. This town is lousy with footpads. They'll steal the boots off a man's feet. You had a gun. Did they take that too?"

"Oh, gawd." The holster was empty.

He staggered outside, and when the morning sun struck him he felt like he'd been hit between the eyes with a hammer. Another groan came from him, and he held his hand over his eyes, slowly spreading the fingers and letting the sunlight in a little at a time.

"Hey, here's a gun. Right here on the ground. Must be yours."

Turning, he saw the livery owner stoop and pick up a sixgun. "Yep," the livery man said. "You musta dropped it."

"Huh-uh. Never dropped a gun in my life."

102

"Must be yours. Got some writin' on it. Let's see. Wells Fargo, and, uh, my eyesight ain't so good."

"It's mine. Lucky me."

"Wonder why they didn't take it? Oh, I'll bet I know. That writin'. They was afraid to be seen with it. Do you work for the Wells Fargo, mister?"

"Used to. Uh, is my horse all right?"

"Sure. You owe me fer his feed."

Looking down at his boots, McCagg grumbled, "I'll pay you. Got to get to my hotel. Which one . . ."

"The Trinidad, I think. I b'lieve that's what you said the first day you was here."

"I'll be back." He staggered toward the hotel.

The hotel clerk, a young man with garter sleeves and a green eyeshade, wrinkled his nose and looked like he was going to spit. "Lost your key, huh?"

"Yeah, I, uh, lost it."

"That'll cost you. And you owe for two days' room rent."

"Two days? Has it been that long?"

"Yep. I was gonna toss your stuff out this morning if you didn't show up, but all you've got is some dirty clothes."

"I'm surprised I've got that. All right, I'll pay you. I've got to get cleaned up, get some more clothes."

"You pay now or go elsewhere."

"All right." He sat in a wooden chair in the lobby and pulled off his left boot, turned it upside down and shook it. A twenty dollar bill dropped into his hand. He put the boot on and handed the bill to the clerk.

"I can't bust that this morning. You'll have to go to the bank. Two doors east."

"Aww, hell."

An hour and a half later he had a bath, a shave and was dressed in the clothes he'd worn to town. The clothes were dirty, but at least they weren't smeared with horse manure. In a working man's cafe he managed to swallow some breakfast. Still feeling weak and groggy, he went back to the lawyer's office. Damnit. Locked. The land surveyor next door told him that Michael T. Haddow had been there, but had left town again.

"I told him about you, and he said you'd have to come back later."

"Did he say when he'd be back?"

"He didn't say. Sometimes he's gone for a week. He said there was another lawyer in town, but there wasn't enough business for two and the other fellow left."

"Aww, hell."

No use waiting. He considered going to the town marshal and reporting the theft of his wallet, but ruled that out. He'd never heard of money stolen from a working man being found and returned. Property? Once in a great while. But cash? It just never happened. Might as well go back to El Moro and the Kleagens.

"Oh, my God." He couldn't help groaning aloud. A man on the sidewalk turned and stared. He'd have to go back with too little money. Not enough to pay for the pump rods and the drill pipe. How the hell was he going to explain it? What the hell was he going to do? If she weren't his baby sister, he'd just not go back. Send her a message saying he had to leave. But he couldn't do that to her. He had to go back. He'd say he was sorry, but his money was lost and he'd have to leave and get a job cowboying on some Texas ranch. Come to think of it, he had friends in Texas. Maybe he could borrow the money and send it to them right away, then pay back the loan from his wages. Or he could borrow from a bank, using the house his mother had left him as collateral. One or the other.

But first he had to go back and explain himself. Gawd, how he dreaded it.

He felt like a man going to his own funeral. All the way back he cursed himself and wished he had died and was going to his own funeral. Then when he thought about it, he was glad he was still alive. He couldn't help thinking about how awful it would have been if he'd had his throat cut back there

104

in that livery barn. The thieves could have cut his throat as easily as not. It would have been terrible, the sheriff notifying Dawnmarie that her uncle, her only relative, was robbed and murdered while he was drunk out of his mind. Alive, he could make it up to her. He'd do it, too, if it took the rest of his life.

He would tell her only that he was robbed. And he would leave with the promise to send her the money right away. He believed he could borrow it. He still had friends.

Skirting El Moro, he rode on to the homestead and got there just before dark. His niece and her husband were glad to see him and welcomed him back. But they knew all was not well.

"You look bad, Uncle Benjamin. Are you sick?"

"Sick at heart," he said, and he told them.

"It don't matter," said Bill.

"He's right, Uncle Benjamin. We have no land anyway."

It took him a moment to realize what she was saying. "What?"

"Sheriff Gantt was here. He brought an order from the judge. We have to leave."

Supper was a quiet one. They all felt as if they were eating their last meal. Finally, Bill Kleagen said, "We've got ten days to go to court and prove our right to the land. But if we lose in court we have to git. That's what the sheriff said."

"Yes," said Dawnmarie. "We can hope for a miracle."

McCagg said nothing. All he could do was silently curse himself for getting so drunk as to pass out in a barn and make himself easy to rob. Were it not for his drinking he'd be in a position to help financially.

They went to bed early. As tired and sick as he was, McCagg still couldn't sleep. By daylight he looked and felt even worse than he had the day before. If that was possible.

Finally, while he sipped his second cup of coffee, he told them what was on his mind. "The judge said you're entitled to a hearing. Maybe he'll give you more time if you ask for it."

Bill nodded, but said nothing. Dawnmarie asked, "What would that accomplish?"

"It'll take a lawyer to argue your side, and with enough time maybe we can get one. But . . ."

"Not enough money. We have a few dollars left. How much do you think it will take?"

"Don't know. But you and Bill need what little money you've got. You can't just load up the wagon and haul off without some money. Here's what I've been thinking, I can go back to Texas and borrow a hundred or so and send it to you. I've got friends, and I can borrow. That way you'll have enough to hire a lawyer or move or do whatever you want to do. You can go to your Grandma McCagg's house in Grand Prairie. It's still empty, and I don't need it. You and Bill might as well live in it."

"It might come to that, Uncle Benjamin, but first . . ." A pause, then, "Bill, what do you think?"

Bill put his coffee cup down and stood. "We don't know that a lawyer could do us any good, but let's go see the judge and find out exactly what's goin' on. I'll go harness the team."

They went first to the sheriff's office, the Kleagens in their wagon and McCagg on his sorrel horse. Sheriff Martin Gantt began shaking his head sadly as soon as they came in the door.

"I apologize," he said. "I didn't want to deliver that paper."

"We're not blamin' you, sheriff," said Bill Kleagen. "We came to town to see the judge about gettin' more time to do whatever we can about this."

"Far as I'm concerned, you can stay 'til you get good and ready to move," Sheriff Gantt said. "That lawyer threatened to get the district attorney to cite me for mal . . . uh, malfeasance, I believe he called it, but I ain't running honest folks off their land. If that's what a sheriff has to do, I don't want to be a sheriff."

"A lawyer?" Dawnmarie asked. "What lawyer?"

"Danged if I know his name. Didn't catch it. He came in here day before yesterday and handed me that paper from the judge and said I had to deliver it and serve notice."

"How about the Arbaughs? Did he have an eviction notice for them too?"

"Yeah, and they're fighting mad. Don't blame them a-tall."

"O-o-h," Dawnmarie groaned, "there's going to be some shooting and some people hurt, maybe killed."

Shaking his head again, the sheriff agreed, "It appears that way."

"I don't get it," McCagg said, frowning. "It doesn't make sense. Did O'Brien and his pals actually hire a lawyer? It doesn't make sense."

"It sure beats me." Martin Gantt lifted his hat and reset it. "They don't look like they'd have two cents to rub together, much less enough to hire a lawyer."

"And," Dawnmarie asked, "what do they want the land for? Do you suppose they're working for the cattlemen?"

"Don't think so, Mrs. Kleagen. I asked around. I don't think the cattlemen are interested in that country. There's nothing to keep them from grazing their stock around there anyhow unless you build some fence."

Bill Kleagen said, "The only cattle I've seen are our own."

"It's a puzzler."

"Well, anyway," Dawnmarie said, "let's go see the judge and find out what we can do."

They had to go to Judge Topah's house and knock on the door. The judge promised to be in his courtroom directly. They went there and waited, sitting on the wooden planks that served as seats. When the judge entered, swinging his walking stick, they stood until he was seated at his heavy desk on the platform.

"Now then, do you have a matter to bring before the court?"

Dawnmarie looked at her husband. He looked at McCagg. McCagg whispered, "It's not my land. It'd be better if one of you did the talking."

Bill Kleagen whispered, "You do it, Dawn."

"Well." The judge was impatient. "Will you stop whispering and speak up."

Dawnmarie stood. "Mr. Topah, we would like to . . ."

"You will address me as Your Honor."

"Oh. Excuse me. Your Honor we would . . ."

"You will first identify yourself."

"Of course. I am Mrs. William Kleagen, this is my husband Mr. Kleagen on my left, and this gentleman is . . ."

"I've met Mr. McCagg. And what do you wish to bring before the court, Mrs. Kleagen." Judge Topah leaned forward and put his elbows on the desk. His features had softened.

"You signed an eviction notice which was served yesterday by Sheriff Gantt. We understand we have a right to a hearing, and we are asking for more time to prepare for it."

"Yes, you do have a right to a hearing, Mrs. Kleagen." The judge was favorably taken by Dawnmarie and was talking like a father. "The eviction order will be stayed, and I will notify the sheriff."

"Why, thank you, Your Honor." Dawnmarie sat.

"Mrs. Kleagen, the hearing cannot be put off indefinitely. How soon will you be prepared? Do you have legal counsel?"

She stood again. "No, sir. I, we, haven't decided what to do about that."

"Very well, a hearing date will be set for, uh, two weeks from today. Will that give you enough time?"

She looked at her husband then at McCagg. McCagg nodded. "Yes sir."

"Very well. This court is adjourned."

"Your Honor." McCagg stood. "I'd like to ask you, if you don't mind, sir, who is the counsel for the plaintiffs?"

"The gentleman who appeared before me was a Mr. Haddow. Michael T. Haddow."

"Uh-oh," said McCagg. "Him."

Chapter Fourteen

The pump rods and the drill pipe had arrived on the train from Denver only that morning, and were at the railroad depot waiting to be picked up. But, Dawnmarie said sorrowfully, the Kleagens didn't have the money to pay for it.

"Take it anyway," Ada Brown said. "Pay me when you can."

"No, we can't do that, Mrs. Brown," said Bill Kleagen. "No telling when we'd be able to pay. I'm real sorry. I hope you can sell 'em to somebody else."

"It's my fault," McCagg admitted. "I'm the one who ordered the stuff and I'm the one who promised to pay. Tell you what, Mrs. Brown, I'm going back to Texas, and I'll send some money to Bill and Dawnmarie, and then they can take the stuff."

"Take it now. Please."

"Aw, thanks just the same, Mrs. Brown, but we don't even know if we own a well."

"Bill, if you don't own one now, you will. Mr. McCagg's homestead will produce water. Take it."

"It's a gamble," said McCagg.

"Then I'll gamble. Besides, I . . ." Mrs. Brown looked down, then at Dawnmarie. "I'm putting the store up for sale. I . . . since Hiram died, I just don't want to run it anymore."

"Oh, Ada. You can't. We . . . we can't get along without your store. The other mercantile doesn't offer . . . Oh, Ada!"

"Take the pipe, Dawnmarie. I want to do this for you. Take it, please."

McCagg allowed he'd help Bill Kleagen haul the drill pipe to his half-section and get started drilling, then he'd hit the trail for Texas. No use putting down the sucker rods. They might have to pull them back up again. If they struck water at McCagg's homestead, they would move there, and Bill would file for an adjacent half-section.

They hauled the pipe to the spot that Bill had picked out. It was in a shallow draw where the grass grew higher than anywhere else, an indication that water had stayed there longer than anywhere else. Bill stood on the wagon with his sledge hammer while McCagg held the first length of pipe perpendicular. Bill hit the top a ringing blow. The pointed, grooved end sank two inches.

"The ground's soft on top," Bill grunted. "Wouldn't it be nice if it was that soft all the way down to water." He hit it again and again, getting into a rhythm that drove the pipe deeper and deeper. He had to stop, eventually, raise his hat and use his shirt sleeve to wipe sweat from his forehead and out of his eyes.

"Let me spell you," McCagg said.

"Naw. We'll screw on another pipe in a minute. Then I can finish the job by myself."

"It'll take a few weeks. Maybe months. You need a breather. Let me spell you."

"Naw. It was my dumb idea."

"Just the same I can't let you do all the . . ." His mouth stayed open, and his eyes squinted to the east. There was a horse over there. And a man.

"Don't look now, Bill, but I think we're being watched. That's . . . why that's one of O'Brien's pals. I recognize the

110

sonofabitch from here."

The man was sitting on the ground, watching McCagg and Bill Kleagen. When he saw he had been discovered, he stood and got on his horse.

"Whatta you reckon he's up to, Ben?"

"Damned if I know. Uh-oh, look out, he's gonna shoot."

A pistol popped, and then the man wheeled his horse and rode away at a gallop, heading southwest toward El Moro. McCagg hurriedly untied his sorrel from the wagon and stepped into the saddle.

"I'm going after that sonofabitch."

"Be carful, Ben."

It was a horse race. The man's brown horse had a good lead, and it was running flat out. The man turned in his saddle and fired. McCagg ignored the shot and talked to the sorrel.

"Go get 'em, feller. Get after 'em."

The sorrel flattened out and ran as hard as it could run, legs pumping, jumping the gulleys, dodging the cane cactus. The man ahead turned and fired two more shots. He had to twist and shoot behind him from the back of a running horse. His shooting didn't worry McCagg.

"Get 'em, feller. Show me you're worth what I paid for you."

Hooves pounding, animal heart pounding, jumping. The distance between the two horses was narrowing. "Sic 'em."

Two more shots came from the man ahead. The gap was shorter.

McCagg took down his catch rope. He muttered, "I ain't pitched a loop for a long time. Wanta catch that sonofabitch alive if I can. Six shots. He can't reload and ride that fast."

Closer.

McCagg tied one end of the rope to his saddle horn and built a loop in the other end. "Pretend he's a cow or a horse or something. Sic 'em, feller." He began whirling the loop over his head to put some power behind it.

The man on the brown horse wasn't looking back now, just spurring hard. The sorrel gained. The gap was closing.

"Go get 'em."

Close now. "Give me another yard, feller. One more yard. Now."

He had the loop swinging over his head, and he pitched it straight out. The loop hit the man across the right shoulder and settled over both shoulders. McCagg jerked the slack out with his right hand, his throwing hand, jerked the loop tight. Took up on the reins.

"Let's yank the sonofabitch off that horse, but not too hard. Don't want to kill the sonofabitch."

The sorrel slowed to a stop, and the man was jerked backward out of the saddle. He hit the ground on the seat of his pants. Hit hard. Lay still. McCagg was on the ground by the time the sorrel had stopped. When he saw the man wasn't moving, had no fight in him, he tied the reins to the rope, close to the bridle bit, to keep the horse from turning away and dragging the man. Then he squatted between his spurs and studied the man's face.

"Yep. You're one of them gunsels that's running with Old Redbeard. You're one of the sonsofbitches."

The man had a three-day growth of brown whiskers and thin brown hair. His hat lay on the ground ten feet away. He opened his eyes, got them focused, and sat up suddenly. The bore of a .45 Smith & Wesson was shoved against the end of his nose.

McCagg grinned. "Hell of a way to treat a feller, ain't it. But, hell, we treat steers that way all the time."

"Huh? Wha . . ." He started to take the rope from around his shoulders, but got only as far as his neck.

"Don't move. Leave it here. Don't move nothing but your mouth. I want to hear some answers to some questions."

"I ain't squawkin'."

McCagg's grin widened. "The hell you ain't. What if I was to shoot off your right ear and then your left ear and

112

then your nose, and . . ."

"Go to hell."

"All right." McCagg stood, backed up two steps and aimed the .45. "If my aim is good all you'll lose this time is your right ear. If I miss I might hit your head. But don't worry, I'm a fair to middlin' shot."

The .45 popped. Blood spurted from the man's right ear lobe.

"Damn. Only nicked it. Well hell, I'll try again. I think I can take off half the ear this time." He squinted down the barrel.

"Wait. Don't." The man put his right hand over the ear, drew it back, studied the blood as if fascinated.

"Feel like answering some questions?"

"Whatta you wanta know?"

"Well now." McCagg squatted between his spurs again, this time a few yards away from the man. He held the Smith & Wesson loosely. "What were you doing just now?"

"I only wanted to see what you two was doin'."

"Why did you want to see that?"

"He told me to watch you. Timothy O'Brien."

"Uh-huh. All right. Now, what does O'Brien and the rest of you want with the Kleagens' homestead?"

"We don't. I mean, O'Brien and the rest of us don't give a damn about no homestead."

"That brings up the next question. You can guess what it is."

"I don't know."

"What do you mean, you don't know? There has to be a reason."

The man was looking at the .45 with narrow eyes. His body was tense. McCagg could read his mind. He was wondering if he had a chance of grabbing the gun and wrestling it out of McCagg's hand.

Grinning again, McCagg said, "Go ahead and try it. I won't have time to aim for your ear and I'll have to put the

113

slug between your eyes."

The body relaxed.

"Like I said, don't move nothing but your mouth. Now, if you don't want the land, why are you trying to get it?"

"He told us to. He's payin' us."

"And that brings up the next question, and you can guess what that one is too."

"I don't know."

"Aw hell." McCagg raised the .45 and took aim at the right ear again. "If you hold still, don't move a hair, I can take the bottom off clean. Get ready, here goes."

"Don't."

"Who?"

"Mr. Haddow."

McCagg snorted, surprised, "Huh? Haddow? Michael T. Haddow? The lawyer?"

"Yeah."

"Well, I'll be doodly damned." For a second, McCagg looked down. It was a mistake, almost a fatal mistake.

The man jumped. Jumped unbelievably fast. He was on top of McCagg before McCagg could get out of his way. McCagg's finger was on the trigger, but the gun was shoved aside. The man had his right hand wrapped around it. Now the gun was between the two men, flat against McCagg's chest with the other man on top of it. McCagg bucked, kicked and tried to roll, but he couldn't loosen the man's grip.

With his free hand, he grabbed at the man's hair and pulled back. Couldn't budge him.

Both men strained, grunted, cursed.

McCagg got the fingers of his left hand in the man's face and clawed and scratched. Still, he couldn't budge him. The new Stetson rolled off, and in desperation McCagg grabbed it with his free hand and threw it in the direction of the sorrel horse. The horse thought the hat sailing toward him was something to fear. It snorted and jumped backward.

114

The rope was still around the man's neck, and he was yanked off McCagg and dragged six feet before the horse stopped backing up.

He was close to death. A gurgling came from his throat. His eyes were squinched tight, and he was barely breathing. McCagg led the horse forward, slacking up on the rope. He untied the rope from the saddle horn, knelt beside the man.

"Damnit," he muttered. "Didn't want to kill him." He took the rope off the man's neck, saw the rope burns. "Hung him. Hung him the same as if he was tied to a tree." Glancing at the horse, he said, "Not your fault, feller. You might have saved my life. He's a stout sonofabitch. My fault. Should have watched him. But what he said took the wind out of me. Surprised the hell out of me."

There were more gurgles and a cough, then a strangling sound and another cough.

"I believe he's going to live. Give him enough time and he'll be back among the living."

After more coughs, his eyes opened. His hand went to his throat.

"You're a tough jasper, I'll give you credit for that. That would have broke my neck."

"Arrgh." He sat up, right hand rubbing his throat.

"Whenever you feel like it, we'll take up where we left off."

"Arrgh." Hacking, coughing. Voice raspy, "You goddamn sonofabitch. You goddamn near hung me."

Rocking back on his heels, McCagg said, "That ain't the way I planned it. What I planned to do is, I planned to shoot off a piece of you at a time."

"You goddamn sonofabitch."

"At least you can talk again. Now, where were we? Oh yeah, you were about to tell me why that lawyer hired you."

"Go to hell."

The .45 came up again. "It would be a dirty shame, after you barely escaped a hanging, to get shot in the head."

"I don't know."

McCagg squinted down the short barrel. "What was that?"

"I don't know. He wouldn't say. O'Brien ast 'im, and didn't get no answer. Said it was none of our business."

"You're lying?"

"I swear it. We tried to figure it out and we can't figure it ourselves." His voice was getting back to normal.

McCagg considered that, then stood and looked around. The brown horse was cropping the grass a hundred yards away. He looked back at the man. Finally, he went to him, lifted his sixgun out of the holster, stuck it in his belt, walked to the sorrel horse and mounted.

"All right, tell O'Brien if I see him out this way, anywhere near here, I'll shoot him on sight. And if I hear of you and your pals giving my friends any trouble, I'll come looking for you."

"I believe you, mister."

"Get on your horse and get."

Chapter Fifteen

There was a lot of guessing in the Kleagen house after supper that night, but nobody could think of a logical reason for what was going on.

"One thing is obvious," Dawnmarie said. "That lawyer, Michael Haddow, wants this land."

"If he's read the law and can make a livin' with the law, it's a cinch he's not goin' to plow and dig and scratch for a livin'."

"He's got to have a pretty strong reason," McCagg put in. "Another question is, why doesn't he just buy these two homesteads. They could be bought."

"Harvey Arbaugh said he's only gonna give 'er another year and if he cain't get a crop he's pullin' out and leavin' ever'thing behind."

"Mr. Haddow could buy it," said Dawnmarie, "but if he can get it for nothing, why put out the money?"

"That's his plan, all right," McCagg allowed. "Use the law to get it for nothing. The only money he's out is whatever he's paying O'Brien and his pals, and I'm betting they work cheap."

"Let's see." Dawnmarie pursed her lips. "The U.S. government sells land for a dollar and a quarter an acre. Two half-sections would cost, let's see, around eight hundred dollars. What do you suppose he's paying those hoodlums?"

"A lot less. But he doesn't want just any land, he wants this land."

Bill shook his head. "I'd ask more than that, now that I've got a well. And this house cost about three hundred in lumber."

"Plus a lot of work."

"So," said McCagg, "he's figured out a way to get it for the cost of hiring some thugs."

"It's ironic," Dawnmarie mused. "The law is supposed to protect people, and he's using it to rob people."

"It's tricky," McCagg said. "Men who know all the tricks of the law can get by with just about anything."

"It appears that way."

"One thing is sure." McCagg drank the last of his coffee. "That lawyer is a thief. A legal thief, but a thief just the same."

"That he is, Uncle Benjamin. He could have come out here and negotiated with us, but he didn't show himself at all."

Bill Kleagen got up, took his coffee cup to the sink, sat again. "He's stayin' out of sight for a purpose. He's sneaky. You cain't trust a sneak."

"The big question is why does he want it?"

"He's got to be workin' for some cowman. Some cowman wants it. This house would make a good line shack, and the river has never gone dry. I'm surprised some cowman hasn't grazed over here already."

"What do you think of that theory, Uncle Ben?"

"That's the only one I can think of. It looks like some rancher has hired the lawyer to buy the land. Only, well, the U.S. land agent said O'Brien's pals have claimed a string of half-sections. Not a big square piece of land, but a strip where there's no water, no nothing. Now that's curious."

Dawnmarie took a kettle of boiling water off the stove and poured it into a dishpan. "Well, someday we'll find out." She turned back to the men. "But I'd give anything to know right

118

now."

Her husband chuckled. "This is somethin' you can put in your book, Dawn."

"Yes, I got a few more things to write about now."

McCagg tilted his chair back on its hind legs. "Unless we can get somebody to argue the law for us, and unless he can out-argue Michael T. Haddow, you'll have nothing to do next winter but write that book."

She smiled, "True. All I'll have to do is have a baby and write a book. But," the smile vanished, "this is our home. Bill has worked terribly hard for it. I can have a baby and write a book right here."

"We'll keep it, Dawn, honey," her husband said.

McCagg decided, when he went outside by himself into the cool night air, that he wasn't going to Texas after all. He didn't want to tell anyone, not ever, but he had another plan.

High, thin clouds covered the western horizon when the sun came up, but they weren't rain clouds. McCagg had the sorrel saddled and had his saddle bags filled with dried beef and Dawnmarie's homemade bread.

"I'll raise some money, and if I can I'll be back. I think I can raise a couple hundred right quick. You-all take care of each other."

She hugged him, kissed him on the cheek, and wiped a tear from her own cheek. "That's in case I don't see you for a while, Uncle Benjamin."

"I've got a hunch you'll be seeing me sooner than you expect."

He rode west to the outskirts of El Moro, then instead of turning south he reined the sorrel north, going around the town. Two miles north, he cut west again for a mile, looked for the rocky ravine that came down from the mountains, found it, rode along its sandy bottom five hundred yards and stopped.

119

The ravine was lined with shale, layers of it, and a twisted cedar grew on top. Under the cedar, he dismounted, and dug with his fingers between the two top layers of shale. Grunting with satisfaction, he uncovered a small canvas-wrapped bundle. Small but heavy. It was too heavy to put in a saddlebag without a counterbalance on the other side, so he tied it on top, right behind the cantle, tied it with saddle strings and short pieces of rope which went from the bundle to the rear rigging rings. Tied it down solid so it wouldn't bounce when the horse jogged.

That done, he mounted and rode out of the ravine and headed south. Again, he went around the town and got on the wagon road that paralleled the railroad. Out of sight of the town, he got down and rubbed dirt on his new Stetson and wiped a dirty hand across his face. He was glad he hadn't shaved for a couple of days. He mounted again and went on.

By keeping the sorrel on a steady trot he got to Trinidad at noon. On the way he passed two buggies, but he only waved, said, "Morning," and kept going. The livery owner was surprised to see him.

"You're not gonna git on another one a them high lonesomes, are you?"

"Don't think so, but then I wasn't planning on it the last time."

His horse cared for, he walked to Commerce Street, leaving the saddlebags with his saddle and carrying the canvas-wrapped bundle in his left hand. The sidewalk was crowded as usual. Repeatedly, he stepped aside to avoid a collision. His first stop was at a pile of newspapers held down by a granite rock. Dropping a nickel in a cigar box beside the newspapers, he took one and scanned the first page.

The story he was looking for was not on the first page, and that gave him hope. If what he feared had happened had happened, it would be front page news. Turning pages, he finally found it, only two paragraphs. His mouth turned up slightly in a tight grin. But now came the tricky part.

At the brick building, at the bottom of the steps that led to the office of Michael T. Haddow, he paused. Paused for a long moment. He recalled advice from Doc Bridges, and tried to remember it word for word:

"Try to imagine you're in the situation you want to make the sucker think you're in. Then behave the way you'd behave if you were in that situation."

All right. He'd arrested a few thieves in his time. He knew how their minds worked. He climbed the stairs.

The office door was locked.

Aw hell.

Then he heard footsteps coming up the stairs behind him. He waited. The man who approached was no one he'd ever seen before. He was puffing from the exertion of climbing stairs, and his fat red face glistened with sweat. Smooth-shaven, he wore a tight collar with a cravat, a finger-length dark coat, a vest, and wool pants with sharp creases down the legs.

"Are you looking for someone?" he asked.

"Uh, yeah." McCagg bit the words off, nervous. "Mr. Haddow, the lawyer."

"I am he." The fat man wiped his face with a white linen handkerchief.

Glancing around quickly, McCagg said, "I wanta talk to you."

"Do you have a legal problem?"

"Uh, yeah."

"Come in." Michael T. Haddow took a long key from a vest pocket and unlocked the door. McCagg followed him in and quickly shut the door behind them. A brief worry frown crossed the lawyer's face when he saw the door closed, but he proceeded to the far side of a big wooden desk, sat in a swivel chair and leaned back. "What kind of legal problem?" His eyes were on the Smith & Wesson.

"Uh." McCagg shifted his weight from one foot to the

121

other and looked quickly around the room. One wall was lined with book shelves, and the shelves were filled with handsomely bound books. "I've got a—another kind of problem."

"What is it?"

"Well, uh, Mr. Haddow, uh, I've been told that sometimes you are in the market for a profit. I mean, a sure profit that the, uh, the law might not approve of."

The lawyer leaned forward and put his elbows on the desk. "Whatever are you talking about?"

McCagg hefted the canvas-wrapped bundle onto the desk. It landed on the desk with a thud. "Are you sure there's nobody else around? I, uh, I've got somethin' here you might be interested in."

"Oh? And what might that be?"

Another quick look around, and McCagg slowly unwrapped the bundle. "Gold."

Chapter Sixteen

At first the lawyer only stared at the brick. He looked up at McCagg, then back at the brick. He swallowed, and said, "Where . . . where did you get that?"

"You heard about the stage robbery?"

It went exactly the way Doc Bridges described it. First a frown followed by a brightening of the face as understanding crept into the mind. Next came a gleam in the eyes, then a narrowing of the eyes, and finally a greedy, cunning look. Michael T. Haddow's tongue flicked over his lower lip, then the lips were clamped shut. He leaned back in his chair. The chair creaked under this weight. He put his elbow on the chair arms and made a steeple of the fingers on both hands. He spoke slowly:

"Are you saying this is one of the gold bars that was stolen in the stage robbery?"

"I ain't admittin' nothin'."

"Are you suggesting that I might be in the market for stolen goods?"

"I ain't sayin'."

"What I should do is turn you over to the sheriff."

"That's what you ought to do." He watched the lawyer's face.

"Hmm. Exactly what are you proposing?"

"Ten thousand dollars."

A humorless smile touched the fat face. "Oh, really. What makes you think it's worth that much?"

"It's worth three times that much. At the Denver mint. Even the newspaper said so."

"Oh? Then I suggest you take it to the Denver mint."

"You know I can't do that."

"Then what good is it to me?"

"Nothin'. Not right now. But in a year or so it will be. Soon's the dust settles from that robbery."

"Hmm. I believe I see what you're driving at."

"Whatta you say?"

"No. No, I don't think so."

"It's a good investment, Mr. Haddow."

"I suppose it is, but . . . there is a risk involved."

"Naw. In a year the robbery'll be forgot. There'll be too many more robberies and murders and stuff. This brick'll be worth thirty thousand dollars."

"No, I don't think so."

McCagg's heart dropped into his stomach. It hadn't worked. He had failed. The lawyer wasn't going to buy it. Hell. Damn. Goddamn. Might as well go. But he had to keep up the act until he got out of town. Slowly, reluctantly, he began to rewrap the brick. "Uh, you're not goin' to the law, are you?"

"I don't know. What would you do if I said I was?"

Hope surged in McCagg. The lawyer was interested. Otherwise he would either go to the sheriff or promise not to, to save his hide.

"Why, I don't know. I'm no killer. I'll just take this and git." He finished wrapping it.

"How about two thousand?"

"Huh? Two thousand? Why, that's robbery."

At that the lawyer threw his head back and laughed. "Robbery? That's funny. Haw-haw." He had no fear of the man before him now. "Haw-haw."

"Listen, Mr. Haddow, I'm desperate. What they call a

desperado. I'll let you have it for five thousand."

"Three thousand five or you can go elsewhere. I'm taking a risk, you know."

McCagg repeated the words as if he couldn't believe it, "Three thousand five hundred? For thirty thousand dollars worth of gold?"

"That's my offer."

"Aww. Goddamn it."

"Take it or leave it."

"Three thousand five hundred cash?"

"Cash. Good U.S. government money."

"Well, you've got me up a stump, Mr. Haddow. For three thousand and five hundred cash dollars it's yours."

"First, I have to have it assayed."

"Huh? Assayed?"

"Of course. Surely you don't think I'd buy gold without having it assayed."

"How can you do that?"

"There's an assayer right down the street."

"But you can't take this down there. He'd, uh . . ."

"Be suspicious? Yes, I suppose he would. Hmm. Here's what I'll do. I'll just take a shaving off this bar and take it to the assayer."

"Then what?"

"Then if it's gold, I'll go to my bank and return with the cash. However, it takes time to process a sample. He probably won't have the assay completed until tomorrow."

"Aww, goddamn it."

"That's the way it is. I'm not so foolish as to buy a brick without knowing what it's made of."

"Yeah, but . . . Tomorrow for sure?"

"For sure."

"You're not goin' to the law?"

"You have my word."

"Well, all right."

"Very well. Now then, let's just take a piece of this." He

reached inside his desk and produced a small penknife.

"Don't take too much. It's worth money, you know."

"Just a small shaving."

"Here. Let me." McCagg produced a larger folding knife from a pants pocket and carefully shaved off an inch-long piece from the brick. Suddenly, he jerked up straight. "Is that someone at the door?"

"There's no one. I have an appointment, but not for another hour."

"I don't wanta be seen with this. I think I heard someone in the hall. Is the door locked?"

"Why, I don't believe so. I'm not in the habit of locking the door while I'm in."

"I ain't takin' no chances. I think I heard somebody."

"Probably the gentleman next door, but if it will make you less nervous, I'll go lock the door." The fat man stood and walked across the room.

Quickly, holding his breath, McCagg took a sliver of gold from a shirt pocket, placed it on the desk and pocketed the sliver he had just shaved from the brick. He didn't have to pretend nervousness. He was nervous.

"Now then." Haddow sat down in his chair again. "I'll take this to the assayer. Why don't you come back tomorrow at, oh, say ten o'clock. The assay should be completed by then."

"Well, I'm, uh, takin' this with me." Fingers trembling, he re-rewrapped the brick. "Uh, Mr. Haddow, I'm uh, I'm busted. Could you let me have a few bucks on account?"

"Need some drinking money?"

"No sir. No sir, I ain't touchin' a drop 'till I git down to El Paso. But I ain't et today."

"Very well." He reached inside his coat and pulled out a thick wallet. "Here's five. I'll deduct it from whatever I pay you tomorrow."

It was too soon to hear from Uncle Benjamin, but Dawnmarie wanted to go to town anyway. She needed a woman to talk to. Ada Brown had always been a good listener, and they had always had a good visit. There was the baby to talk about and there was Uncle Benjamin.

She hoped he wouldn't mortgage Grandma McCagg's house. It was his now, and he could do with it as he pleased, but she had always hoped that one day he would tire of his wandering adventurous ways, find a good woman and live in that house. He hadn't mentioned mortgaging the house, but she was afraid that that was what he had in mind.

She wanted to go to town, but couldn't. Bill had taken the team and wagon up to Uncle Benjamin's half-section and was pounding away on that drill pipe. A dreamer. Dreamed of striking water, erecting some windmills and buying some cattle. A sigh came from her as she kneaded bread dough on the kitchen table. Yes, Bill was a dreamer. But he didn't just sit and dream. He worked and dreamed. She wouldn't have him any other way. She sighed again. She hoped to God he didn't work himself into an early grave for nothing.

And there was Ada to worry about. Selling the store. Where would she go and what would she do? Bill, Uncle Benjamin and Ada. And the baby. Dawnmarie had a lot to think about. Worry about.

So far, everything had gone the way Ben McCagg had hoped. Glancing skyward as he rode north, he said, "Thanks, Doc."

Oh, he'd let the pettifogger gyp him down to three thousand, but hell, it was free money. And he'd taken it from a thief. No doubt at all now that Michael T. Haddow was a thief. A legal thief. The worst kind. The kind that made the law something to sneer at. But — McCagg chuckled to himself as he rode north — wouldn't that sonofabitch be in for a hell of a shock when he tried to sell that brick. Would he wait a year or would he think of a good lie to tell at the

Denver mint? No, come to think of it, he'd find out sooner than that. They were bound to meet again in El Moro. In court, probably.

Chuckling aloud now, he said, "I can't wait."

But the chuckle died when another problem came to mind. He wanted to get back to Dawnmarie and Bill right away, but they'd know he hadn't had time to make a round trip to Texas. Maybe he could tell a lie. Well, not a lie, but a half-truth. Like, he'd run into a man he knew in Trinidad and talked him out of some money. He didn't have to name the man. If Dawnmarie tried to pin him down he'd be vague. Not lie, just not tell the whole truth either. He had the money now to go to Pueblo and hire a lawyer. He could pay for the drill pipe and the sucker rods, and even order a couple of those windmills. Wouldn't that be something? And if a lawyer couldn't do any good, he had enough money to buy off that O'Brien. Sure, offer him some cash and he'd back out of his claim on the Kleagen homestead, and Dawnmarie could hurry to the land office and sign the papers the legal way.

Yeah, he grinned to himself as he rode north, thanks to a crooked lawyer, things were looking good.

Dawnmarie cracked the long whip to keep the horses on a gallop. "I'm sorry, I'm sorry," she cried. "Please hurry." The two horses were running their best, pulling the bouncing, rattling wagon toward El Moro.

She looked back at Bill. He was in pain and bleeding. She'd done all she knew how to do and she had to get him to town. "Please hurry." The horses were already badly winded, but they were doing their best.

It was gunfire that had awakened her that morning. Bill was up at daylight as usual, outside to see to the animals. At the first shot, she jerked upright in the bed. At the second shot, she was running for the door in her long nightdress

128

and bare feet.

"Bill," she had cried. "Bill."

She had found him on the ground near the edge of the arroyo, eyes squinched tight with pain. "I'm shot, Dawn, honey."

"Where, Bill?" She had dropped onto her knees beside him and cried when she saw the blood. "Oh, Bill. Bill, honey." Quickly, she'd torn off his shirt, ripped the buttons off. She'd tried to lift him, couldn't. Paying no mind to the rocks cutting her bare feet, she had run to the house and yanked a book from a shelf. Doctor Miller's Home Medicine. She'd read the table of contents hurriedly, and groaned. Nothing about a bullet wound. She'd grabbed a clean towel and tore another towel into strips and ran back to her husband.

"Bill, honey, I'll put a compress on it and get you to town. Maybe we can catch the train to Trinidad and a doctor."

Gritting his teeth, he had gasped, "They were waitin' over there, Dawn, across the river. I didn't see 'em at first."

The wound was on his left side, just above the belt. She tied the folded towel in place with the cloth strips, then ran to the corral. Thank God the team was quiet and gentle as she buckled the collars around their necks, slid them down to their shoulders, then threw the harness on and buckled the hames around the collars. "Whoa, boys. Whoa now." Her fingers trembled as she rigged up the driving lines, and she criticized herself. "Damnit, Dawnmarie, you've got to do this right. Stop shaking, now. Just do it, damnit." She had never sworn before.

The off horse stepped obediently over the wagon tongue, and she fitted the end of the tongue into the ring on the neck yoke then quickly hooked the tug chains onto the singletrees. "Whoa, boys."

Still running in bare feet she'd yanked the mattress off the bed and laid it in the back of the wagon, and went to her husband.

"Bill, honey, I've got the team hitched to the wagon, but I can't carry you, honey. Can you . . ."

Voice strained with pain, he'd mumbled, "Sure, Dawn. I can make it."

With her arms under his shoulders, she'd lifted him, using more strength than she realized she had, and got him in the wagon, lying on the mattress. She gathered the lines and yelled, "Hit up. Hit up, there."

Chapter Seventeen

The two horses had run as far as they could go when the light wagon rattled down the main street of El Moro and stopped before the mercantile.

"Ada," Dawnmarie screamed. "Ada."

Men gathered, curious.

"What is it, Dawnmarie? What in the world . . . Oh, my. What happened?"

"Bill was shot. Has the train left yet? I've got to get him to a doctor."

"I don't know. Run," Ada Brown shouted to the gathering. "Get the sheriff. Tell him to stop the train." A man left on the run. To Dawnmarie, she said, "I'll get some clean bandages. I'll be right back." She disappeared into her store.

A man said, "The train's still in town, ma'am. Can I help you get him over there?"

The two horses were standing with their heads down, spraddle-legged, sides heaving.

"Go to the train. Please tell them to wait." She picked up the lines, yelled "Hit up," but the spent team couldn't move.

Ada Brown came back, carrying a clean white square of cloth and a spool of white ribbon. With the help of another man, she climbed into the wagon, took off the bloody bandage and wrapped the clean one around the wound. "How do you feel, Bill? We're going to get you to a doctor."

A weak grin split Bill Kleagen's lips. "With all the purty women I've got on my side, I cain't lose." His eyes squeezed tight with pain and his jaw muscles bulged.

"The team can't go any farther, Ada. We'll have to carry him."

"I'll be right back." Ada Brown ran into her store again.

Sheriff Martin Gantt hurried up, buttoning his suspenders, carrying his gunbelt over his shoulder. He panted, "Why, it's . . . it's Mrs. Kleagen. And . . . Bill Kleagen."

"I've got to get him on the train and to a doctor in Trinidad. Please, stop the train."

"I'll do 'er, Mizz Kleagen. You men, carry him." Martin Gantt left on the run.

"Here." Ada Brown was back with a narrow canvas cot. "Let's put him on this."

A small crowd had gathered, and help was plentiful. Four men lifted Kleagen gently onto the cot and six men picked it up and ran with it. It was two blocks to the railroad depot, and the men were winded to the point of collapse themselves by the time they got there.

A huge black engine on six thirty-seven-inch driver wheels sat on the track, puffing and hissing steam. The engineer in a striped cap with a red bandana around his throat leaned out of the cab. Behind the engine were five freight cars and two passenger cars. Passengers had their faces stuck to the windows, trying to see what was happening.

"In here." The conductor wore a black bill cap and had brass buttons on his coat. "Bring him in here." He stepped aside as the men carried the cot into the nearest passenger car.

"I'll telegraph ahead," Sheriff Gantt said. "I'll have a doctor waiting at the depot." To the engineer, he yelled, "Roll that thing."

"Here, Dawnmarie." Ada Brown held out a coat and a pair of slippers.

Not until then did Mrs. William Kleagen realize she was still in her nightdress and bare feet.

Hissing like an angry beast and chug-chug-chugging, the big engine spun its drive wheels on the rails. It blew its whistle wildly, blew puffs of smoke from its smokestack and moved forward. Rail cars jerked in a chain reaction until the last car was moving. Slowly at first, then faster.

El Moro was alive when McCagg rode down the main street. Men and women were standing in little groups, talking and waving their arms. They all stopped talking when he rode past, and a couple of men pointed at him. He tied up at the hitchrail in front of the Pinon Mercantile and stepped inside. The store was filled with people, but nobody was buying anything. Ada Brown's head jerked up when he came through the door.

"Mr. McCagg. Where have you . . . ? Have you heard?"

"Heard what?"

She pushed through the crowd and stopped in front of him. "Bill Kleagen was shot."

"What?" His heart jumped into his throat. "Who . . . how . . . ?"

"He's alive. We put him on the train to Trinidad. He's with a doctor by now."

"In Trinidad? How bad was he shot?"

"He was shot in the side. I think the bullet was still in him. He was awake, but in pain. I don't know . . . I'm no doctor, but I have hope."

McCagg croaked, "Dawnmarie?"

"She's fine. I don't know how she did it, but she hitched a team to the wagon and brought him to town. Poor thing, she was still in her nightdress and had no shoes on. The team's at the livery. Somebody took them over there."

"In Trinidad. Can we . . . where's the telegraph office?"

"In the depot."

133

Spurring the sorrel, McCagg rode at a dead run to the depot, hit the ground before the horse came to a stop and ran inside. He sent a telegram to the sheriff at Trinidad and asked him to wire back news of William Kleagen's condition. The last line read: "Tell Mrs. Kleagen I'm in El Moro." He signed his name.

He rode slowly back to the mercantile, eyes downcast, silently cursing himself. Damn, damn, damn. I should have been there. I shouldn't have left. I should have plugged that red-bearded sonofabitch when I had a chance. I shouldn't have gone to Trinidad. I should have . . .

Inside the store, the crowd had thinned, and Ada Brown said, "Come back to the kitchen, Mr. McCagg." He followed her into the back room and sat heavily in a kitchen chair. "Like some coffee?"

"Naw. I should have been there. I shouldn't have let it happen. All I can do is wait for an answer to my telegram. I'll go back to the depot pretty soon. I wonder if Dawnmarie needs anything. Maybe I ought to go back to Trinidad. Get a fresh horse and go back." He looked up at Ada Brown with pain his eyes. "What do you think I ought to do?"

She sat at the table across from him. "You wired the authorities in Trinidad to find out how Bill is?"

"Yeah."

"Then you should wait for an answer."

"Yeah, I reckon."

"Mr. McCagg. Ben. You can't blame yourself. You couldn't have been there. You had to do whatever you did."

"Yeah."

"You've got more than enough time for a cup of coffee and something to eat."

"Naw. I've got to get back to the telegraph office."

"Rest a minute, Ben. Let me pour you some coffee."

The coffee was strong and good, but he gulped it down, then rode back to the depot. It was a clapboard frame box of a building with a long gable roof and tall dirty windows.

"No." The telegrapher sat at a big desk with the telegraph key in front of him. They key was silent. He looked at McCagg over half-lens glasses. "You wired the sheriff and somebody had to deliver it to the sheriff and he has to find out which hospital your friend is in and send somebody there to find out how he is and get back to the sheriff and the sheriff has to send somebody back to the depot to send a message back here. Better be ready to wait a while."

"Yeah. I'll wait right here."

Every time the telegraph key started clicking out a Morse code, McCagg got up from his hard bench and went to the telegrapher's desk. "No," he was told. "This's from Denver." Or, "No, this's from Cheyenne."

The sorrel horse was tied outside, but he hadn't traveled far that day and wasn't tired. McCagg tried to figure out what to do. Someone had to go to the Kleagen place and see that the animals were cared for and see that O'Brien and his pals didn't take over the place. What would he do if he found them there? Try to shoot them out by himself or get help from the sheriff? Would the sheriff help?

The telegraph key started clicking again. The telegrapher was writing down a message. McCagg got up and hurried over.

"No. From Denver again. I'll holler if there's anything for you."

More worried and nervous by the minute, McCagg sat. He was sitting with his head in his hands when Ada Brown came in. "Hear anything yet?" she asked.

"No. Nothing."

"It takes time. I came over because I want to help. Some friends, my neighbors, are driving a two-horse buggy down to Trinidad and they're waiting for me in case I want to go down."

"Dawnmarie would appreciate that."

"We'll have to wait and see what the situation is."

Again, the telegraph key started clicking. The telegrapher

began writing it down. Both McCagg and Ada Brown watched him intently, hoping.

"Ben McCagg. Here it is."

In long fast steps he was at the desk snatching the note from the telegrapher's hand. "UNCLE BEN BILL ALIVE DOC OPTIMIST I STAYING MERCY HOSPITAL BROKE STOP."

Silently, he read it and handed it to Ada Brown, trying to decide what to do, reaching a decision. The animals could wait. The homestead could wait. Dawnmarie needed money, and he'd ride back to Trinidad. That was the only thing to do. But Mrs. Brown changed his mind.

"I'm going. My neighbors are waiting. I'll lend her some money."

"What about your store?"

"It's open. No one will steal from me. I've had folks take what they wanted when I wasn't there and leave the money on the counter. No one has ever stolen from me."

Digging into his pants pocket, McCagg pulled out a thick sheaf of folding money. "Here. Give her this." He didn't count it, just handed over a bunch of bank notes.

"I'll be there before sundown. She'll be fine. Pray for Bill." Mrs. Brown turned to go, then, "Ben, please don't do anything reckless. Bill didn't say who shot him. Take care of yourself, Ben." And she hurried outside where a man and woman were waiting in a buggy with two handsome bay horses hitched to it.

He watched them go, the bay team striking a trot as they turned onto the main street and headed for the southbound wagon road. They'd be there soon. Mrs. Brown was a good friend. Dawnmarie would be all right. It was Bill he had to worry about. The doctor was optimistic. Doctors were sometimes wrong. He'd check with the telegrapher often.

"It's going to be a long day, feller," he said to the sorrel as he climbed into the saddle. "But you're young and strong." His next stop was at the sheriff's office. Empty. That left only one place to go.

Riding east and north, across the broad land, across the shallow draws, around the cane cactus, keeping the river on his left, McCagg felt the hot August sun beating down on his back. A drop of sweat ran down his face from under the new Stetson. Big black flies were biting the horse on the neck and shoulders, and the horse was constantly shaking its head and shivering its hide in defense. McCagg took his hat off and used the brim of it to brush a fly off the animal's right ear. He used his hand to brush flies off its neck and shoulders.

"Goddamn flies," he muttered. "Drive a horse crazy."

He reined up five hundred yards from the Kleagen place, and studied everything about it. Bill's saddle horse was in the small pasture he had fenced off. The milk cow's calf was in with him, and the cow with a swollen bag stood near the pasture gate. The cabin door was shut. No other horses were in sight and no men. His gaze moved next to the river and the few cottonwoods that grew in the arroyo created by the river. He couldn't see into the arroyo from where he was, so he reined the horse in that direction. He stopped. A man was riding out of the arroyo. One man. He looked familiar. It was Sheriff Martin Gantt.

Chapter Eighteen

The sheriff saw him coming and his hand went to the sixgun on his right hip. Then he recognized McCagg and he relaxed and hooked his thumb in the gunbelt.

"Howdy, Ben," he said when McCagg rode up.

"Howdy. See anything interesting?"

"Well," Martin Gantt half-turned and looked back across the river, "plenty of tracks, and these." He dug three spent shell casings out of his shirt pocket. "They waited over there, and they'd been there a spell. Soon's Bill Kleagen came outside where he was a good target they opened up."

McCagg dismounted, took one of the empty cartridges and examined it. "Forty-five-sixty. Winchester repeating rifle."

"That's what I'm guessing."

"Know anybody who carries that kind of gun?"

Shaking his head sadly, Martin Gantt said, "Yeah. Too many Winchesters around. These won't prove a damn thing."

"Naw. Reckon not. And Bill didn't say who shot him?"

"No. And that might be my fault. I just plain didn't ask. I was too busy getting him on the train and I didn't think about it till it was too late."

McCagg was looking across the river. "He probably didn't get a look at the shooter anyway. Plenty of cover over there.

I don't reckon the tracks told you anything?"

"Two men. Rode up in the dark and waited for daylight. At least one smokes cigarettes. But a lot of men do that nowadays."

"Not what you could call conclusive evidence, is it?"

" 'Fraid not."

"Well, without physical evidence you have to think about a motive, and who do you think has a motive?"

"That's not hard to figure out, but without physical evidence the judge will throw the case out of court."

"Uh-huh." McCagg looked across the river, looked at the eastern horizon, looked at the sheriff. "Care for a cup of coffee and some chuck? I ain't ate since early this morning. Dawnmarie's probably got some bread or something in there."

"I ain't ate a-tall today," the sheriff said, dismounting. "Too big of a hurry to get out here and see what I could see."

"I've got to turn that calf out so it can suck. That, or milk the cow, and I ain't fond of milking cows."

"The horse seems to be in good shape except he's lonesome. He was glad to see my horse. The team's in town, at the livery."

Inside, they found two loaves of bread. They found butter in a water barrel outside. "I can cook something if you want it, sheriff."

"Naw. This'll do 'til I get home to my woman."

McCagg built a fire in the cookstove, filled the galvanized coffee pot with water, dumped in a handful of coffee and put it on the stove. While they waited for it to boil, they ate big hunks of bread smeared with butter. "Much as I hate to milk cows I do like the butter," McCagg said around a mouthful.

"My sentiments exactly. My woman buys milk and butter from a neighbor who milks two cows."

After the coffee had perked a while, McCagg got up and poured two cups full. "Even got cream for the coffee. Want some?"

"Sure. Can't let the cream spoil."

They sipped coffee. Then McCagg said, "Speaking of a motive, what do you think?"

"The first thought that popped into my mind was Old Redbeard and his cohorts. But on second thought, they've got that court order, and although the judge granted a temporary injunction, I don't think they're in any hurry to take over. I went over to the Arbaughs a couple of hours ago, and they hadn't been bothered for a week or so. Scared hell out of them when I told them Bill Kleagen had been shot. They think they're next."

"What're they going to do about it?"

"They're forted up. They're going to fight, court order or no, and they ain't got an injunction. They haven't been to court a-tall."

"What're you going to do about it?"

Martin Gantt didn't answer. Instead, he blew into his coffee cup to cool its contents, took a sip, studied the table top. "You know, this whole thing is the biggest damn puzzle I ever heard of. Those gunsels went to a hell of lot of trouble to get a legal claim in these two homesteads, and they've claimed a string of half-sections southwest of there. They ain't farmers. They're hoodlums and nothing else. It's hard to believe they really want these homesteads."

"They want them. Let me ask you something, do you know a Trinidad lawyer named Haddow? Michael T. Haddow?"

"I've met the man."

"What do you think of him?"

"Hmm. Well, I ain't had much experience with lawyers, and I know there's good and bad in every profession, but, uh, to tell the truth, I wouldn't trust him any farther than I could throw him uphill."

"All right, now, I'll tell you something. I'm not toting a badge any more and I can do things a lawman can't do, and . . ." McCagg told about catching one of O'Brien's

140

henchmen and shooting off a piece of his ear, and what the man had said about Michael T. Haddow. He didn't tell about skinning the lawyer out of three thousand dollars.

"Good Lord." Martin Gantt shook his head. "This whole damn thing has got my brain tied up in a knot. That lawyer wants this land, and he doesn't plan on buying it. Now, what the holy hell does he want with it?"

"Does he want it himself, or is he working for somebody?"

The sheriff answered that question immediately. "He's working for somebody. He ain't about to get his hands dirty on a piece of worthless land."

"Who? How about a cowman?"

"Naw. I know every cattleman in this end of the state, and they ain't the kind to hire a lawyer. If they wanted this land they'd either buy it or just graze on it anyway." Martin Gantt studied his coffee cup. "Who? I just plain don't know."

"Yeah. Well." McCagg stood. "Anyway, if you can find that jasper with a piece of his ear missing, you'll have a suspect in Bill Kleagen's shooting. He was probably waiting over there to get even with me. He didn't know I wasn't here."

The sheriff stood too. "I'll head back to town now and see if I can find him. Here, I'll help wash the dishes. Least I can do."

"Naw, I'll do them. I've got to stick around a while anyway. I'll borrow Bill's horse and ride over to El Moro this evening 'case there's a message at the telegraph, then I'll come back here for the night."

"I'll let you know if I learn anything."

" 'Preciate it."

He turned the sorrel into the horse pasture and caught and saddled the bay. When he crossed the river he knew he wouldn't find anything. Martin Gantt's footprints were mixed with the shooters', and it took a while to figure out

141

whose were whose. When he did he followed the flat-heeled tracks to where horses had been hobbled, and followed horse tracks until he was sure they had come from and gone back to El Moro. There was no doubt in his mind who was responsible for the shooting. He had a terrible urge to go to town and get them in his gunsights. But he'd let the sheriff do it the legal way. If he could. Then if the legal way didn't work he'd do it the illegal way.

Stomping around the yard, he kept a wary eye on the horizon and the river arroyo. It was good a place for an ambush, but Bill and Dawnmarie weren't thinking about that when they'd picked this spot. They shouldn't have to think about that, now that the Indians were corraled. He studied the well rods lying beside the house and wondered if he could install a well by himself. Naw, not until this whole mess with Redbeard, Haddow & Company was settled.

Smiling grimly at his thoughts, he wondered if a company was behind the land jumping. A cattle company, maybe. From out of state. Texas? New Mexico? Some company that wanted to stay out of sight and keep its plans secret until the land was theirs. Why a secret? Well, maybe the homesteaders, when they found out somebody wanted their land, would jack up the price. As it was, the land could be bought cheap. Except Bill's and Dawnmarie's. Bill had a dream, and wasn't about to sell. Now with Bill hurt, maybe Dawnmarie would sell.

Aw hell, what was he thinking about. The company didn't have to buy it. It was theirs anyway. They used the law to get it for practically nothing. Unless he could out-lawyer them. And he couldn't do that until the day of the hearing.

Hmmph. For a time it had looked like it was going to be a duel between lawyers. That was before Bill was bush-whacked by some bloodthirsty, trigger-happy sonofabitch. Now it could easily turn into a gun duel.

Another grim smile touched McCagg's lean face, and he fingered his moustache. Let the lawyers do their lawyering,

142

but one way or another the Kleagens were going to win this duel.

Late in the afternoon, he mounted Bill's bay horse and rode to El Moro, getting there just before dark. No message at the telegraph. Next he went to the mercantile to see what he could see. It was unlocked, but there were no people inside. On a long counter was a couple of one dollar bills and a note. Idly curious, McCagg read the note.

"Miz Brown. I took some flour and sugar and left two dollars. If this is not enuff I'll settle with you later. Josephine Ledbetter."

McCagg had to smile. It gave his spirits a lift. It wasn't the lawyers and judges and politicians who kept society together. It was folks like Josephine Ledbetter. In his years as a lawman he'd seen all kinds of scum and crud, and knowing folks like Dawnmarie and Bill, Mrs. Ledbetter and Ada Brown made him feel better about the world. Too bad The Creator had to sprinkle the earth with thieves, cutthroats, and sneaky sonsofbitches, but that's the way it was. They had to be dealt with like the rattlesnakes and rabid skunks. Eliminated.

Realizing that what had started as a pleasant thought had turned into a sour one, McCagg called himself a cussed sorehead, and went out to his horse. Mounted, he rode to the sheriff's office, and found only the deputy Joel in. Sitting. With his feet on the desk.

"The sheriff ain't here." His manner, his sneering way of talking irritated McCagg.

"I can see that. I don't reckon you'd know where he is?"

"He's somewhere investigatin'. That's all I know."

"What's your name?"

"What? What's my name?"

"I didn't think you knew." With that, McCagg turned on his heel and went outside.

***

143

It was lonesome in the Kleagen house. He could feel the presence of Dawnmarie, and thought about what a lucky man Bill was for having her. She'd harnessed and hitched the team in her bare feet and nightdress. Got her wounded husband in the wagon with sheer willpower and hauled him to town. Didn't care about herself, only her husband. A good woman. Pretty, smart, educated, but able and willing to do what needed to be done on a frontier homestead. A man who had a good woman was a lucky man.

Before he blew out the lamp, he checked Bill's old rifle. It was a Henry, Civil War Yankee gun. It was so old the stock was bleached and the long octagonal barrel was shiny in places. But the magazine tube, in spite of being made of tin, seemed to be in good condition, and the loading mechanism worked. Those old rimfire forty-fours were among the first metallic cartridges made and they had been known to misfire. He shoved sixteen of the short cartridges into the front end of the magazine tube and got the gun ready to shoot. It was better than nothing.

The mattress was missing from their bed, but he didn't want to sleep in their bed anyway. It would have been an invasion of their privacy. Besides, he wanted to be in the room with the door. He had a chair propped against the door and a dishpan on the chair. He made his pallet under the window. Any try at forcing the door open would shake the chair and dislodge the dishpan, and anybody who crawled through the window would land on top of him. Either way, he'd come out of his sleep with the Smith & Wesson in his hand.

Lying in the dark, he heard a coyote yap-yapping somewhere, and a hoot owl in one of the cottonwoods along the river. "Hoo hoo-o-o, hoo-hoo," it went. He liked hearing them. It was better than the damnable racket on the streets of Denver.

At dawn he was up, staying low until he'd studied the country across the river and crept to the arroyo and studied

144

that. No men or strange horses in sight. His sorrel and Bill's bay were cropping the buffalo grass in their small pasture, and the milk cow and her calf were nearby. Milk in a tin bucket hanging in a water barrel was sour and he threw it out. The butter was still good. He fried some bacon and made some cowboy biscuits and ate well. He washed the dishes and left the kitchen as clean as he'd found it. That was an unwritten law, and, he thought with a wry grin, he might sometimes ignore the written laws, but he'd obey the unwritten ones.

As he saddled the sorrel, mounted and headed for El Moro, he had two things on his mind: he wanted to find a message from Dawnmarie, and he wanted to know what Sheriff Martin Gantt had learned about the shooting.

If anything.

Chapter Nineteen

The telegrapher started shaking his head when he saw McCagg come through the door. "No telegram. Nary a word."

That could be good news. He tried to convince himself of that. If Bill had died she would send a telegraph. But then maybe she would wait until she could come back on the train with the body and tell him in person.

Aw hell, a man could drive himself crazy worrying. He had to do something. He would see the sheriff.

"He ain't here," Deputy Joel said, taking his feet off the desk and sitting up straight as if ready to fight. "And I don't want any smart aleck horse shit from you or any damn body else."

"All right, all right." McCagg stood in the doorway and hooked his thumbs in his gun belt. "Just give me a hint as to where he went."

"Down to Trinidad. Took the train first thing this morning. Wants to talk to that jasper that was shot."

"Uh-huh. If he went on the train he'll come back on the train and he won't get back till tomorrow morning."

"Keereck. The trains pass one another in Trinidad."

"Uh-huh. Thanks. 'Preciate it."

He could go to Trinidad himself. That's what he ought to do. The sorrel wasn't too leg weary and could make it in a few hours. Better than waiting around and doing nothing. But there was that lawyer. As far as Michael T. Haddow knew, McCagg was on his way to El Paso, and it wouldn't do to accidentally meet him on the streets of Trinidad. Of course he'd have to come face to face with the lawyer sooner or later, and he was looking forward to it, but he didn't want it to happen in front of Dawnmarie and Bill. Aw hell, to hell with that sonofabitch. He got on the horse, rode out of town and headed south. Two miles from town he met a buggy pulled by a pair of handsome bays, and he recognized Ada Brown and her neighbors on the padded seat under the canopy. The man hauled up the team.

"Ben." Ada Brown leaned forward in the seat. "Bill's going to recover. The doctor said the bullet missed the vital parts."

A broad smile split McCagg's lean face. "That's the best news I've heard in many a year. How's Dawnmarie?"

"Tired, but fine otherwise. She sat up all night with Bill. He was in pain most of the night, but he finally slept and he was sleeping well when I left. I rented a room for Dawnmarie near the hospital, and I finally talked her into going to bed herself. Are you going down?"

"I was. But maybe I'd better let her sleep. Is the doctor sure Bill's going to live?"

"As sure as he can be. Bill bled a lot, and the wound was painful and he was suffering from shock, but he's a healthy young man and the doctor said he'll pull through. He'll be on his feet in a week or so, but it'll be a long time before he can do any hard work. That's what the doctor said."

"He won't have to do any work till he's good and ready." The sorrel was stamping its feet and shaking flies off its head and neck. The bay team was fidgeting too, wanting to get home and in the shade of a barn where the flies weren't so bad. "Reckon I'll nose around town a while and go back to the homestead. The sheriff went down on the train to find out if Bill saw who shot him."

"He didn't. He saw somebody, but he didn't get a good

147

look. That's what he told Dawnmarie."

McCagg felt like swearing then, but he couldn't swear in the presence of women. "Sheriff Gantt made a trip for nothing, then."

"Come to the store, Ben, and I'll fix you some dinner."

"I'll do that if I can. Might not be in town, however."

He followed the buggy back to town, but left it when it turned toward the mercantile. On the chance that Dawnmarie had wired him, he went again to the railroad depot and the desk of the United States and Mexico Telegraph Company. "I know I'm making a pest of myself," he said, "but . . . ?"

"Nope." The telegrapher peered at him over his half-lens glasses. "All I got here is a telegraph for Judge Topah. And I ain't got nobody to deliver it to him."

"Can't it wait?"

"When folks send telegraphs they're in a hurry."

"You can't take it yourself, huh?"

"Naw. I'm afraid to go to the toilet. Can't leave this here desk."

"Well, if somebody's in a hurry, I'll take it to him. I know the judge."

"You sure I can trust you?"

McCagg shrugged. "It's nothing to me. If you want, I'll take it. If you don't, I won't."

"I got no choice but to trust you. Here." He folded a sheet of yellow paper and handed it to McCagg. "The judge might have an answer. If he does he can come over here or send it with somebody."

McCagg put the folded sheet in a shirt pocket with no intention of reading it. Until . . .

"It's from a lawyer in Trinidad. Says urgent."

All right, he thought as he got on his horse, it's prying into somebody else's business, but maybe not. Maybe it's my business. Maybe it's Dawnmarie's and Bill's business. All right, so I'm prying. As soon as he was out of sight of the

148

depot, he reined up, unfolded the sheet of paper and read the handwritten message.

JUDGE TOPAH RE KLEAGEN PROPERTY URGENT ARRANGE HEARING SOONEST ARRIVE TOMORROW STOP MICHAEL HADDOW ATTORNEY AT LAW.

Uh-oh. That lawyer was going to meet with the judge. Bill was in a hospital and Dawnmarie was with him. Somebody had to be there to represent the Kleagens. He was the only one. Thinking of it brought a grin to his face. "Well, whatta you know," he said to the sorrel, refolding the paper. "As the Chinaman says, here's where the dung gets flung." He pointed the horse toward the judge's one-room courthouse, and grinned to himself. "Hell, who knows, it might be fun."

His Honor had gone fishing over west of town somewhere, his plump gray-haired wife said. With the sheriff out of town there was no legal business to take care of. "When he retired and we moved down here from Denver, he was planning on doing nothing but fishing and enjoying the clean air. Then he got bored and got elected judge. He doesn't get paid much."

"When he gets home, give him this, will you, Mrs. Topah?"

The Curly Wolf was wide open. A beer and a short conversation with the bartender would be a good way to kill time. He had to kill time, what with the sheriff gone and Dawnmarie and Bill in Trinidad. Besides he and the bartender had something to talk about. For instance, were O'Brien and his cohorts in town? Did he know where they slept and ate? Had he seen the man with a piece of ear missing? Bartenders heard all the news and knew everything. Hell, he might even have a suspicion about who wanted all that land east of town on the Picketwire. He'd go in and have one mug of beer. One and no more.

Dismounting, he tied the sorrel to a hitchrail, shifted his gun belt into the best position for . . . for what? If the man he'd roped and shot was in here, he'd be in for a fight. Well hell, he'd never run from a fight before. But, damnit, he had to stay clear of trouble for a while. At least until tomorrow. Or until Dawnmarie and Bill got home.

Aw hell.

Reluctantly, he turned around and got back on the horse. A beer would have tasted mighty good, but, well there'd be other times.

Now he had to get out of town. Either that or let Ada Brown fix him something to eat. And that wouldn't do. She might get the wrong idea. Good looking woman and all that, but . . . naw.

On his way back to the Kleagen place, he reined the sorrel south toward the Arbaughs. He intended to ask them if they had seen anything of O'Brien. But when he topped the rise and saw the cabin, he was seen, and Harvey Arbaugh hurried into the cabin and slammed the door. The next thing McCagg saw was a man's face at the window and a gun barrel.

He's scared, McCagg said to himself, and a scared man is a dangerous man. He might recognize me and remember me and he might not. Best leave him alone. Turning his horse north he went far around the Arbaughs and headed for the Kleagens.

Nothing had changed. Bill's bay horse nickered at the sorrel, glad to have some horse company, and the milk cow grazed a hundred yards downriver, her calf at her side. He warmed up the biscuits left over from breakfast, and fried some bacon. Biscuits and bacon made good sandwiches. But what about supper? Ada Brown? He'd bet she could cook.

Naw.

He spent the rest of the day outside. The water barrels were warm. Needed fresh water. Bill had hauled the barrels up from the river in his wagon. The wagon and team were in town. McCagg carried a bucket of water from the river, and realized why Bill had worked so hard digging a well. He kept his eyes on the western horizon and the river arroyo. For supper he had a can of peaches, bread, butter and coffee. After supper he arranged his chair and dishpan and went to bed.

Tomorrow the sheriff would be back, and maybe he'd learn something. Not from Bill, but from somebody else. Tomorrow the lawyer Michael T. Haddow would be in town, and they'd meet again.

Tomorrow the fur would fly.

Chapter Twenty

The big steam engine began tooting its whistle a half-mile from town, then came puffing and blowing steam past the depot. It stopped fifty feet down the track with the engine under a water tank that stood on high wooden legs. The passengers who got off had to walk a ways on a wide brick apron to the depot. McCagg hung back out of sight behind a freight wagon. Sheriff Martin Gantt was the first one out of the passenger car, and he cut across the depot yard and headed for the north side of town as fast as he could walk, carrying a leather valise. Next came the redheaded O'Brien, and this surprised McCagg. What was O'Brien doing in Trinidad? After him came Michael T. Haddow, dressed in a white shirt with a stiff collar and cravat, a long coat and creased gray pants. He carried a small leather suitcase. The lawyer and the redhead talked a moment, then went separate ways. McCagg hung back. He didn't want the lawyer to see him yet. Not yet. But he did want to talk to the sheriff. He hung back and watched the lawyer head for the one hotel in town, and the red-headed, red-bearded one walk on past the hotel and out of sight around a corner.

Hoping the sheriff was going to his office, McCagg rode his sorrel horse over there. The office was empty. Waiting, he heard the steam engine's whistle toot twice, and a few minutes later the big engine huff-huffed its way north. He waited, then went to the cabin used as a courtroom. It was locked. Back at the sheriff's office, he found it still empty.

"Oh, mister," he said to a passing railroader. The man stopped and shifted a lump in his mouth from the left side to the right. "Do you happen to know where Sheriff Gantt lives?"

"Yaa-ow. Reckon I do. Lives over north in a white house. 'Bout four blocks north. Only two houses on the block and other'n's brown. Can't miss it."

"Obliged," McCagg said. " 'Preciate it."

The house was easy to find. It was a shotgun house, the kind the railroads liked to build. So named because the rooms were on either side of a hall, and a man could throw a rock through the front door and out the back door. It wore a fresh coat of white paint. A white board fence surrounded it. In back were a corral and stable, also white. McCagg tied the sorrel to a hitchrail just outside the fence, opened a narrow wooden gate and approached the house. He hoped the sheriff wouldn't mind being bothered at home.

But the sheriff wasn't at home. A middle-aged woman in a long dark dress and white apron answered his knock. She wiped her hand on a muslin towel.

"I apologize for bothering you, ma'am, but I'm hoping to find Sheriff Gantt here."

"He just left. Came home, grabbed a clean shirt and a piece of bread and hurried right back to the depot."

"He did? Uh, my name is McCagg. Benjamin McCagg. Do you happen to know where Mr. Gantt went?"

"To Denver. Said he had to ask some questions of somebody there."

"To Denver? To ask questions?"

"That's what he said. That's all I know."

"Oh. Well, I sure do thank you, Mrs. Gantt."

"You're welcome."

Horseback again, McCagg's mind percolated with questions. Denver. Who in hell did he want to question in

153

Denver? Did it have anything to do with Bill Kleagen getting shot? Naw. Couldn't be. Not way to hell up in Denver. But he was going up there to question somebody. Who? Why?

He left his horse in a pen at the livery and walked down the path in front of the Curly Wolf, the sheriff's office and the mercantile. When he passed the hotel, he took a look inside, but saw only the clerk, writing something in a book. Cutting through the vacant lot near the saloon, he saw the judge coming and right beside him was the lawyer. Two fat men. The judge swinging his walking stick, and the lawyer carrying a sheaf of papers. McCagg hung back.

They walked down the alley, stopped long enough for the judge to use a key to unlock the courtroom door then went inside. McCagg shifted his gunbelt and holster, lifted his hat, ran a hand over his thinning hair, reset his hat and walked with swift steps to the courtroom. There, he paused two seconds, pushed the door open and entered.

Judge Topah was at his desk on the platform. The lawyer stood in front of him, saying something. The judge's head jerked up. He frowned at being disturbed. Michael T. Haddow's head swiveled around.

"Mr. McCagg," the judge said, "do you have something to bring before the court?"

"Yessir, I do."

Haddow's face had turned white. It changed to red. He sputtered, "McCagg? Why you . . . you're . . ." His fat hands fluttered like wounded birds.

"Have you gentlemen met?" the judge asked.

Smiling, McCagg said, "Yes we have, Your Honor." To Haddow, he said, "Do you want to tell him where and how we met?"

"Why . . . why. You're, uh . . ."

"Yep. It's me. Have you got something to report? Right here's a good place to report it."

"Mr. McCagg, enlighten me," Judge Topah ordered.

"Whatever are you talking about?"

"Your Honor, Mr. Haddow and I met in Trinidad a few days ago. I know he represents the plaintiffs in their legal action against the Kleagens, and when I saw him here I guessed that he is here in connection with that case."

"Yes?"

"As you have no doubt heard, Your Honor, Bill Kleagen was shot and is now in a hospital in Trinidad. Mrs. Kleagen is with him. I'm here on their behalf."

"Any objection, Mr. Haddow?"

"Yes. I mean uh . . ." The lawyer ran a finger around the inside of his stiff collar, cleared his throat, and went on. "Your Honor, my clients want to get on with their business, and I am requesting that you set aside the preliminary injunction and have Mr. and Mrs. Kleagen removed from property that does not belong to them."

"Mr. McCagg?"

"You set a hearing date, Your Honor. We'll be ready to argue the law on that date."

"Your Honor." The lawyer's voice was back to normal now. He had regained his composure. "The wheels of justice are moving too slowly here. Time is of the essence. My clients have a right to their claim under the Homestead Act as amended in 1864, and wish to start working the land immediately."

McCagg asked, "What are they going to do this time of year?"

"Why, I, uh, Your Honor, am I to be interrogated by this gentleman?"

"Sounds like a fair question."

"Why, I'm no farmer myself. But believe me when I say they want to get started making the necessary improvements on the land."

"I did set a hearing date, Mr. Haddow."

"May I point out, Your Honor, that my clients and I were not present to argue against the injunction."

155

"Hmm. You have a point. However, the defendants have a right to a hearing. Mr. McCagg, do you know when either Mr. or Mrs. Kleagen will be available?"

Shifting his weight from one foot to the other, McCagg answered, "I can't say, Your Honor. I just don't know."

"A week?"

"Well, maybe Mrs. Kleagen."

"Do they plan to have legal counsel?"

"Yes sir. If I can find one."

"Very well, one week from today this case will be resolved. No delays. Is that satisfactory, Mr. Haddow?"

"Well, Your Honor, I . . . oh well, yes, that is satisfactory."

"Very well. Is there any other business to come before the court? Then this court is adjourned."

McCagg left first. He waited outside for the lawyer. He didn't have to wait long. Michael T. Haddow marched fearlessly up to him. "You, sir, are a thief. You owe me three thousand dollars."

At that McCagg had to laugh. "The hell you beller. You're a bigger thief than I am. Being a lawyer, you know it's against the law to buy stolen property. Go ahead, report me."

"That brick, it's . . ."

"It might make a good weight for something or other."

"You will regret this." The lawyer's round face went hard and his voice turned deadly. "I promise you, McCagg, or whatever your name is, you will regret this." He turned on his heel and walked down the alley toward the hotel.

McCagg watched him go and knew he meant what he said. That, he mused, is one dangerous man. O'Brien and his pals are thieves and probably killers, but they're dumb kittens compared to him.

Yes sir, that is one very dangerous sonofabitch.

Chapter Twenty-one

McCagg had to know. He had to ask the bartender in the Curly Wolf. He shifted his gun belt and holster and stepped through the open door. He couldn't help being relieved when he saw only one other customer in the place. It was someone he'd never seen before. The bartender put down his *Rocky Mountain News* and came over.

"Ben McCagg," he said by way of greeting. "How's your nephew? Is he, uh . . . ?"

"He's alive. The doctor said he'll live."

"I'm glad to hear that. I never met the man, but I hear he's honest and a hard worker. Any idea who shot him?"

"No. I was wondering if maybe you heard something."

With a shake of his head, the bartender said, "Nothing. No hint of any kind. Sheriff Gantt was in here asking the same question."

"Seen anything of O'Brien lately?"

"Hasn't been in here for a few days, and that's odd. Him and his crew usually hang around in here more than anywhere else."

"Any idea where they're staying?"

"No idea a-tall myself, but when the sheriff left here I got the notion he knew, and that's where he was headed. You lookin' for 'em?"

"No, not now. Just curious. I'd sure like to know where

they were the morning Bill Kleagen was shot."

"You want a beer or a slug of whiskey? It's on the house. The first one anyway."

"Uh." For a long moment he couldn't take his eyes off the beer keg and the whiskey bottles on a shelf behind the bartender. "Uh."

"I know what your trouble is. I've seen a hundred men like you. You can't take one drink without havin' to have another'n and another'n."

He couldn't. Just couldn't. Not with that lawyer in town hating his guts. He had to stay sober. Some other time, but not now. "Uh, thanks just the same, but some other time."

A grin lit up the bartender's face. "Good for you. I'm a damn poor businessman, but I'm glad you said no. I thought I ought to offer you one on the house, but I'm glad you didn't take it."

McCagg swallowed a dry lump in his throat, and forced his eyes away from the liquor. "Seen anything of a man with a piece of his ear missing?"

"No. The sheriff asked the same thing."

"You don't know where the sheriff went when he left here?"

"No idea a-tall."

"His wife said he took the train to Denver this morning. Have you heard anything about somebody or something in Denver?"

The bartender gave it some thought and shook his head. "No, 'fraid not."

"Hmm. Well, thanks just the same."

"Any time."

No use asking the deputy, McCagg thought as he walked to the depot. The deputy wouldn't tell him the way to the nearest toilet. Inside the depot, he got another negative shake of the head.

"Nary a word."

His stomach reminded him it was noon. It also reminded

him it was tired of his cooking, and could use a good woman-cooked meal. Well, there was Ada Brown. Her invitation was probably still good. And there was the cafe. Ada Brown would no doubt put on a better feed. Or he could go to the mercantile and buy some groceries, some canned oysters or something that didn't need cooking. If he did, Ada Brown would probably invite him to her kitchen in back of the store. Why not?

Well, if he took her up on it, she might invite him next to her rooms upstairs, and that might lead to something else. So what? A man needed a woman now and then, and Ada Brown wasn't bad to look at. A little plump, but with nice cushiony tits and a round bottom.

He stood in front of the depot and thought it over. Finally, he grinned to himself. A few words of advice he'd heard from a cowboy a long time ago came to his mind:

"Don't catch nothin' you cain't turn loose."

Ada Brown was a widow, lonely. She'd be easier to catch than to turn loose.

The sorrel hadn't been fed at the livery, just penned, but McCagg saw with satisfaction that Bill's team was eating hay in another pen. He saddled the sorrel and rode out of town, going northeast. Hanging around town was useless. The sheriff was gone, and the next court hearing wouldn't take place for a week. Tomorrow he'd get on the train and go to Pueblo, find a lawyer and arrange for him to represent the Kleagens in court. Meanwhile?

"Well," he said to the sorrel, "you've got your buffalo and gramma grass and I've got, let's see, there's spuds and turnips, beans, flour, sugar, coffee, baking soda, and hell, if I can't make out on that I ought to starve."

He slept outside that night, not wanting to be trapped inside if Michael T. Haddow sent his hired gunsels to kill him. Either Haddow wanted to shoot him and get the Kleagens out without waiting for a court order, or the men who shot Bill Kleagen had intended to shoot McCagg. In the dim light of dawn, they could have been mistaken. He didn't know. There were too many things he didn't know.

So McCagg carried his quilts and blankets down into the river arroyo. He spread them out under a cottonwood near the water where he would be hard to find and where he could hear anyone sneaking up. He kept the old Henry loaded with one in the chamber. All he had to do to fire it was cock the hammer back. It was best that way. The mechanical sound of a cartridge being jacked into the firing chamber would carry far in the prairie night and would give away his position.

"Let the sonsofbitches come," he muttered, as he pulled off his boots and covered himself with a blanket.

They didn't come. He lay awake most of the night expecting them, but there were no human sounds at all. River water lapped softly at the banks, the night breeze stirred the leaves of the cottonwoods, and a cow lowed for her calf somewhere east. The horses blew through their noses in the fenced pasture up on the bench. Nighttime was a good time for grazing animals. At night there were no flies. The hoot owl was back. He heard it swoop down, and heard the squeak of a field mouse when the owl caught its supper. No clouds, just a million stars. Lying on his back, he looked up between the tree branches and located the Big Dipper, the Little Dipper, the Milky Way and the North Star.

At times he dozed but when the first hint of daylight came he was awake. It was this time of morning that Bill Kleagen was shot. It could be their favorite time of day for an ambush. Moving silently, he pushed down the blanket and pulled on his boots. He listened. It was quiet now. Gradually dark shapes turned lighter, became clearer. Soon it was daylight. With the dawn came the birds, singing their songs in the cottonwoods. Still, he waited—until finally the sun showed itself over the low eastern horizon. It just popped up, big and bright, spreading warmth over the prairie. The day was going to be another hot one.

He rode Bill's bay horse to El Moro, giving his sorrel more grazing time. The grass was getting scarce in the horse pasture, and it took longer for a horse to eat its fill. Bill was going to have to move the fence to fresh grazing ground. McCagg went around the Arbaughs' place, crossed the draws and got back on the two narrow tracks that served as a wagon road. His first stop was the depot.

"Nope. Nary a word," the telegrapher said.

"How often does the mail come in?"

"Ever' day. From the north early in the mornin' and from the south just before noon. Ada Brown sorts it."

Decision time again. He wanted to be at the mercantile when the mail was sorted in case Dawnmarie wrote him a letter. But while the mail was being sorted, he wanted to be on the northbound, headed for Pueblo where he could hunt up a lawyer. Could he do both? Maybe. If he could talk Ada Brown into coming to the depot and sorting through the mail right here, she could hand him his letter if he had one and he could board the train. They'd have time. The train didn't stop in El Moro any longer than it had to, but it did have to take on water here.

He left the bay horse at the livery and made certain it was fed good hay. He walked from there to the mercantile. Ada Brown was going over some papers when he came through the door. She looked up and smiled.

"Good morning, Ben."

"Morning, Mrs. Brown."

"Ada. Call me Ada."

He wasn't sure he wanted to be on first name terms with her, but how could he refuse? "All right, Ada." He told her about his plans for the day and asked her help.

"Of course. Someone usually brings the mail over here, but I'll be at the depot waiting for it today and I'll look through it immediately. I'm happy you're hiring a lawyer. That's the civilized way to settle disputes. Would you like some coffee? Have you had breakfast?"

161

"Well, uh." She scared him. The thought of her wanting to get more than just friendly was scary. She would be hard to refuse. But he could think of no excuse for declining her offer of coffee. "Uh, I've had breakfast."

"How about some coffee? I've already got the pot on."

"Well, uh, if you're sure I won't be putting you to any trouble."

She was cheerful and pleasant, and offered him some doughnuts she'd baked just the night before. When she got up from her chair to open the oven, he couldn't help looking at her nice round bottom. He had to breathe a silent sigh of relief when a customer entered the store and she excused herself. While she was gone, his gaze went to the stairs that led to the second floor rooms. What was her living room like? And her bedroom?

Aw hell, Ben McCagg, when this mess is over you're going back to Texas and get a job ramrodding a cow outfit, or as a peace officer, or something like that.

She was gone a long time, and he was getting restless. He ought to be doing something, but he had nothing to do until the train got to town. When finally she came back she was all smiles. "I think I've found a buyer."

"A buyer? Oh yeah, you said you wanted to sell out."

"Yes. A couple from Pueblo read my ad in the newspaper. They're very much interested."

Just to make conversation, he asked, "What will you do then?"

"I don't know. My husband and I worked awfully hard to have something, this store, and I'll get enough for it that I won't have to do anything for a long time. Still . . ." Her face furrowed into a small frown. "It's going to be hard doing nothing. I don't know."

Not wanting to pursue that subject any further, he stood, thanked her for the coffee and doughnuts, and allowed, "The train ought to come rolling in pretty soon. I reckon I'll go over to the depot and hang around."

"I'll be there when the train arrives."

The sun was hot on his shoulders when he walked down the street to the railroad. He deliberately kept from even looking in the direction of the Curly Wolf. When he walked past the hotel he took a look in the lobby, half-expecting to see Michael T. Haddow. Only the clerk was there. At the depot, the telegrapher glanced up, then went back to reading his newspaper.

"Expect the northbound soon?"

"She's on her way, right on time." He turned a page.

McCagg took a seat on a wooden bench and prepared to wait. It occurred to him he'd have to buy a ticket. "Where's the ticket agent?"

"Out back." He yelled, "Hey Walt. Passenger."

That's when the telegraph key began clicking. It seemed to be clicking faster than usual. It seemed to be demanding immediate attention. The telegrapher put down his newspaper and listened. He picked up a pencil and began writing. Slowly. A word at a time. His eyebrows went up and his face turned white.

Oh God, McCagg thought. It's bad news from Trinidad. Oh no. No, no.

When the key stopped its click-clacking he was at the telegrapher's desk. "Is it from Trinidad?" He stopped breathing as he waited for an answer.

"No. It's from Denver." The telegrapher was excited. His face registered a mixture of excitement, then worry and fear.

McCagg was relieved. But something was wrong. "What? Bad news, you say?"

"Damn, I reckon. It's from the chief of police in Denver. It's about Sheriff Martin Gantt."

"What?"

"He's dead. Sheriff Gantt is dead."

Chapter Twenty-two

McCagg told Ada Brown when she came in. Ada Brown dropped heavily onto a wooden bench. "Oh my," she groaned. "Oh my. Poor Mrs. Gantt."

"Somebody's got to tell her," the telegrapher said. "I'll go tell the deputy. I can leave my desk for an emergency like this. But somebody's got to tell Mrs. Gantt."

"That's the deputy's job," McCagg said. "Does the telegraph say how Martin Gantt died?"

"No. Just that a man identified by his badge and papers as Sheriff Martin Gantt of Trinchera County died in Denver last night."

Ada Brown's face was pinched. "Could there possibly be a mistake?"

Shaking his head, the telegrapher said, "No. The message is from the chief of police."

"Oh my. Oh my."

"I've got to sign off and then go hunt up the deputy." The telegrapher went back to his desk and tap-tapped on the telegraph key a few seconds, then stood and put on his cap.

"I'll tell Mrs. Gantt," Ada Brown said.

"You don't have to do that, Ada. It's the deputy's job."

"No. I know her. She . . . she needs a friend, a woman. I'll go."

"I'll write you a copy of the message." The telegrapher went back to his desk.

McCagg followed them outside, then stood and watched them go in separate directions, the telegrapher in his railroader's overalls and cap and Mrs. Brown in a long dress and wool shawl. He felt that he ought to do something, but he didn't know what. It was none of his business. The sheriff was a good man, a good lawman. Honest. A friend to the honest people and not afraid of the lawless. It was sad. But lawmen took their chances. Nobody knew that better than McCagg. He'd seen them die. He'd felt the breath of death himself. Still, it was sad.

He had to talk to somebody. Ada would be gone for a while. The deputy was the last man he wanted to talk to. That left the bartender at the Curly Wolf. McCagg ambled in that direction.

"Beer."

"You look like you had to shoot your best horse."

"Huh-uh," McCagg said, guzzling the beer, glancing around the big room. Two men were drinking and talking at a table. One, a railroader, was standing at the bar, looking at him curiously. McCagg didn't recognize them. "Listen."

The bartender leaned close.

"Listen, a telegraph just came in from Denver. I happened to be over at the depot waiting for the northbound. Sheriff Martin Gantt is dead."

"Holy hell." The bartender jerked up straight. "Dead? Martin Gantt? Holy hell."

"What's that you say?" The railroader down the bar had heard. The two men at the table were looking at the bartender.

"Another beer." McCagg drank half of that, then told everyone about the telegram. "That's all anybody around here knows," he said, finishing the beer. "Just that telegram."

"It's that damn Denver traffic," someone said. "Hell, a feller can't get across the street up there without gettin' run over by a beer wagon."

That reminded McCagg that his mug was empty. "Hit 'er again," he said.

"Wa-al, the Denver papers'll tell all about it, you bet. The papers'll git here on the southbound in the mornin'."

"Yup. We'll know about it then."

McCagg heard a train whistle somewhere. It tugged at his mind. He was supposed to do something. What? Hell. "Hit 'er again."

Men's voices swirled around him, speculating, swearing. "Good feller, Martin Gantt. Never find another'n like 'im."

Everything was swirling.

"McCagg. Hey, Ben McCagg." The bartender was in front of him, leaning across the bar.

"Huh?" With an effort he got his eyes focused.

"There's a lady wants to see you. Outside. Ada Brown. She sent a feller in to tell me to tell you."

"Ada? Outside?"

"Yeah. She's waitin'."

"Oh, Gawd." He forced himself to take his elbows off the bar and stand up straight. He wiped his mouth with the back of his hand, hawked, swallowed, pulled his hat down and blinked. He squared his shoulders and forced himself to walk to the door, to walk straight.

She was waiting on the path near the saloon. He expected a scolding. Instead, she smiled. A forced smile, but a smile just the same. She knew he'd been drinking and she smiled. "Ben, you've got a letter from Dawnmarie. I thought you'd want to know right away."

"Oh, I, uh, a letter?"

"From Dawnmarie. Why don't you come to the store, to the kitchen, to read it."

"Oh, uh, all right." He did his best to walk in a straight line. She stayed beside him, talking. Concentrating on his walking, he didn't know what she was saying. It seemed like a mile, but finally they were in her kitchen and she was stoking the fire in her cook stove.

"I'll put the coffee on. Here's the letter."

With fumbling fingers he got the envelope open and took out

166

the letter, unfolded it. He squinted, blinked and got his vision clear enough to read. It was a long letter.

"Dear Uncle Benjamin," it began. "I am very happy to tell you that Bill is doing fine. My main problem now is keeping him in bed until the doctor says he can get up. He will have to stay in bed a few more days. I am thinking about taking the train to El Moro day after tomorrow. That would be the day after you receive this letter. I will stay only one day and come back here until Bill is able to travel. Bill has something he wants to tell you. I know what it is but he got me to promise not to tell. He said you won't believe it until you see it."

The letter went on for three pages. She told about Sheriff Gantt coming to visit Bill and about the sheriff saying he was going to see the lawyer named Haddow about something. She told about Trinidad and how the city had grown. The letter closed with: "Give my regards and my thanks to Ada. She has been a wonderful friend. And thank you very much for the money. Wherever did you get so much? I will probably see you soon.

"Love Dawnmarie."

He started to refold the letter, but instead handed it to Ada Brown. "Here. I know Dawnmarie wouldn't mind if you read it."

"Are you sure? I don't want to pry into family matters."

"Naw. She'd want you to read it."

As he drank a cup of coffee, his hands began to shake. He allowed Mrs. Brown to serve him a big bowl of hot potato soup, and after he ate he felt better. It was pleasant in the kitchen, but a terrible urge to unload some of that beer prompted him to excuse himself and head for the livery barn. He expected a lecture from her about his drinking, but all she said was:

"Take care of yourself, Ben."

On the way back to the Kleagen place, riding Bill's bay horse, he cussed himself for drinking. What a dumb thing to do. Then suddenly he realized something. He realized he had stopped without finishing his last beer, or whiskey or whatever

167

it was. Yeah, he was on his way to getting falling down drunk, and now, two hours later, he was stone cold sober. Wouldn't it be great if he could have a sociable drink now and then without getting stinking. He proved he could stop when he wanted to. Yeah, he had actually stopped in the middle of a drink.

All he had to do was want to.

It wasn't much of a supper. He had never liked to cook. When he was younger, cowboying on some of the big outfits in Texas and batching in cow camps, he had always grabbed an axe, the morrals or something to do his share of the work without doing the cooking. Washing dishes was something else he didn't like, but it had to be done.

For the second time, he spread his quilts and blankets on the ground in the river arroyo, carefully picking up every little stick and rock before he unrolled the quilt. Again, he took off only his boots, and he kept the Henry and the Smith & Wesson within easy reach. High, thin clouds blocked out the moon and some of the stars on the east, but held no promise of rain. For a time he lay awake, listening to the low splashing of the river and thinking of Dawnmarie and Bill, their homestead, Bill's dream of going into the cattle business and Dawnmarie's plan to write a book about the pioneering McCagg family. If he was going to be in a book he had to quit getting drunk. He didn't want to go down in history as the boozer of the family. He didn't realize he was asleep until something woke him up.

He awakened suddenly, every sense alert, nerves tight. What was it?

Moving slowly, carefully, he pulled on his boots, got to his knees and put the Smith & Wesson in its holster. He picked up the Henry and put his thumb on the hammer, ready to cock it and fire.

He listened, breathing in shallow breaths. His own heartbeat and the gentle splashing of the river were the only sounds. It was too damn quiet.

Then he heard footsteps. Up on the rim of the arroyo. And a low grunt as somebody strained with something. Then it was quiet again.

They were up there. Was somebody down in the arroyo? If he moved, could he do it without making a sound? Not likely. But he had to move.

Standing, heart thumping, he took a step, then another. He put each foot down slowly and carefully. He stopped and listened. Footsteps again up near the house. They thought he was in the house.

Gripping the Henry, thumb on the hammer, finger on the trigger, he took another step and another. He had to climb out of the arroyo. No, not all the way out, but far enough that he could see the house. Clouds still hid the moon and eastern stars. He couldn't see a thing.

A horse blew through its nostrils. The sound came from west of the house. A horse stamped its feet. How many were there? He had to move. Carefully. Take it slow and easy.

His right boot came down on something that wasn't solid. Immediately, without putting any weight on the boot, he picked up his foot and put it down eight inches farther ahead. He believed he was now on the path that led from the river to the arroyo. Though he couldn't see it he could feel it with his left hand. The ground wasn't so steep. No weeds or grass on the path. No sticks or rocks. He could look over the rim of the arroyo now, but he couldn't see anything. It was darker than a stack of black cats.

Quiet again. He listened. He heard something, but didn't know what. Something liquid. Had somebody reached into a water barrel? Naw. Why would they do that? Ears straining, he heard footsteps again. A match flared, briefly lighting up a dark face under a dark, wide-brim hat. For two seconds the man was a good target, and McCagg raised the rifle. Stopped. Stopped with his heart in his throat.

The house was on fire. And footsteps were coming his way. Running right at him.

Chapter Twenty-three

Before he knew it the man was almost on top of him. Without raising the rifle to his shoulder he cocked the hammer back and squeezed the trigger. The old Henry roared and kicked back in his hands. The man ran into him, knocking him down. He dropped the rifle and grabbed the Smith & Wesson. But the man kept going, rolling. Rolling, crashing through the brush to the bottom of the arroyo.

McCagg didn't know whether the man had been hit. He didn't wait to find out. He rolled himself off the path, against a steep bank. A lead slug smacked the ground where he'd been and a rifle cracked at the same instant. The shot had come from up near the house, not from down in the arroyo.

When he crawled to where he could again look over the rim, McCagg saw flames creeping up the outside wall of the house near the door. He wanted to run over and try to put out the fire, but if he did he would be in the firelight and a perfect target. He had to put out the fire. He couldn't.

Watching the flames, he guessed somebody had sloshed coal oil on the front of the house and touched a match to it. Their plan was to burn him out. One man would get down here where they could pick him off when he came out the door. Another would get around in back where he could watch the window. How many were there? At least two. One down in the arroyo and one somewhere near the house. The one in the arroyo could be dead or badly hurt. It was the other one he had to worry about.

The flames lit up the front yard and the water barrels. One barrel was nearly full and the other about a quarter full. A bucket and a drinking dipper hung from one of the barrels. If he could get up there he might be able to put out the fire.

He'd be shot, trying.

He had to try. It wasn't in him to just stay here and watch the house burn down. Dawnmarie and Bill had worked hard to build that house.

Leaving the Henry and holstering the sixgun, he scrambled back to the path, climbed to the top, put his head down and ran. Expecting a bullet to tear into him, he ran to the full barrel, yanked the lid off, grabbed the bucket, filled it and sloshed it on the flames. He filled the bucket again, and heard the first shot. Trying to ignore the shooting he splashed another bucket of water on the burning house and filled the bucket again. The next bullet hit the bucket, punching a hole through both sides. Water squirted through the holes, wetting McCagg's right pants leg. He splashed the remainder of the water on the flames.

A rifle slug tore through the right side of his shirt. He filled the bucket again. A hot iron seared his left ribs, and the shock caused him to let the bucket slip from his fingers. Acting from instinct, he dropped to the ground, then realized he was in the firelight, and rolled away from the flames into the darkness. It took a moment, but when he thought about it he knew he hadn't been hit hard. He was fully conscious. He could move both arms and legs. When the next bullet came his way, searching in the dark for him, he got up, picked up the bucket, filled it and sloshed more water on the house. The flames were dying. Another bullet hit his gun belt. It felt like a hammer blow.

Now he dropped the bucket, straightened his gun belt and

ran around the corner of the house where the bullets couldn't reach him.

As he peered around the corner, he felt as though a hot branding iron were being held to his left side. The fire at the house was weak now on the wet wood, but he knew if it kept burning it would find dry wood and flare up again. He couldn't let that happen. He couldn't get shot again either.

The burning in his side made it hard to think straight, yet he had to think. He couldn't just stand here. Forget the pain. It was long way from his heart. He had to find a way to completely extinguish the fire at the house.

Now there was movement between the house and the arroyo. The Smith & Wesson in his hand, he snapped a shot in that direction. Someone shot back at him, but the bullet didn't come close. He fired again at the muzzle flash. He heard footsteps running and saw a dim shape moving west. It disappeared in the darkness. He listened.

A horse snorted and stamped its feet. A man cursed. Then there were hoofbeats going away, and it was quiet again.

Quickly, he holstered his gun and splashed water on the flames until they were out and it was so dark he had to grope for the water barrel. Then he dropped the bucket, went to the edge of the arroyo and waited for something to happen.

Sitting in the dark, he waited. Like the flames at the house, the flame in his left side had died. Now all he felt was a dull ache. Waited.

Come on, daylight.

He could hear the horses, his sorrel and Bill's bay, moving in the horse trap. Another horse to the west whinnied in a low gasp. Whinnied again.

The horse had to belong to one of the men. Its owner hadn't left. He was the man who had rolled down the arroyo. That meant he was still there. Dead or hurt so bad he couldn't walk. His partner had abandoned him. Run off without him. There was no sound from down there, only the quiet slapping of river water against the banks.

Hurry up, daylight.

Hours passed. His left side was numb. Broken ribs? Who knows. It couldn't be a fatal wound or he would have lost consciousness by now. Instead he was wide awake. The horse over west whinnied again, got no answer. Probably hobbled. The fire at the house had died completely.

As before, daylight started with a faint glow on the eastern horizon. Slowly, it spread. Darkness turned to vague black shapes, which gradually became definite shapes. The house first, then the water barrels, the arroyo and the cottonwoods. Finally, he could make out the horses, his sorrel and Bill's bay, and another horse over west. Hobbled, all right. A short-backed brown horse. He'd seen that horse before. He waited until the light was good and he stood. When he moved, he moved carefully. If there was a man in the arroyo, he could be conscious and just waiting for Mc-Cagg to show himself. Whoever he was, if he was alive, he had plenty of time. All he had to do was make himself hard to see and wait.

It wouldn't do to walk down the path. That's what the man would be watching. McCagg went around the house, crawled through the fence surrounding the horse trap, and climbed down into the arroyo from the east. The birds were singing in the cottonwoods. Working his way slowly upriver, he saw the man.

Dead. No doubt about that.

The body lay on its back with the right leg doubled under it. Both arms were out wide. It wasn't a position a man would choose to lie in. A sixgun was in a holster on the right side. McCagg stood over the body and recognized it. The dead man had a piece of his right ear missing. Just a red nick from the earlobe. There was no blood, only a red spot in the middle of the chest. The man had died without bleeding, an indication that he had died almost instantly. When the heart stopped, the bleeding stopped. The Henry forty-four had stopped the heart.

Satisfied that no other human was near, McCagg walked up the path to the house. There was some fire damage, but nothing that couldn't be fixed. Bill would have to pull off the charred boards and replace them with new lumber. A square gallon can lay near the cabin, and when McCagg picked it up he could smell kerosene. Boots had tromped across Dawnmarie's garden. Inside the house, there was no damage at all.

Taking off his shirt, he inspected his wound. An ugly red groove cut across his rib cage, but it was obvious that the bullet hadn't entered his body. Apparently it had grazed his skin between two ribs, leaving a wound that would heal. That is, if it didn't get infected. He had to do something for it. A bottle of carbolic powder stood on a kitchen shelf, and he mixed it with water and bathed the wound. Now he needed a bandage to keep it clean. He didn't want to rummage through their personal stuff, but he had to find something. In their bedroom, he opened two drawers of a dresser before he found a clean man's undershirt. He soaked that in carbolic water, placed it on the wound, then tore a laundered flour sack into strips and used the strips to tie around his chest and hold the bandage in place. The bandage was wet and it soaked through his shirt, but he knew it would soon dry.

He cleaned out the ashes in the cook stove, carried them outside in a bucket and gathered some firewood to cook breakfast. But he couldn't stop thinking about that dead man, and skipped breakfast. On his sorrel he rode to El Moro, wincing when the horse stepped on low ground and jarred his left side. What had happened had to be reported to the sheriff. Sheriff? Hell, the sheriff was dead too. That left the deputy. It had to be reported.

The sheriff's office was empty. Of course, McCagg thought, the sheriff's body probably had arrived on the morning southbound, and the deputy had to do something

174

with it. What he would do with it, McCagg didn't know. The cafe down the street caught his attention, and so did Ada Brown's mercantile. Mrs. Brown would probably be with the sheriff's widow. No use going there. He didn't want to go there anyway. He untied his horse and was leading it to the cafe when he saw Ada Brown coming. She saw him.

Mrs. Brown was sad. "That poor woman. I wish I could do something for her."

"She's taking it hard, huh?"

"Very hard. Her nearest neighbors are with her. The funeral will be tomorrow. The body is laid out in nothing more than a wooden box. We volunteered to help get him dressed in his best shirt and coat, but she didn't want us to see him undressed. She did it herself. Poor woman."

"It's too bad." McCagg shook his head sadly. "I liked him. He struck me as a good lawman. Not too many really good ones around." That reminded him of the deputy, and he asked Ada Brown if she knew where he was. The deputy had helped carry the body in its box to a wagon and then into the house. She hadn't seen him after that.

"Why, Ben? Did something happen?"

"Well." He didn't want to tell her. She watched his face, knew something was on his mind. He read worry and real concern in her eyes. Maybe telling her wouldn't be so bad. "Well, they tried to burn down the Kleagen house last night, I, uh, traded some shots with them."

"Oh my." Her hand went to her throat. "Who, Ben?"

"I don't know. It was dark. I put out the fire before it did any damage."

"You traded shots with them? Are you hurt?"

"Naw." He didn't tell her about the dead man. But he couldn't help glancing down at his left side.

"Are you sure?"

"Yeah."

"Have you had breakfast?"

"Well, no, but . . ."

"Come with me to the store. I'll fix something."

"Aw. I don't want to be any bother."

"Ben, you're a relative of Dawnmarie's and that makes you a friend of mine. Let me fix you something, won't you?"

Leading the sorrel horse, he walked with her to the store, tied the horse to a hitchrail outside and followed her to the kitchen. There, she added coal to the stove, fried some bacon and eggs and placed it on the table before him along with some fresh doughnuts. He didn't realize how hungry he was until he started eating. He didn't stop until the plate was clean and the doughnuts were gone.

While he ate she sorted the mail that had come on the southbound that morning. There wasn't much. Then she unrolled the half-dozen newspapers from Denver, glanced at a headline in the *Rocky Mountain News* and gasped.

"Ben." She hurried to the table and put the newspaper in front of him.

"Look. Look here. Sheriff Gantt was murdered."

Chapter Twenty-four

It was on the bottom half of page one. The headline, in big bold type, read: RURAL SHERIFF MURDERED. The story began:

"The body of a man identified as Sheriff Martin Gantt of Trinchera County was found in an alley on Capitol Hill last evening, and authorities said a bullet wound was discovered in the back.

"Authorities did not know what Mr. Gantt was doing in Denver, and they refused to speculate about what he was doing at the state capitol. The body was found by a stroller about six o'clock. There was no evidence of robbery, authorities said.

"The dead sheriff's office will be notified by telegraph this morning and the body will be sent by rail to El Moro. Denver police will begin questioning patrons of Capitol Hill lounges and saloons this morning."

Ada Brown said, "The Denver newspapers always get here a day late."

"Yeah." McCagg put the newspaper down and frowned. "Did you, uh, did anybody see a bullet wound in the body?"

"No. Apparently someone in Denver cleaned it before putting it in a box. But poor Mrs. Gantt. She will have seen it by now."

"It's too bad. A d-darned rotten dirty shame." He continued frowning at the table. "I wonder if his murder has anything to do with what's going on around here. The newspaper said he wasn't robbed."

"No, just shot in the back for no apparent reason."

"There has to be a reason."

His thoughts were interrupted by a train whistle south of town. "That's the northbound," Mrs. Brown said. "Dawnmarie is coming."

The big black locomotive with its diamond-shaped smoke stack huffed its way under the high water tank, leaving the one passenger car fifty feet from the depot. A brass-buttoned conductor was the first out, and he placed a metal stool under the steps to make it easier for the passengers to step down. Two passengers were waiting to get on, and one of them was a well-dressed Judge Clarence J. Topah, his gray beard neatly trimmed. He nodded at McCagg and McCagg nodded back. Dawnmarie was behind a man in a wrinkled business suit. McCagg met her halfway, and took a cheap cardboard suitcase from her hands. She put her arms around his neck, hugged him and stepped back.

"Bill is doing better every day. He wants to come home and get to work. The doctor said he'd better stay at least three or four more days. How are you, Uncle Benjamin?"

She was as pretty as ever. The rest had been good for her. Somehow she made him proud, so bright and pretty with her oval face framed by dark brown hair and her straight nose and mouth. He smiled with genuine pleasure at seeing her.

"I'm just fine, Dawn. Do you want to go back to the homestead? I'll get the team and wagon." He'd tell her about the shooting on the way home. Then he remembered the dead man in the river arroyo, and said, "Or maybe you'd rather stay in the hotel tonight, seeing as how you're going right back to Trinidad tomorrow."

"Is everything all right at the homestead? Did anything happen?"

178

He'd have to tell her about the fire, the body in the arroyo and the sheriff's murder, but not now, not here. "Let me rent you a room at the hotel. We can eat at the cafe."

"All right, but I'd like to see Ada first. She'd be hurt if I didn't visit her."

"Right now?"

"Might as well. I haven't got much to carry, as you can see."

If he didn't tell her, Ada Brown would. Except that Mrs. Brown didn't know about the dead man at the homestead. While Dawnmarie was visiting Mrs. Brown he'd hunt up the deputy. No, he'd have to stick with her long enough to tell her himself. But not out here in the street. "All right. She'll want to talk to you." They walked side by side, him carrying her suitcase.

The women hugged, and Ada Brown led her to the kitchen and said, "Sit right down and I'll fix you something. You too, Ben."

He sat and listened to the women talk about Bill and the hospital. When there was a lull in their conversation, Mrs. Brown looked at McCagg with wrinkled brow and said, "Did you tell her about Sheriff Gantt, Ben?"

"No, uh . . ." He told her. Almost everything. The fire at the house, the shooting, everything but the dead man. "The house ain't hurt much, Dawn. It'll need a few new boards is all."

"Uncle Benjamin, are you sure you weren't hurt? How could there be so much shooting without you getting a scratch?"

Grinning a crooked grin, he said, "I move too fast. You'd be surprised how fast I can jump when the bullets fly."

She gave him a look that said she wasn't sure she believed him, then switched the subject. "Poor Mrs. Gantt. Can I do anything for her? I don't know her, but I appreciated Mr. Gantt and I'd like to do something."

"I'm going back over there after we eat and you can go

179

with me. Mrs. Gantt likes to hear good things about her departed husband."

"Of course. But it's too early for dinner. Why don't I check into the hotel and come back later?"

"Hotel? Listen, I've got two bedrooms upstairs. You're more than welcome to stay in one of them tonight."

McCagg said, "Whatever you want to do you do, Dawn, it's fine with me. I'll go back to the homestead tonight and look after things. First, I have to find that deputy and report what happened. But I was wondering, did Sheriff Gantt say why he went to see the lawyer, Michael Haddow?"

"No. He asked Bill who shot him, and Bill couldn't give him a clue. I apologized for Bill and said I was sorry he'd made a trip for nothing. Mr. Gantt said he had another man to see in Trinidad and he named Mr. Haddow. He didn't say why he wanted to see him."

McCagg mulled that over. "He went to see Haddow and then went to Denver as fast as he could get there. He was murdered in Denver. He wasn't robbed. He was murdered for some other reason."

"Uncle Benjamin, do you think . . . do you think Mr. Haddow . . . Uh, he is the one who is trying to get our homesteads away from us, ours and the Arbaughs."

"All I can say is it's strange." Turning to Mrs. Brown, he asked, "Did the body have any papers with it? I mean the stuff that was in his pockets when he was found?"

"There were some things in a cardboard box. I don't know what."

"I'd like to see them. Do you think Mrs. Gantt would let me see them?"

"Why, I don't know. Do you think you might find a clue as to who murdered Mr. Gantt?"

McCagg shrugged. "Who knows? I just can't leave things as they are. And I don't trust that deputy."

"I'll tell her that, and I'll tell her that you are a former law officer."

"When you go over, I'll go with you. Right now, I'll try to find the deputy." As he put on his hat and left, he saw Dawnmarie reaching for the newspaper to read what little it had to say about the sheriff's murder.

Still no one in the sheriff's office. Well, McCagg thought, a lawman couldn't just sit in an office. He had to be out on horseback, talking to people, making himself known. The door of the Curly Wolf was wide open as usual. McCagg glanced at it, and his mouth went dry. Oh no, he told himself. Not at all. No sir. Not with Dawnmarie in town. No siree. With nothing else to do he went back to the mercantile.

The women visited as they cooked a noon meal of sausage soup and corn bread. Mrs. Brown had to interrupt her cooking twice to wait on customers. Dawnmarie was sorry she was selling the store, and said, "I hope you stay in El Moro. I'll miss you something terrible if you don't."

"I don't know yet what I'll do. I know now how my husband felt when we sold the farm and left Kansas. Footloose and restless. We came out here, saw a need for a store and built one."

"It's the best thing that ever happened to this town."

"It's been good to us, this store. It's just too much for me alone. Too much heavy lifting. And I can't afford to hire help."

Another customer came in. While Mrs. Brown was gone Dawnmarie stirred the soup. "It will be grand to eat a home-cooked meal again. Restaurant meals are all right, but they'll never be as good as home cooked."

McCagg sure couldn't argue with that, but he added, "Make that a woman home-cooked meal. I've never met a man who could do what women do at a cook stove."

After they ate they walked together to the widow Gantt's house. McCagg stayed outside near the white board fence while the women went in. Soon Dawnmarie came to the door and beckoned to him. He told Mrs. Gantt that he

181

recognized a good lawman when he saw one and he knew right from the beginning that Martin Gantt was one of the best. Though her face remained stiff and unsmiling, he could see that she appreciated hearing it.

The body was laid out in a wooden box, in a clean shirt and dark coat with the hands down at its sides. McCagg wanted to ask about the bullet wound, but didn't know how to do it. It wasn't important. If the newspaper said there was a bullet wound in the back there was a bullet wound in the back.

"Mr. McCagg." The widow was facing him. "Ada tells me you would like to look through the things Martin had in his pockets. I'll get them for you." She left the parlor and went to another room. When she came back she handed him a small cardboard box.

"I'm much obliged, Mrs. Gantt. I'll put everything back." He took the box out on the porch and opened it. A Colt thirty-eight caliber sixshooter in a belt holster, the kind of gun that didn't weigh much and would be comfortable to carry. A folding knife, sharp. A calfskin wallet with forty-two dollars in it. A handkerchief. A silver star with a circle around it and an engraved message: "Sheriff Trinchera County, Colorado." Nothing more. He went through the two compartments in the wallet, found a folded piece of paper carrying the message: "In the event of my death or injury please notify my wife, Mrs. Carrie Gantt in El Moro, Colorado."

McCagg shook his head when he read it, and muttered, "Damn."

In the other compartment he found another folded piece of paper with three words written on it: Rampart Reclamation Co." Carefully, he put everything back the way he'd found it and took it inside. Again he thanked the widow. He left, walking slowly, head down, thinking.

Rampart Reclamation Co. What and who in hell is that?

The deputy was in this time. He bristled when McCagg

entered, and McCagg felt like a strange dog that was about to be chased out of the yard by another dog. He hooked his thumbs in his gunbelt and stood in the doorway. "I've got something to report." He told about it.

"Well now." Deputy Joel tilted his chair back on its hind legs. "You say they tried to burn the house down." McCagg nodded. "And you say you shot one of 'em." Another nod. "And the body's still where it fell."

"Right again." He had an urge to say something cynical, like, That's good thinking, Deputy. But he didn't.

"They shot at you."

"One of them did."

"They shot first?"

"No, I shot first."

"Well now. How come?"

McCagg told all about it again, in detail. "The evidence is there if you care to look at it."

"Yep." Deputy Joel stood. "I sure do want to look at it. I'll get some help and a packhorse and bring the dead man back here."

"I don't think a packhorse will do. You'll need a wagon."

"Why?"

"You've heard of rigor mortis?"

"Yeah. So what?"

"The way I understand it, after a man has been dead a while the blood settles in the joints and congeals. That makes the joints stiff, and that makes it damned hard to tie the body on a packhorse."

"Huh?"

"Of course if you want to wait until tomorrow, the congealed blood will have decomposed enough that you can bend the arms and legs again."

"You know all about that stuff, huh?"

"Not all about it. I'd like for you to inspect the place and move the dead man today before the Kleagens go back."

"Are you tellin' me how to do my job? I'm sheriff now, and

183

I tell you what to do. You don't tell me."

"Sure, sure. If you want me I'll be in town until late this evening and then I'm going back to the homestead. If you want, I'll help you bring the dead man in."

"I don't need no help from no goddamn smart aleck Texican."

"Sure, sure." McCagg turned around and sauntered away.

Deputy Joel yelled after him, "And don't go nowhere till I tell you you can."

He took the sorrel to the livery barn, put him in a pen and fed him some hay. He gave the livery owner a five dollar bill. "This is for the sorrel and the Kleagens' team." At the store, he found Mrs. Brown waiting on a customer and Dawnmarie in the kitchen reading the newspaper. She looked up. "I offered to sit with the widow, but she has neighbors who know her better and they're going to stay the night with her."

"It's too bad." He dropped into a kitchen chair. The wound in his left side had started to sting again. He wished he could change the bandage, but he didn't want Dawnmarie to know about it. He'd fix it at the homestead. "Dawn, have you ever heard of a company called the Rampart Reclamation Company?"

"No. Why?"

"Sheriff Gantt was carrying a piece of paper with that name on it. I don't know whether it means anything."

Frowning in concentration, she repeated, "No. I've never heard of it."

"I wonder if it's some company in Denver and I wonder what kind of company it is."

Still frowning, she said, "I can't imagine."

He hated killing time. Thoughts of the Curly Wolf came to his mind repeatedly throughout the rest of the day. Silently, he cussed himself for even thinking about it. He could go back to the Kleagen place. But the deputy would be there and he didn't want anything to do with him. He visited with his niece, and asked her what Bill wanted to tell him. She reminded him that she had made a promise. They talked about the book she was going to write, and how she would have plenty to write about. The women decided they would have supper early so McCagg could eat with them and get back to the homestead before dark. He was more than glad to go along with that plan.

They were cooking something that smelled delicious, when the deputy came in the front door.

"I just got back from the Kleagen claim," he said to Ada Brown, "and I'm lookin' for Ben McCagg."

McCagg heard him and came out of the kitchen. "Yeah?"

Immediately, the deputy drew his sixgun, pointed it at McCagg with the hammer back and said:

"You're under arrest for murder."

Chapter Twenty-five

He had no chance. The deputy's gun was pointed at his middle and it didn't waver. McCagg glanced back at Dawnmarie who was right behind him, and at Ada Brown. Both women had questions on their faces.

"You're gonna come with me," the deputy said, "and I don't want no fuss. You give me any trouble and I'll blow a hole in you."

No use asking why. McCagg had killed a man. It was self-defense, but the deputy was always looking for an excuse to lock him up. Deputy Joel kept the sixgun pointed at his middle as he carefully stepped close and lifted the Smith & Wesson from its holster.

"That's the second man you've killed in this county, and you belong in jail, mister. I'm gonna see you go to prison this time."

"Uncle Benjamin," Dawnmarie said, "who . . . what happened?"

He turned half-around. "I didn't tell you because I'm not proud of killing men, but one of the two who tried to burn your house ran at me and I shot him."

"He didn't have his gun out of its cradle," the deputy said. "He wasn't no threat to you."

"It was dark. All I could see was somebody touching a match to the house and somebody about to run into me. He did run into me. He didn't expect me to be where I was."

"You're under arrest and that's that. March." Joel waved his gun in the direction of the door.

For two seconds the gun wasn't pointed at McCagg, and he wondered if he could move fast enough to grab it. If he could move fast enough he could grab the barrel of the gun with his left hand and clip the deputy in the jaw with his right elbow. Hit him in the face a few times and he could take the gun away from him.

Naw. Not with women present. He had no choice but to go to jail.

As they left, Ada Brown said, "I'll go see the judge, Ben."

Same old jail. McCagg thought grimly that it was getting to be a second home to him. He thought too about something somebody said back when he was a Ranger: Every lawman ought to spend some time in jail. Every lawman and every judge. Then they wouldn't be so quick to lock men up. Well, he sure as hell knew what it was like. And he sure as hell didn't like it.

Deputy Joel wouldn't allow Dawnmarie and Ada Brown to bring him his supper. "Ain't nobody gonna see 'im 'til I say so and I ain't ready to say so."

McCagg could hear their conversation, and he heard Dawnmarie say, "Judge Topah will have a different viewpoint."

"That judge is plumb out of the county."

Ada Brown said, "He'll be back on the southbound in the morning. He'll have something to say about this."

"You ladies have got to git on out of here now. This ain't no place for ladies, and I got a duty to keep the peace in here."

Dawnmarie yelled, "Uncle Benjamin, we'll talk to the judge first thing in the morning."

His supper was cold mashed potatoes and a piece of meat a dog couldn't chew. "Tougher than a boiled owl," McCagg grumbled as he gave up on it.

Sit. Walk the floor. Lie on the wooden bunk. Walk the floor.

It was around midnight when he heard voices outside. Men's voices. Angry. "No, you can't come in here." That was Deputy Joel's voice rising from inside the sheriff's office.

A man yelled from outside, "We're a-comin' in. He's killed two men in a week and we ain't gonna let no judge turn 'im loose."

Good God, McCagg thought, a lynch mob. He went to the cell door and looked between the bars. Light from one lamp showed Deputy Joel standing by the outer door. The door was shut, but it didn't look strong.

The man's voice came through. "We're gonna see he don't kill nobody else."

"The law'll take care of him," the deputy yelled. "You can't come in here."

The danger didn't soak in at first, and McCagg looked between the cell bars as a mildly interested party. Then, when the door crashed open with a splintering of wood, he suddenly realized he was the target of an angry, bloodthirsty mob that meant to kill him.

Five men poured through the door, all wearing black bandanas around their faces. One had red eyebrows, and McCagg recognized the redheaded O'Brien. Deputy Joel wrestled with the men, but was soon knocked down and disarmed. A man in overalls grabbed the key ring from the deputy's desk and they all gathered in front of the cell.

"McCagg," Red Eyebrows said, "you've killed your last man." The cell door was unlocked.

There was no escape. Five pairs of rough hands grabbed for him, grabbed both arms and legs. He kicked, jerked his arms, arched his back, butted with his head. Swore. They had him helpless. So helpless that they carried him. Carried him feet first to the door. Deputy Joel was standing again, protesting. He followed the mob outside. He was ignored.

"I've got the rope," a man said.

"Carry 'im to the depot, to the telegraph pole."

"Yeah, we'll hang 'im from a pole."

McCagg kicked, swore, "You sonsofbitches. You goddamn sonsofbitches."

"Shut up, or I'll punch your face in."

"Don't hit 'im. I want 'im wide awake. I wanta hear 'im beg."

"Go to hell, you goddamn sonsofbitches. Rot in hell."

"You're the one's goin' to hell, mister."

He was carried. The street was dark, but he could see at least five men. He kicked, bucked, twisted. It did no good.

Gunshots.

From somewhere in the dark they came. Two shots, three, four.

"Jeesuz. Some damn body's shootin'."

"Where?"

Two more shots.

"Jeesuz."

Their holds loosened.

Another shot boomed, and another.

"God damn."

"From over there. Over there in the alley."

Their holds loosened more. Now the mob was shooting back, shooting into the dark.

McCagg kicked, twisted, felt his legs come free, kicked, broke loose, ran.

Men were between him and the livery barn. He couldn't get to a horse. Run. Where? His legs weren't made for running. But run he did — right back inside the sheriff's office.

The lamp was putting out enough light that when he slammed the door he could see the latch had been ripped out. Straining and grunting, he shoved the heavy desk against it. A shoulder hit the door from outside, moved the desk a few inches. Again, someone rammed the door.

McCagg rummaged with hasty fingers through the desk

189

drawers until he found his Smith & Wesson. He blew out the lamp and backed up against the wall next to the door, flat. The next blow moved the desk a few more inches.

"Let me try," a man said. "Shit, let's hit it together."

The Smith & Wesson popped, bucked in McCagg's hand.

"Jeesuz, he's shootin' through the door."

Guns fired outside, and bullets tore through the door, smacking against the far wall. One ricocheted off a cell bar.

"Pour it to 'im." Gunfire was so fast and furious that, for a few seconds, it sounded like one continuous boom.

McCagg flattened against the wall, held the Smith & Wesson across his chest pointed it at the door and fired again. Shooting stopped outside.

"Jeesuz, he's got all kinds of guns and ammunition in there."

"God damn it. Can't see 'im. Can't see where he is."

"Stay away from the Goddamned door. He can shoot right through it."

McCagg's lips skinned back from his teeth. "Come on, you bloodthirsty yellowbellies," he muttered. "I've shot better men than you. Come and get me."

The shooting had stopped, but men were still out there. He could hear them talking. Then it started again, fast, bullet after bullet. They made splinters out of the door. But no one tried to open it. McCagg hugged the wall and watched lead slugs smack harmlessly into the far wall. It stopped. He waited.

Men pushed on the door and moved the desk. McCagg reached across his chest and fired. Someone cursed. The door was open about a foot now, but McCagg was on the other side, the hinged side. No one dared put his face up to the opening and look in.

There was more talk, more cursing. Then quiet.

He couldn't leave. He was trapped in there. Men were waiting for him to open the door and come out. They would shoot him to pieces. All he could do was wait for something to happen. Nothing happened. It was quiet. Maybe they'd given up and left. Maybe. Maybe not. Wait.

"Damnit," McCagg muttered, "seems like all I do is wait in the damn dark. But," he let out a long sigh, "if that's what I have to do to stay alive, that's what I'll do."

While he waited he tried to guess at who had fired from across the alley. Was it townsmen who didn't approve of vigilante justice? Or was it . . . suddenly his heart froze. No, it couldn't be. But the shots had come from that direction, from the alley behind the . . . "Oh no," he groaned, "not Dawnmarie and Ada Brown. Oh, God no." The mob had returned the fire. They could have been hit. He groaned again, "Oh no. Not them."

He wanted to get out of the sheriff's office and get over to the store and find out. He had to. Now.

Holstering the Smith & Wesson, he pulled the desk away from the door and opened the door wider. He stood back. Nothing happened. He opened the door still wider, wide enough to squeeze through.

And he realized he could see across the street. The buildings, the store, were visible. Daylight was coming. No one was in sight. No one.

And then a white figure came out of the store. Dressed in white. Dawnmarie. She came across the street, looking carefully in all directions. She stopped in front of the sheriff's office and took another long look. Then:

"Uncle Benjamin?"

He lifted his new Stetson from a peg on the wall, put it on and stepped through the door. Relief released the tension in her eyes.

"I'm as good as new, Dawn."

Her shoulders slumped with relief. "Thank God."

Standing in front of her, he put his hands on her shoulders. "Was that you who fired from the alley?"

"Yes. Me and Ada. She had her late husband's rifle and I had his pistol. We didn't aim at anyone. We just fired those

191

guns to divert their attention."

"It worked. You saved my life. You could have been killed."

"We were scared half to death, but we had a plan. When they shot back we ran behind the mercantile and ran in through the kitchen door and bolted the door. We heard so much shooting over here, we were worried sick."

He put his arm around her shoulders and together they walked to the mercantile. Ada Brown was waiting on the step. "Thank God you're all right, Ben."

"You saved my hide, Ada, you and Dawnmarie." It occurred to him that he had not called her by her first name before.

"The southbound will be here any minute and Judge Topah is supposed to be on it."

"That reminds me," McCagg said as a train whistle sounded far away, "I'm still under arrest."

"That's the southbound."

"Know what I'm going to do? I'm going back to jail."

"Back to jail? Uncle Benjamin, you can't do that."

"Why not, the mob is gone, and I am under arrest, you know. I wouldn't want to do anything illegal."

He grinned. "But this time, I'm keeping my gun."

Chapter Twenty-six

Inside the sheriff's office, he stepped through the cell door and closed it. With nothing to fear now, he lay on his back on the bunk and put his hat over his face. The wound on his left side throbbed, and he knew he would have to clean it again soon. A half-hour later Deputy Joel came in.

The deputy had his head down, worry wrinkles on his face, and when he looked up and saw McCagg he stopped as if he'd run into a wall. "Huh? What? What are you doin' here?"

Standing, stretching lazily, McCagg grinned and drawled, "I'm your prisoner, remember. You must have had an entertaining night."

"I did all I could. I couldn't hold back a mob by myself." He eyed the forty-five on McCagg's right hip but said nothing about it.

"Sure, sure."

"Nobody can blame me for what happened."

"Sure, sure. Where's my breakfast?"

"I'll, uh, I'll go git it." Joel left.

McCagg lay back again and put his hat over his face. In another half-hour the deputy was back with a platter covered with a cloth. McCagg ate this breakfast of hotcakes and syrup. The coffee was only lukewarm. When he finished, he opened the cell door, put the plate on the floor outside the cell, stepped backward inside and shut the door. In another half-hour a man came in.

"Joel, the judge said to bring the prisoner to court."

"Aw shit. All right." He stepped to the cell door, opened it and said, "Come on out, McCagg. Give me that gun."

"No."

"What?"

"No. Hear?"

"You're my prisoner. You can't go to court with a gun."

"You gonna stand here and argue or do what the judge said?"

Joel hesitated, calculated his chances, said, "If you try to run I'll shoot the shit out of you."

Grinning, McCagg drawled, "If I decide to run I'll put you down first."

Dawnmarie and Ada Brown were there and so were a dozen townsmen and women. The judge sat at his desk on the platform. McCagg marched up to the front of the room.

With a stern expression, Judge Topah said, "Deputy, why are you holding this man?" His eyes went to the forty-five on McCagg's hip and back to the deputy.

"I arrested him for murder, Your Honor. He killed a man at the Kleagen homestead."

The stern eyes went to McCagg. "What do you say in your defense, Mr. McCagg?"

He told all about it again, admitted the dead man hadn't fired a shot, but said he was definitely a threat.

Back to Joel. "What evidence do you have, deputy?"

Joel had to tell about finding the Kleagen house damaged by fire, about finding a can that smelled as if it had contained kerosene, and about finding the body of an unidentified man in the arroyo.

Back to McCagg. "You said you were shot at while you were putting out the fire. Seems to me you were a good target at the time, and yet you don't seem to be any the worse for it."

"Well, uh, Your Honor, I . . . could I see you in private?"

"Anything you have to say will be said in open court."

"It isn't what I have to say, Your Honor, it's what I have to show. A bullet wound."

"Hmm. Is it on a part of your anatomy that can be shown in court?"

"Well . . ." He pointed with a finger to his left side.

"Hmm. Seems to me it wouldn't be indecent for you to pull your shirttail up."

He did. Glancing first at the audience. They were watching, waiting, eyes wide. Slowly, he pulled the shirttail out of his pants and raised it above the bandage. Reluctantly, he untied the strips of flour sack and uncovered the wound. It was still red and hadn't started to heal.

Dawnmarie gasped, "Uncle Benjamin, why didn't you tell us?"

The stern look fixed on her. "There will be no more outbursts." The judge's features softened, and he added, "Although I can understand your concern, Mrs. Kleagen." To McCagg he said, "Seems you were wounded." To Joel he said, "What do you say to that, deputy?"

"Well, uh, all I can say is he shot a man who hadn't drawn his gun."

"Under the circumstances and considering the evidence presented, I find there is no reason to bind the defendant over for trial. Deputy, release the prisoner. Now then." He kept his stern look on Joel. "What about the altercation at the jail last night?"

Joel seemed to shrink inside his clothes. "I tried to protect the prisoner, Your Honor, but there were too many of 'em."

"Did you recognize any of them?"

"No, Your Honor, they all wore masks."

"Hmm. I want it understood that I will brook no vigilante justice in my jurisdiction. Deputy, I want you to learn the identities of the culprits and bring them before me."

"Yes, Your Honor."

"Case closed. Does anyone else have anything to bring before the court?"

He was embarrassed. Even when Ada Brown excused herself and left the kitchen, he was embarrassed. But Dawnmarie scolded him and said he was being silly, and she'd seen men barechested before. Finally, he unbuttoned the two lowest buttons and raised his shirt above the wound. Didn't take it off, just raised it. While he sat in a kitchen chair, Dawnmarie washed the red wound and put a clean bandage on it. "There," she said. "It doesn't look too bad." Immediately he pulled his shirt down and tucked the tail under his belt. If he'd had any privacy he'd have unbuttoned his pants and tucked the tail down where it belonged.

Instead he said he believed he'd get his horse and go back to the homestead to make sure everything was still there. "While I was in jail, somebody could have carried off everything you own."

"Stay for dinner, Uncle Benjamin. Ada likes to cook and you don't cook so good yourself."

Grinning, he allowed, "Can't argue about that."

"I'm worried about Bill. I mean I'm worried about Bill worrying about me. I told him I'd be back today, but after what happened last night I couldn't leave. I'm afraid he'll be worried and try to get out of bed and come home to find out what happened to me. And there's the funeral this afternoon. I promised I'd go."

"Send Bill a telegraph, Dawn. Somebody will deliver it to him."

"Yes," she said, brightening. "I didn't think about that. I'm not used to all these modern conveniences. That's what I'll do."

But before she could leave, Mrs. Brown came back to the kitchen. "There's a man out here, Dawnmarie. He said Judge Topah wants to see you."

196

"The judge wants to see me? Whatever for? I was just going to the depot to send a telegraph to Bill."

McCagg said, "I'll send the telegraph. I'll tell Bill you're fine and dandy and not to worry."

"Well, I am curious. Thank you, Uncle Benjamin." She put a dark wool shawl over her shoulders and left through the front door.

McCagg ambled over to the depot. He was stared at by everyone he passed on the street. He was stared at by the telegrapher.

"Say, ain't you . . . ?"

"Yeah. I'm a tough old bird." He dictated a message:

BILL DAWN FINE DON'T WORRY STAY PUT BEN

Then he ambled to the livery barn and saw that his sorrel and Bill's team had been fed and watered. After that he had to find out why the judge wanted to see Dawnmarie, and he went back to the store. She was sitting at the kitchen table with her face in her hands.

"What did he want, Dawn?"

She was near tears when she looked up, and she shook her head sadly. "He said he went to Pueblo where he can use a big law library, and he could find nothing in the law that gives us legal right to our homestead. He said he has always practiced corporation law, and a lawyer who knows more about land laws than he might find a loophole or something, but he could find nothing himself. Squatters' rights do not prevail on land that has already been opened for homesteading."

"Oh-o-o." McCagg sat down heavily.

Dawnmarie twisted her hands in her lap. "We're going to lose our claim, aren't we, Uncle Benjamin? We're going to lose it."

"No." He looked down at his boots, then looked up at Dawnmarie's tortured face. "No," he repeated. "Law or no law. Nobody's gonna take it away from you."

Chapter Twenty-seven

Leaving Dawnmarie at Ada Brown's, he rode the sorrel back to the homestead, getting there just before dark. He'd had a good supper, and to the sorrel and Bill's bay horse, he said. "I'm gonna take you fellers downstream where the grass is tall enough to feed a herd of buffalo."

He made hobbles out of an empty feed sack and hobbled the horses where they could eat their fill. Tracks made by a light wagon ran past the house and down into the arroyo. They crossed Dawnmarie's garden.

In near darkness, McCagg walked down the path to the river, to where the dead man had been. He could see where the body had lain. No blood. The man hadn't suffered.

Nothing had been disturbed inside the house. Lighting a lamp, he checked the Henry again, trying the loading mechanism. It worked. He had been afraid that dropping it in the arroyo had dented the magazine tube, but there was no damage.

In spite of having his sleep interrupted two nights in a row, he didn't feel like going to bed. Sitting in the light made him uncomfortable, though, and he blew out the lamp. After everything that had happened, he felt safer in the dark. One of Michael T. Haddow's thugs was dead, but there were more. Five men had broken into the sheriff's office last night and tried to hang him. Two or three of them might have been townsmen, toughs who could be talked into doing something like that. Still, that left at least two men on Haddow's payroll.

Sitting in the dark, he went over in his mind everything he had learned, everything he had heard. Sheriff Gantt being murdered in Denver. The Rampart Reclamation Company. Squatters' rights meaning nothing in this territory. A smart lawyer with experience in land laws might find a way to make it mean something, but probably not. And then he remembered that with everything happening, he hadn't gone to Pueblo to hire a lawyer. Had to do that. Had to do that in the morning.

Thinking of the law and lawyers gave him a sudden surge of hope. Michael T. Haddow knew the law. If the law didn't protect nesters, Haddow had only to wait a few more days and win the battle in court. He didn't want to wait. He'd sent his thugs to burn down the house and eliminate the Kleagens' most capable ally. Why didn't he just wait?

Did he do that to get even with McCagg? Or—

"Aw hell," McCagg muttered. He laid out his pallet under the window again. Eventually he dozed off.

By the time he got to the depot in El Moro the southbound had gone and the northbound was due in about an hour. McCagg left the sorrel at the livery and bought a ticket to Pueblo. Two other passengers were sitting on the hard benches, waiting, both well-dressed men. McCagg walked outside, down to the water tank, squinted up at it and wondered how they got water up there. Can't get water to run uphill, he mused silently, and looked around for a pump. It was behind a tin shed. There was a steam engine to provide the power and a small pump with flywheels on each side. That's what Bill needs, he said to himself, a steam engine to do the pumping. Or a windmill. Yeah, that's what he wants, a windmill.

With nothing else to do he went back inside the depot and sat opposite the two well-dressed men. One was short, squat, with a billygoat beard, and the other was small, thin, and smooth-faced. The short one was recalling the times he'd had to travel by stage coach from Denver all the way to Trinidad to sell dry goods, and the thin one only nodded his head, seemingly not very much interested.

"What line are you in, if you don't mind my asking?" said the short one.

"Oh, I'm in my own business." He clearly didn't want to carry the conversation further.

"In your own business? Now, that's the way to live. One of these days I'm gonna quit working for other people and get into a business of my own. Yes sir, that's the way to make money, not working yourself to a frazzle for other folks. What kind of business are you in?"

"Why, uh, the reclamation business."

"The reclamation business? Now that's interesting. What . . .?"

"Excuse me, sir, I must visit the, uh, toilet." The thin one stood and headed for the door.

The reclamation business. The words stuck in McCagg's mind. Rampart Reclamation Co. He walked over to the telegrapher and asked, "You wouldn't happen to know who that gentleman is, the little skinny one?"

"Nope." Reluctantly, the telegrapher looked up from his *Police Gazette*. "All I know is he's waiting for the northbound. Came in on the southbound and asked what time the northbound will get here."

"Sounds like he's meeting somebody then."

"Said he was expecting somebody from Trinidad. Somebody named Haddow. Must be that lawyer feller."

Right then McCagg went to the ticket agent and cashed in his ticket to Pueblo. This was going to be a meeting he wanted to see. He stood back where he wasn't too conspicuous and waited. When the northbound puffed and hissed its way to the water tank, he stood back and watched Michael T. Haddow get out of the one Pullman car and shake hands with the little thin man. They talked a moment, a serious conversation with

200

Haddow shaking his head repeatedly, then walked away toward the hotel. McCagg watched them go and started to follow, but out of the corner of his eyes he saw another man step out of the Pullman. This man was walking funny, a little bent at the waist, with his left elbow tight against his side and his forearm across his stomach.

Aw for . . . McCagg went to him. "Bill, what the hell are you doing here?"

Bill Kleagen's face was pinched. He spoke with quick tense words: "Where's Dawn? What happened? Why . . . ?"

McCagg cut him off. "Dawn's fine. She's in Trinidad right now looking for you. Didn't you see her?"

"No. She's . . . she's in Trinidad?"

"Yeah. She was supposed to be on the southbound. Didn't you get my telegram?"

"Telegram? No. She's all right? You sure?" His face was pale and he was gripping his left side with his elbow.

"Has to be. She stayed in town yesterday and last night because of some things that happened, but she was supposed to head back to Trinidad first thing this morning. What are you doing here? Ain't you supposed to be in bed?"

"I'm doin' fine. I had to come back and see if anything happened. I reckon I just missed seein' her in the Trinidad depot. I got on the train as soon as I could and sat down. You say something happened?"

"Yeah, but Dawn and everybody is all right. Tell you what, let's get you a room at the hotel. You don't look so good."

"Where's my team and wagon? Is anything wrong at home?"

"Everything's fine. Some things happened, but you've got to sit down someplace, get some rest. You ought to be on your back in bed. I'll tell you all about it as soon as we get you in bed. Wait here a minute and I'll check to be sure Dawn got on the train this morning."

He was gone only two minutes and when he came back he was smiling. "Yep. The ticket agent said she boarded the southbound. The telegraph feller said he didn't know why my telegram wasn't delivered to you, but he said they sometimes can't find anybody to deliver a message. Come on, let's get you over to the hotel. When Dawn sees you're not in the hospital, she'll get back here as quick as she can. She'll be just as worried about you as you are about her. I wish I could holler that far."

With McCagg's help, he made it to the hotel, signed the registration book and climbed sorely to a second floor room. Inside, McCagg said, "Now you flop down on that bed and don't move. Have you ate today? I'll go get you something from the cafe."

"Naw. I'm not hungry. Listen, Ben, there's somethin' I wanta tell you."

"Dawnmarie said you had something to tell me, but it can wait. You look like you need some rest."

"No, this is somethin' else."

"Get on that bed, will you, Bill?"

He sat on the edge of the bed and pulled off his boots, then lay back. "Listen, Ben, I've been thinkin'."

McCagg opened the one window in the room. The room held only the bare necessities. There were a narrow bed, a small table, a wash basin, a pitcher of water, a towel, a bar of soap, and a hall tree to hang clothes on. "I'll go see Ada Brown and tell her where you are in case Dawn sends a telegram to her to try to find you. In fact, I'll go to the telegraph feller and see if there's any word from Dawn. If there is, I'll send a message back."

"Ben, will you listen to me?"

McCagg sat on the edge of the bed. "Yeah, all right, but Dawn is probably worried sick."

"I've been thinkin'. You know how Dawn likes to read the newspapers? Well about a year ago she read somethin' to me about the German farmers up at Greeley. You know, a town north of Denver somewhere? Well they irrigate a lot of land, and they can grow just about anything. The newspaper said the land was worthless until somebody dug a big ditch."

"Yeah." He wished Bill would stop talking so he could go to

the depot and question the telegrapher.

"Well, last summer I seen some fellers that looked like government men or somebody like that. They had on those hats with the peak-ud tops, you know. They both wore the same kind of clothes. They were trampin' around the river banks."

"Yeah, I've got to get over to the depot. Dawn's worrying about you." McCagg stood.

"Ben." Kleagen sat up, face white, then lay back again. "Aw, I'm prob'ly crazy. Wait 'till Dawn gets here, and if she thinks I'm wrong I'll shut up about it."

"Fine. I'll go to the depot first and then I'll get you something to eat." McCagg went to the door, opened it. "You stay put, now."

The stairs squeaked as he walked down, turning his feet sideways so his spurs wouldn't catch on them. It reminded him of the last time he'd walked down those stairs, looking forward to seeing his niece again. Seemed like months ago, but it couldn't have been more than a couple of weeks. If that long.

The clerk wasn't at his desk, and the lobby was deserted. McCagg headed for the door, then had an idea. Taking a good look around and seeing nobody, he went to the clerk's desk and tried to read the registration book upside down. Couldn't. After another glance around he turned the book his way. Three names: Michael T. Haddow, Trinidad, Jerome B. Whitney, Denver, and William Kleagen, El Moro.

Jerome B. Whitney from Denver. In the reclamation business. In town to conduct some business with Michael T. Haddow.

McCagg would have given anything to find out what their business was. And as he walked to the depot, he tried to figure out a way to do it. Whatever their business was, it had to do with the Kleagen homestead.

He would have bet on it.

Chapter Twenty-eight

There was a telegram, all right. But it was for Ada Brown, and the telegrapher had sent it with the mail sacks over to the mercantile. Ben reckoned that Dawnmarie had wired Mrs. Brown because she didn't know exactly where he was. He headed for the mercantile as fast as he could walk.

"I was just leaving," Ada Brown said. "Dawnmarie is waiting at the telegraph office for an answer, and I didn't know what to say. Is Bill in town? Is he all right?"

"Bill's all right. A little weak, but all right, I left him at the hotel, and I think he'll stay there. Want me to wire Dawn?"

"Thank God. I guessed he was here, but I wasn't sure. Yes, if you would please. She would rather hear from you."

"I'll do that right now."

"Does Bill need anything? How about food? Can I take him something?"

"I was going to get him some chuck from the cafe, but . . ."

"I'll take him something. Which room is he in?"

"Two oh four."

"I've made some soup with potatoes and bacon, and I'll take some right over."

As McCagg walked again to the telegrapher's desk he couldn't help thinking about that soup. It reminded him that it was noon and his breakfast had been early and light. He could use some of that soup himself.

DAWN BILL HERE RESTING EASY COME BACK BEN

After he'd written the message on a sheet of paper and handed it to the telegrapher, he cracked, "Between the sheriff and us, we're giving you something to do."

Grinning, the telegrapher said, "You-all've shore got me guessin' at what's gonna happen next."

"You never know. Your guess is as good as mine."

He stopped at the livery and saw that his sorrel and Bill's team were fed, then went back to the hotel. Ada Brown arrived at the same time, carrying a tray covered with a clean cloth. "You go in first, Ben, and if it's all right I'll come in."

Bill was resting, but awake when Ben opened the door and looked in. "Somebody out here's got something for you, Bill." He stepped back and let Mrs. Brown enter. She set the tray on the small table and uncovered it. There was a big bowl of steaming soup, a spoon and knife, two thick slices of bread and a jar of preserves of some kind.

"Do you feel like sitting up, Bill?"

"Yeah. Yes, ma'am. Boy," he said, eyes wide, "that's just what I need."

McCagg watched him hungrily as he ate every bit. He looked at Ada Brown with hungry eyes, and drawled, "Well, reckon I'd better get something at the cafe."

"Ben McCagg, you'll do nothing of the kind. But you'll have to come to my kitchen. I couldn't carry enough for both of you."

Leaning back on the bed with a contented sigh, Bill Kleagen said, "Nothin' like a good meal to make a feller well. Give me a little more time now and I'll be chasin' rabbits with the hounds."

Mrs. Brown said, "Don't overdo yourself, Bill. Dawn-marie will be back tomorrow. You just stay here. I'll bring you some supper." To McCagg she said, "Come with me, Ben, and I'll wipe that hungry look off your face."

He followed her out like a lost puppy.

Well-fed now, Ben McCagg couldn't get his mind off the little thin man from Denver. He considered going up to room two-oh-six at the hotel—Jerome B. Whitney's room—and asking him. Asking him what? Well, about The Rampart Reclamation Company. And what his business was with Michael T. Haddow. What did it have to do with a string of homesteads that cut across a big bend in the Picketwire River?

Uh-oh. Suddenly, he remembered the map he'd seen in the land agent's office. That's what the string of home-steads did, cut across the bend in the river. And what was it Bill had said? Something about an irrigation canal somewhere. That could be it. But how does a feller go about proving it? Just ask? How do you do that? Doc Bridges would have known how. How would Doc do it?

He tried to think it out while he walked back to the hotel and up to Bill's room. There are times, Doc had once said, when a man has to put all pretensions aside, be himself and not try to fool anyone. Just lay the cards on the table and let everyone see them.

Instead of stopping at Bill's door, McCagg took a few more steps and stopped in front of room two-oh-six. He planned in his mind what he was going to say. With Dawnmarie's love of reading and Bill's suspicions, the puzzle was almost solved. Only a few questions were unanswered. The thing to do was to present it all to Mr. Whitney and see what happened. If he was right, the man from Denver couldn't deny it. Not without lying in his teeth. Would he? McCagg knocked lightly on the door.

When he came out a half-hour later, he reckoned the puzzle was solved but not the problem.

Bill Kleagen was sitting up when McCagg went back to room two-oh-four. "Bill, you started to tell me something, but I was too worried about Dawn to listen. And Dawn said you had something to tell me."

"Yeah, Ben, I have. I hit water on your claim. Sure as shootin'. Only about sixty feet." He sat up straighter, his face bright. "There's water out there, Ben, and there's windmills to pump it up. With water, you can graze cattle and do just about anything."

"Yeah, but you said something else, and it turned out to be important. Damned important. You . . ."

He was interrupted by a knock on the door. McCagg opened it and when he saw who was there his hand went instinctively to the Smith & Wesson.

"I was told that William Kleagen is in here," said Deputy Joel.

"Yeah."

"I've got a paper for him. I've got another'n for Harvey Arbaugh and a couple other fellers."

"What kind of paper?"

"It's a subpoena signed by Judge Topah. You'd better git outta my way while I serve it. If you don't you're interferin' with an officer of the law."

McCagg stepped back and let the deputy enter, but kept his eyes on him. Joel went to the foot of the bed, unfolded a sheet of paper and handed it to Bill Kleagen. Kleagen took it, stared at the handwriting on it a moment, then looked at McCagg.

"If you can't read," Joel said, "then I'm required by law to read it to you." He took the paper from Kleagen's hand, and read:

"To Mr. William Kleagen. You are hereby summoned into the Trinchera County Court of the Honorable Judge Clarence J. Topah on August twenty-one at one-thirty p.m. to testify in litigation concerning Timothy O'Brien versus William Kleagen."

"August Twenty-one?" McCagg asked. "Why that's uh . . ."

"That's tomorrow. Tomorrow at one-thirty in the afternoon. If you don't show up, you'll, uh, you'll forfeit somethin'."

"But the judge set a hearing for, let's see, a couple of days from now."

The deputy was shaking his head. "All I know is the judge told me to serve these papers, and that's all I give a shit about. You have been served." With that, Joel turned on his heel and left the room.

"Well, I'll be damned," McCagg muttered. "That goddamn lawyer must have talked the judge into moving the hearing up. And I never did go to Pueblo and hire a lawyer to argue for us. Damn, damn. Bill, if I was to bend over, would you kick me? I ought to be kicked 'til I can't walk. Why in hell did I keep putting that off? Damn me anyway."

Fear drained swiftly out of her mind and body when Dawnmarie read the message from her uncle. So swiftly it left her weak in the knees. She went out onto the sidewalk and leaned against a brick building for a moment. Bill was resting easy. Then the relief was followed by resentment. Why did he leave the hospital? Why did he cause her to make herself sick worrying about him? He wasn't well enough to travel. Why didn't he stay in bed? The answer, when she thought about it, was simple, and the resentment left her mind. It was because he was worried about her. She didn't come back when he expected her to and he was convinced that something had happened to her. He couldn't just lie in bed and worry.

Well, he was resting easy, and Uncle Benjamin was

208

with him and so was Ada. If her uncle didn't know how to take care of him, Ada did. Now she had to get back to El Moro. It was much too far to walk. If she had a horse she could ride. She didn't have a horse. Or, if she were a man she could walk out to the northbound road and hope someone came along in a buggy and offered her a ride. Only a man could do that. Not a woman. She'd have to wait for the train. Wait until morning.

Now that she didn't have to worry about Bill, she worried about everything else that had happened. An attempt to kill Bill. Two attempts to kill Uncle Benjamin. A hearing coming up in court. Would they by some miracle be able to keep their homestead? Keeping it was terribly important to Bill and to her, but not as important as keeping Bill and Uncle Benjamin alive. And they would fight. They both would. Someone would be killed.

How was it going to end?

Restless and anxious, she walked the length of Commerce Street and back, bought a newspaper and went to a hotel. It was a long day. A long night. She couldn't sleep, worrying.

At daylight she was at the depot and soon after that she was on her way north, watching the scrub pine, cedars and pinon go by, listening to the clackity-clack of the wheels going over the fishplates that held the rails together. At times, when the wind shifted, black smoke from the engine obscured the view, but she didn't mind. She was thankful for the railroads. What a change they had made in some people's lives.

He uncle was there to meet her, and he hurried her to the hotel where Bill was sitting on the edge of the bed. Uncle Benjamin stood out in the hall while she and her husband hugged and kissed. Bill was looking better, but still weak. Then her uncle came in and they talked.

The hearing was today. Not in two days, but today. Uncle Benjamin apologized all over the place for not going to Pueblo and hiring a lawyer. But her spirits climbed when he told about his conversation with a gentleman named Jerome B. Whitney of Denver. In fact, Dawnmarie was so excited at the news she couldn't sit still. She jumped up and kissed him on a leathery cheek.

"You've solved it. Now we know all about it."

But even after Mr. Whitney visited with them in Bill's room and repeated what he'd already said, her uncle was worried. "I keep remembering what the judge told you, about how land that has been opened up for homesteading can't be claimed by just squatting on it. The law has to be followed, and Bill didn't do it. No matter what else has been going on, the law has to be obeyed. That's all a judge cares about. The law is his god. Nothing else matters."

And later, while Mrs. Brown served a meal in her kitchen to Dawnmarie, Bill and McCagg, he was still nervous. It was the first time Dawnmarie had ever seen him nervous. He repeatedly apologized for not having a lawyer to argue for them in court. "If we had a smart lawyer he might find a hole in the law. We need a professional talker to talk for us."

She tried to calm his fears. "If the judge is as much concerned about justice as I think he is, it isn't hopeless." She stood. It was time to go.

Mrs. Brown said she would stay at the store and hope, maybe even pray.

Dawnmarie said, "Don't worry, Uncle Benjamin. I have a feeling we won't need a lawyer.

"In fact," she had to smile, "it's quite possible that the lawyer, Michael T. Haddow, will need a lawyer."

Chapter Twenty-nine

Everyone was there but Harvey Arbaugh. Michael T. Haddow and Jerome B. Whitney were flanked by the red-bearded Timothy O'Brien and the husky John Cannon. Another man whom McCagg recognized as one of the O'Brien bunch was with them. Deputy Joel stood at the back of the room, arms crossed, glaring at everyone. Bill and Dawnmarie Kleagen came in with McCagg right behind them, keeping an eye on Haddow and Company. Bill Kleagen was walking straight now that he'd rested from his train trip. His color was better. Also present was the U.S. Land Agent Bruce Thiede, carrying a roll of maps.

The judge was ten minutes late, and McCagg would have bet he planned it that way. Making everyone wait for him showed how important he was. When he finally entered, everyone stood until he'd taken his seat behind the heavy desk on the platform. He looked at some papers on the desk and then out at the men and the woman waiting patiently. Clearing his throat, he said, "The people's court of Trinchera County, Colorado is now in session. It appears the first matter on the docket is O'Brien versus Kleagen. Are the litigants present?"

Michael T. Haddow stood. "I am here representing Timothy O'Brien, Your Honor." Bill Kleagen looked at his wife. She whispered something to him and patted his arm. He stood, looking embarrassed, and said, "I am William Kleagen."

"Mr. Kleagen," Judge Topah looked at him sternly, "are you represented by counsel?"

"No sir."

"Very well. Be that as it may. Mr. Kleagen, you were not present when I set a hearing date for August twenty-three. Have you any objection to moving the date up to today?"

"No sir."

"You have a right to object, you know."

"Yes sir."

"Are you sure you would not rather wait until you can retain legal counsel?"

"Yes sir."

"Very well. Mr. Haddow, present your case."

The lawyer stood, buttoned his coat in the middle, cleared his throat and began. The case was a very simple one, he said. His client had a legal right to the parcel of land in dispute simply because it was open for homesteading and no one else had claimed it. He called upon the land agent, Bruce Thiede, who agreed that the name of William Kleagen had never been recorded in connection with a claim under the Amended Homestead Act of 1864. He also said that Timothy O'Brien did register for a half-section of land on the north bank of the Purgatoire River in Township thirty-four, South in Range fifty-nine, West of the sixth Principal Meridian, on the south half of section five. He sat.

"Mr. Kleagen, how do you answer?"

It was clear that Bill Kleagen would rather be somewhere else. Almost anywhere else. His wife patted his arm, and he stood again, shifting his weight from one foot to the other. "Well, uh, sir, Your Honor, we, my wife and me — I — believe we can show that Mr., uh, O'Brien and Mr. Haddow have used fraud and deceit to get our land." He looked down at his wife for her approval. She nodded and smiled.

The judge's eyebrows rose. "You can? Proceed."

Bill Kleagen stammered, "Well, uh . . ."

"Mrs. Kleagen." Judge Topah shifted his gaze to her. "Perhaps you can speak better for the Kleagen interests."

Standing, she said, "Your Honor, my husband is plenty capable of presenting our case." She sat.

"Very well. Proceed, Mr. Kleagen."

Bill Kleagen stammered again, and finally started talking. "Uh, sir, we believe Tim O'Brien has no interest at all in farming and only filed a claim because he was paid to by Mr. Haddow. Mr. Haddow represents a Denver company called the Rampart Reclamation Co." He looked down at his wife. She smiled. He went on, his voice picking up strength.

"Mr. Whitney here is president of the Rampart Reclamation Co., and he told us all about it. The company has plans to . . ."

Michael T. Haddow jumped to his feet. "Your Honor, I object to any disclosure of private plans. The Rampart Reclamation Co. and its economic plans are not an issue here."

"Mr. Haddow," the judge fixed his gaze on the lawyer, "I'm not sure I agree with your objection. If private plans of a Denver firm are somehow connected with this litigation, then I want to hear what those plans are." His gaze went to Jerome B. Whitney. "Mr. Whitney, do you have any objection? You are Mr. Whitney, are you not?"

"Yes, Your Honor, I am Mr. Whitney, and no, I have no objection."

"Very well. Mr. Kleagen, proceed."

"The company is six businessmen who believe they can build an irrigation canal across a long bend in the Picketwire, excuse me, the Purgatoire River. One end of the canal will have to be dug on our claim and the other end on the half-section claimed by Harvey Arbaugh. It's the only place where an irrigation canal can be dug. The six businessmen are honest men, and they hired Mr. Haddow to buy the claims from us and to find ways under government laws to get the rest of the land they need. They hoped they could get some of it through the Homestead Act and more under the Desert Reclamation Act. They, uh . . ."

Bill Kleagen paused and shot a glance at Jerome B. Whitney, who nodded at him.

"They, uh, expected Mr. Haddow to buy our claims, but Mr. Haddow saw what he thought was a way to get them for nothing. He planned to pocket the money he was being given to buy them."

"Objection." The lawyer was on his feet, red in the face, and stomping mad. "This is pure conjecture. There is no basis for this kind of accusation. I resent this and I object strenuously."

"Mr. Kleagen." The judge looked down his nose. "You will refrain from conjecture, that is, from giving your opinion about someone else's plans. I assume that you can corroborate what you have said about Mr. Whitney and the Rampart Reclamation Co."

"Yes, sir. Mr. Whitney himself has said he will tell you the same thing."

"Very well, proceed."

"Well, uh, Mr. Haddow ran into some trouble. First, you were not so quick with an eviction notice. You probably didn't . . ."

"Objection. We're not dealing with probabilities here."

"Mr. Kleagen, tell the court what you know to be true, not what you think is true."

"Yes, sir. Another problem was Sheriff Martin Gantt. The sheriff didn't hurry out and drive us off our land the way Mr. Haddow expected him to. He told us he wasn't going to do that, not even if he had to give up his badge. Another problem was Harvey Arbaugh. He told Tim O'Brien he would fight to the death before he would give up his claim. My wife and I agreed that we would fight them any way we could. Then my wife's uncle, Benjamin McCagg, came to visit. Ben is an ex-Texas Ranger and he's got several commendations for bravery. He promised he would stay until the problem was settled and he would fight too."

He had to pause, look at his wife, at McCagg, at Whitney. Satisfied that they agreed with him, he went on: "There was some shootin'. Tim O'Brien, John Cannon and some of their pals shot at Harvey Arbaugh's cabin, and Harvey shot back. Then they picked a fight with Ben McCagg in the Curly Wolf saloon, but he was faster with a gun than they were. While this was goin' on, Mr. Haddow was worried. He was worried because he had until today to get the land the Rampart Reclamation Co. needed. He was desperate. Somebody ambushed me and shot me in the side early one morning. I didn't see who did it, but I can guess."

"Objection. Your Honor, how much of this prattle by an illiterate man must we be subjected to?"

"Illiterate or not, he has a right to be heard. Mr. Kleagen?"

"Next, two men tried to burn our house down and kill Ben McCagg. Ben was too smart for them, and wasn't in the house. He shot and killed one of the two men and put out the fire. He was shot himself, but he survived too. The final day for gettin' control of the land is here. This hearing is Mr. Haddow's last chance."

The young man stood bareheaded in front of the judge's desk with his back to the others and tried to think of what to say next. Not knowing what else to say, he suddenly sat down.

A long silence followed. Wooden benches creaked as men shifted their weight. McCagg was proud of his niece's husband. He wouldn't have believed Bill Kleagen could say that much at one time. Dawnmarie had her hand on her husband's arm. She was smiling at him. The judge was the next to speak:

"Mrs. Kleagen, have you anything to add?"

"Your Honor." She stood, slender and pretty. Dignified. "I believe my husband has presented our case. He has shown the court how a greedy man tried to use the law to steal from honest working people. My husband has shown the court how that man resorted to violence when his plan wasn't moving fast enough and he was under deadline pressures. Men have

215

been killed. Sheriff Martin Gantt, a fine gentleman, was murdered after he learned that the whole thing was somehow connected with the Rampart Reclamation Company and had traveled to Denver to learn more. Someone was sent on the same train, from here or from Trinidad, to make sure he didn't come back. My husband and my uncle were both wounded. I . . . I'm not so presumptuous as to tell Your Honor what the law is, and I'm not sure I know anyway, but I believe that when fraud and deceit are used, the law is on the side of the victims."

A small smile turned up one corner of the judge's mouth, then quickly disappeared. The stern expression returned, "Mr. Haddow?"

The lawyer was already on his feet, his face livid. He shot a venomous, threatening glance at the Kleagens, and sputtered, searching for words. Then he visibly forced himself to be calm. It took a moment, but when he spoke he spoke in a professional manner:

"This is preposterous, Your Honor. There is not one shred of evidence to corroborate Mr. Kleagen's testimony. Mrs. Kleagen has in effect accused us of murder. This is so ridiculous as to be unworthy of consideration. In fact, I object to everything Mr. and Mrs. Kleagen said. It was nothing but conjecture, and . . ."

"Most of it can be corroborated or denied very easily, Mr. Haddow. Would you care to have Mr. Whitney testify?"

"Well, I, uh . . ."

"Or Mr. O'Brien? I see he is present along with Mr. Cannon."

"Very well, Your Honor, I would like to have Mr. O'Brien stand and testify."

The red-bearded one stood, awkwardly, hat in his hand, looking at Michael T. Haddow, puzzled. The lawyer said, "Mr. O'Brien, tell the court, did I employ you to file a claim on the land in dispute?"

"Well, uh . . ."

Before he could go on, the judge interrupted, "Let me warn you, Mr. O'Brien, it is a crime to give false testimony. If you do not tell the truth here you can and will be prosecuted and jailed."

O'Brien sat down so fast he almost fell down.

"Anything further, Mr. Haddow?"

"Your Honor, I can only say that testimony from Mr. and Mrs. Kleagen is pure conjecture and has not been proven. With that in mind, I am certain Your Honor will find for the plaintiff."

"Ahem. Very well. I am going to take this matter under advisement, and in the meantime I am going to wire the district attorney and request that he conduct a full investigation. When that investigation is completed, I will rule on this matter. Not one day before. Now, is there anything further to come before the court?"

Chapter Thirty

McCagg was watching the wrong men. He saw the sudden shifting, the quick eyeball messages between Haddow, O'Brien, Cannon and the other one. He saw Deputy Joel suddenly stand straight, spraddle-legged, right hand close to his gun butt. He took it all in, stood facing them and was ready.

But he wasn't watching the lawyer.

He didn't see Michael T. Haddow reach inside his long coat and draw out a silver-plated, short-barreled revolver. Not until it was too late.

"Hit the ground," he yelled. But not until the silver-plated revolver popped loud enough to sting everyone's eardrums. Not until a hastily fired bullet smacked into the judge's desk.

Judge Clarence J. Topah dropped behind the desk immediately. Dawnmarie and Bill, Jerome B. Whitney and Bruce Thiede stood with frozen faces, not understanding what was happening.

The lawyer's revolver was self-cocking and he aimed it again, this time at Bill Kleagen.

"Get down," McCagg yelled, jumping over a bench and grabbing at the lawyer.

Dawnmarie and Bill hit the floor a split-second before the gun popped a second time. Then McCagg had the lawyer around the neck, wrestling with him, grabbing at the gun. Another pistol shot exploded, and the room was filling with gunsmoke. McCagg felt the bullet zip past his head as he twisted the revolver out of the lawyer's hands, twisted the lawyer around between him and O'Brien.

"Get behind the desk," he yelled, still wrestling with the fat Michael T. Haddow. Another shot exploded, and the lawyer went limp, a dead weight in McCagg's arms.

With the silver-plated revolver in his left hand and his left arm around the lawyer's throat, McCagg dragged him backward, using him as a shield. He had the Smith & Wesson in his right hand. He fired from the hip. The explosion rocked the courtroom. Gunsmoke was getting thicker.

Redbeard spun around, and fell onto his knees.

Two more shots, and McCagg felt a slug thud into Haddow's body. He continued dragging the body backward, up onto the platform. Another shot. It zinged past McCagg's left ear. Out of the corner of his eyes he saw Bill Kleagen pick up one edge of the heavy desk and, with Dawnmarie's help, tip it over. Then he was near the desk, and he dropped the dead man and dove headfirst behind it.

A shot knocked the heel off his left boot.

Bullets thudded into the heavy desk top but didn't penetrate it. The explosions were punishing everyone's ears and gunsmoke was burning their noses. In a glance, McCagg saw five people huddled behind the desk. Including Judge Topah. The judge was on his knees, and he began talking, yelling:

"Stop this at once. I will tolerate no violence in my courtroom. Stop it, I say."

A slug smacked the desk. The judge jerked back.

They were in a bad spot. Sooner or later, a bullet would find its way through the desk top, or around it, and someone would be killed. How many men were out there? O'Brien was down, but that left two of Haddow's hired thugs. And there was Deputy Joel.

McCagg dropped the lawyer's gun, cocked the hammer back on his own gun and peered around the end of the overturned desk. Splinters flew off the desk next to his face as a pistol popped. He fired at a dim shape.

"I will not tolerate this," the judge yelled. "I will brook no . . ." Another shot smacked the desk. "Shoot, man," the judge yelled. "Shoot the bastards."

Peering carefully around the desk wouldn't do it. That only made him a target. He had to move fast and shoot fast. He was gathering his courage and nerve, when another gun fired, this one close to him. A glance showed Bill Kleagen holding the dead lawyer's revolver, firing another shot over the top of the desk and ducking behind it again. His shooting drew fire.

McCagg's mind yelled, NOW.

He rolled over once, away from the desk, and fired from flat on the floor. He fired at the first man he saw, and the man staggered backward and fell. A bullet splintered the floor two inches from McCagg's right shoulder. The Smith & Wesson barked again and again.

Gunsmoke was so thick now it was hard to see through. McCagg squinted, trying to see. No one was moving. He had the hammer back, ready to shoot again at anything that moved. Nothing moved.

A man yelled, "Don't shoot. It's over. They're all down." The voice came from the back of the room near the door. "Don't shoot."

It was Deputy Joel.

At first, no one moved. No one was convinced that the danger was over. McCagg squinted, finally saw the deputy, shifted his gun in that direction.

"Don't shoot."

"Come here," McCagg yelled. "Come up here where we can see you."

A form moved in the gunsmoke. It was a man's form. It came closer.

"Drop that gun," McCagg said, no longer yelling.

"I'm a legally constituted peace officer and I don't have to drop my gun. I'm ordering you to drop your gun."

"Drop that gun or I'll drop you." /

Deputy Joel didn't drop his gun, but he holstered it and stepped up onto the platform. The judge stood. Everyone stood. Bill Kleagen still held the dead lawyer's revolver.

They looked at each other. They looked at the desk, at the bullet holes, at the bullets embedded in the desk top. They squinted through the smoke at the dead men. One of them raised up, groaning, and fell flat again. The fat body of Michael T. Haddow was sprawled on its back near the desk where McCagg had dropped it.

Gradually, the smoke cleared. Judge Topah wiped his eyes with a white handkerchief, blew his nose, and said, "I had hoped, now that we have a court of law, that this sort of thing would no longer happen in Trinchera County, but . . ." He spread his hands with resignation.

Then, with authority back in his voice, he barked, "Deputy, you have your job to do."

"No, he doesn't," McCagg said.

"What do you mean, Mr. McCagg?"

Locking eyes with the deputy, McCagg said, "He just stood there. While you were shot at, while everybody was shot at, he just stood there and didn't do a damned thing. He's the sorriest excuse for a lawman I ever saw."

"And," Dawnmarie added, "I'm not so sure he wasn't taking money from Mr. Haddow. He did nothing to keep a lynch mob from trying to hang Uncle Benjamin. I can't prove it, but for lots of reasons I don't trust him."

"Perhaps," the judge said thoughtfully, "the DA should include you, deputy, in his investigation. I am asking that you give up your weapon and your badge until the investigation is completed."

Mouth open, unbelieving, Deputy Joel stared at the judge. Finally, he shrugged, lifted his sixgun out of its holster and started to hand it barrel first to Judge Topah.

McCagg yelled, "Watch it."

Joel's thumb was on the hammer, pulling it back. McCagg squeezed the trigger of his .45. The firing pin punched an empty shell. Judge Topah saw death coming, and his face went slack.

A pistol popped. Popped again.

The deputy staggered back, spun around, dropped his six-gun and tried to run. He took four steps and fell face down.

Bill Kleagen's eyes were as big as coffee cups as he watched the deputy fall, looked down at the silver-plated revolver in his hand, looked at his wife. He stammered, "I didn't want . . . I never shot a man before. I didn't want to. Not ever." He seemed ready to cry.

Dawnmarie put an arm around his shoulders. "It's all right, Bill, honey. It's all right."

He let the pistol fall from his hand as he stood with shoulders drooping. His wife stood in front of him, talking to him quietly.

"Ahem. Well, I've got to restore order now." Judge Topah straightened his coat and the cravat at his throat. "I'll have to deputize someone." Looking at McCagg, he said, "Mr. Mc-Cagg, you are the best qualified, but you are not a resident of Trinchera County. Bill Kleagen, you are still recovering from your wound. I'll find someone. I'll find someone and get some help and we'll restore order." He stepped down from the platform and walked with dignity to the door.

They watched him until he was outside, then followed him. A crowd had gathered outside, attracted by the gunfire. Judge Topah was picking volunteers. The crowd gathered around the door, trying to look in.

"Step aside," the judge said. "Step aside now. My deputies have work to do."

Talk was scarce in Ada Brown's kitchen. Dawnmarie and Bill seemed to be numb from all that had happened. Dawnmarie told Ada about it, speaking in a flat, dull monotone, saying no more than she had to. Ada served coffee.

After a while, Bill got up and said he was going to get the team and wagon. "Let's go home, Dawn, honey."

"I'll get the team," McCagg said, and left. When he drove the wagon up to the store's front door, the Kleagens were ready. "Are you coming, Uncle Benjamin?"

"Not now, Dawn. Here." He took a roll of bills from a pants pocket, peeled off two bills and handed the rest to her. "Don't argue with me now. Use this, you and Bill, however you think best. I'll see you-all later."

"Uncle Benjamin, you're welcome to go home with us. You're always welcome." Her husband added, "Come home with us, Ben."

"I'll see you-all later. I'm not saying when, but it'll be soon. That's a promise."

Dawnmarie looked back at him as they left, the wagon rattling over the rough dirt street. When they were out of sight, McCagg hitched up his pants and looked toward the Curly Wolf.

Why not? He wanted it, and he had earned it. No reason in the world he shouldn't have it. He started in that direction, walking with a limp now that one boot heel was missing, thinking about how good a glass of beer would taste. Beer, hell. Whiskey. That's what a man needed after a dirty job was done. Yeah, whiskey. He licked his lips in anticipation.

Her voice slowed his steps. "Oh, Mr. McCagg. Ben."

Aw for . . . Reluctantly, he slowed, stopped and stood still without looking back.

"I've got a nice rib roast in the oven, Ben, and I could use some help consuming it."

Damn.

"I can't eat it all myself, and it would be a sin to waste it."

Goddamn.

He looked over his shoulder at her, looked at the saloon, back at her.

She was standing on the step, her face dead serious. "Wouldn't that be better, Ben?"

"Aw," he muttered.

"Wouldn't it, Ben?"

"Aw hell."

"Think about it, Ben."

He thought about it. He stood with his head down, thinking about it.

He turned around.